blitz

allie lasky

prologue

· · ·

Tucker

I MUST BE GOING CRAZY. There is no way in the history of the world that my high school ex-girlfriend is on my college campus. I've imagined her before. It's not the first time my mind has played tricks on me.

I could have sworn I saw her on Saturday. But I know—I *know*—that Mason Prince would never step foot onto Massachusetts State University at Newton's campus. More than that, she would never show up at a football game and sit in the front row and wear my jersey, not after the way she ended things.

Over the last two and a half years since we broke up, I've imagined her beside me, talking to me and keeping me company. I've pretended she's been in the room more than once. It must have been that hard hit in Saturday's game.

Wait. I didn't get hit. Fuck. What's going on? Is it a brain tumor? I blink a few times. No, I'm pretty damn sure that's Mason across the dining hall, sitting with a group of athletes, laughing and having a grand old time.

It must be the stress of finals week. She is safe and sound at Georgetown, going out with a new guy each weekend and partying all the time. She's not here. I've checked out her social media a few times. I would know if she had moved to Newton. She's dating some guy on the Georgetown tennis team and looks disgustingly happy.

And she's certainly not here for *me*. She made it brutally clear she didn't want to be with me anymore the night before I left for college. No, that relationship is dead and buried; there is no resuscitating it.

A familiar laugh carries across the room, and I almost drop my peanut butter sandwich. That sounds... it really does sound like her. And it looks like her.

But it can't be her.

Sam, my best friend's girlfriend, sets her hand on my arm. "Are you okay, honey?"

With a lump in my throat, I nod. "I'm fine."

"It's okay to not be okay, Tuck," she says quietly.

I crane my neck. Someone is sitting in between us now, so I can't see Mason's look-alike anymore. It's not like I'm going to go over there and *talk* to her. What would I say? You look like the ex-girlfriend I've been pining after for two and a half years? Talk about pathetic.

one

. . .

Tucker

I NEVER SAW the blitz coming. Winter break passed much too quickly. Before I'm ready for it, I was back on campus doing all of the things I don't want to do. Classes. Homework. Papers.

With football season over, it's time to buckle down and focus. I have two months of relative peace before spring ball starts up. It's just enough time to get into trouble. Good thing I'm taking a full course load and then some, working for a clinical study, and still finding time to work out with the team three times a week and lift weights another four times.

I am so fucking exhausted, and it's only the first week of the semester. I have to look to the future: to graduation, to grad school, to moving on with my life and making something of myself.

Thursday, January 12th starts out like any other day. I work out in the weights room with the rest of the defensive squad. Have breakfast in the dining hall with my five roommates and Sam, Miles's girlfriend, who likes to hang out with us. Go to my classes: anthropology, developmental psychology, and abnormal psychology. Grab lunch in the ASC. Study until it's time to meet with my clinical advisor.

The Social Skills Assessment Center is located on the fifth floor of the Humanities and Social Sciences building. It's a nondescript room in the middle of the psychology department, beige everything. The walls, the carpets, even the tables are beige.

I open the door and run smack into a smaller feminine body. I set out my hand to steady the person I've set off course and recoil in shock.

It's been two and a half years since I last saw Mason Prince in person. Two and a half years since she broke up with me in a text message. She didn't even have the decency to pick up the phone when she stomped all over my heart. She's supposed to be in DC. Why is she here in Boston??

"Hey, King," she says quietly, not looking at me. "I like the beard."

She looks the same and yet completely different. Her long, wavy, dark hair is natural and pulled back in a jaunty pony-tail. Her chocolate brown eyes are as rich as ever. Her brown skin glows with health. She's a looker; she always has been.

"Mason."

I hate the way my dick notices her supple curves. She's always been lithe, lean. At twenty, she's a fully grown woman, even more gorgeous than she was when I fell in love with her at fourteen.

She winces. "So you still hate me?"

"I don't hate you. That would require me to have any level of feelings for you." My words are as cold as the bitter stone that used to be my heart.

"I deserve that," she says, her eyes trained on my neck. I swallow thickly and her mouth drops open. Her pretty pink tongue comes out to wet her lips. My traitorous dick twitches in my jeans.

"Why are you here?"

"I go here now. I transferred to Newton."

What happened to Georgetown? She never gave me a real

reason for dumping me two days before I left for college, but I can't discount the distance between DC and Boston played a part.

"I go here now. I decided it was a better fit," she says.

Did she come here for me?

I don't know how I feel about that. I love her, I've loved her since I was too young to know better, but a part of me will always hate her for the half-life she cursed me into living. I don't need to drink unicorn's blood to be tethered to her, unable to properly move on. There are so many unanswered questions between us.

My heart hammers in my chest like I've just done ten laps around the field in full gear. "Why are you *here*?"

"It's good to see you."

"I can't say the same."

"King…"

"Don't call me that," I snap.

I can't let her make me remember the good times, when all she's done is condemn me to a lifetime of bad.

"I'm volunteering here," she says. "There are people here in need of help. I can help."

"You should leave."

"I just got here."

"No, you should leave Newton. Transfer somewhere else. Anywhere else."

She forces a laugh. "Surely we can share the same university. It's been two years."

And a half.

"Oh, good, you're both here," a voice says, and we both jump at the sight of Professor Alvarez, the director of the assessment center. "We can get started."

I chance a glance at Mason. She looks as confused as I feel. "Get started?"

"You two will be staffing the center on Monday and Wednesday afternoons," she says, like it's a given.

It's true that my afternoons are wide open. I don't have any classes scheduled those days. After our weight lifting session at seven and my morning classes, I'm free the rest of the day to review tape or get in a second workout. Or do my homework.

Mason gulps. Loudly. "The two of us?"

"Plus a few graduate students getting their hours in," Professor Alvarez continues agreeably.

The assessment center provides services to school-aged children, teenagers, and adults with and without diagnoses. It's open to the community, not just the university's students and faculty. It's mainly staffed by graduate students getting in clinical hours with a few undergraduate volunteers—like me—to do the boring work, like checking in clients, preparing their diagnostic paperwork, and doing any grunt work the grad students require.

Professor Alvarez shows us to our desks, two seats side by side, behind a wide reception desk. The online check-in system is easy enough to understand. The database is slightly more complicated.

"We'll go over the appointment system in depth later," Professor Alvarez says.

"Great," Mason says with a bright smile on her face. She's always been bubbly and cheerful, pulling me out of my dark funks when things got to be too much.

I wish it were anyone else in the world sitting beside me right now. I'd even take Tony O'Rourke, the big man on campus and resident bully who has never not once had a kind word for anyone ever, over being trapped in a small office with my ex-girlfriend. And now we're going to spend several hours a week together, every week. I'd rather have a prostate exam—without lube.

Every minute is excruciating, sitting here beside her, smelling her clean citrus soap and something else uniquely Mason. My traitorous eyes rove hungrily over her form. She's filled out a bit, her shape curvier than it was before. She's grown up. She's probably still running. I hope she's still running.

We're released after a quick two-hour orientation.

"Do you want to—"

"No." I want nothing she's offering.

Her face falls. "Right. Yeah."

I turn to go.

"See you tomorrow," she yells at my back.

I raise my middle finger in goodbye. I can hear her scoff behind me. I don't care.

I never wanted to see Mason Prince again. I never wanted to spend another moment in her presence. And now we're stuck together.

It's only five o'clock. There's plenty of time for me to hit the football gym across campus. I grab a new set of workout clothes from my locker and change before I can talk myself out of it. The gym is nearly deserted. There are two rookies deadlifting in the center of the room. I nod to them and head to the treadmill. At my size, I can't run very fast or very far without my knees and ankles protesting. Still, I set the machine to a punishing pace and prepare to get my ass handed to me.

She's here. She's at Newton.

Did she follow me here?

I never wanted to see her again. I never wanted to think about her ever again. I can't go down that road. Once that box is opened, I'll never be able to close it again. I loved her. She destroyed everything good about my life. Now all the memories of the best moments in my life are tainted.

She loved me, but she didn't love me enough to want to make it work.

My hips ache. My knees throb. My ankles sting. Still, I keep going, running through the pain. It reminds me that I'm alive. I have breath in my lungs. My heart beats a thousand beats a minute. I'm alive. I'm alive. I'm alive.

I can live without her. I've been doing just fine for the last two and a half years. I can survive with her being back in town. I can get through this. I let out a roar of—I don't know, triumph? Frustration?

"That's right, man," one of the rookies says. "You tell 'em."

I hit the five-mile mark, and the machine decides it's had enough of my brutal strides. It powers down into a cool down automatically. Hands on my hips, I try to catch my breath. I don't feel better.

But I don't feel worse, and sometimes, that has to be enough.

two

. . .

Tucker

THE GUYS ARE SITTING at our usual table in the back of the dining hall when I roll up. I take my usual seat with a grunt. Maybe a five-mile run with no warm-up wasn't the best idea.

"Oh, honey," Sam says, her small hand on my arm. "Are you okay?"

"I'm fine."

"Okay." She looks me over, then my plate. "If you want to talk, I'm here for you."

"Thanks, but I'm fine. Nothing to talk about."

My plate is laden with three servings of spaghetti and meat sauce and two portions of garlic bread. No vegetables, no salad. I'm not interested in health today. I don't care if the school nutritionist yells at me for ditching my macros. My whole world is falling apart at the seams. I can eat a little bit of pasta if I want to.

The guys talk around me. Well, Amir, Greg, and Barrett talk. Wes reads his book. Miles and Sam play footsie under the table, lost in each other's eyes. It should be sickening. It's not.

I miss the days when Mason and I used to be like that. We

had the world at our fingertips, our whole life ahead of us. And she decided going to frat parties and hooking up with strangers was more important than our life together. So, no, I don't miss her. I miss the idea of what we had, the lie I believed.

I need a peanut butter sandwich. That will make everything better. I push back my seat, and Sam scrambles to her feet.

"I want ice cream," she announces loudly. "You coming with me?"

I don't trust my voice, so I nod. She wraps her arm around my elbow and leads me through the dining hall.

"What are you in the mood for?"

Wordlessly, I point to the sandwich bar. She looks up at me with such innocence in her eyes. So trusting.

"You can talk to me, you know," she says, manhandling me. I let her drag me through the different food stations. People are probably staring, this curvy softball player pulling a giant football player behind her. I don't care. "I'm here for you."

"No, you're not."

Sam rolls her eyes. "Just because I'm dating Miles doesn't mean you and I aren't friends, Tuck."

I grunt, spreading peanut butter over a slice of bread.

"Just think about it," she says, making her own sandwich with the chunky nectar of the gods. This confuses me.

"You don't like peanut butter."

"No, I don't, but I know someone else who does," she says. Her eyes drift over to our table, and a sappy smile takes over her face.

"So you two… you're good?"

"We're solid," she says, smooshing together the two halves of her sandwich and grimacing. "This is so gross. How do you like this?"

I take a bite of my sandwich and nearly groan. It's good. It's so good.

"Come on, big guy," she says, wrapping her hand around my elbow again. "I still want ice cream."

We're standing at the soft serve station when I see her. Mason. She's eating alone, her headphones on and a thick textbook open in front of her. Her lips move as she reads to herself. Her makeup is natural, emphasizing her rich brown eyes and sharp cheekbones, her high forehead and prominent nose and mouth. She looks more and more like her Korean-American grandmother every day. Mrs. Prince could have been a beauty queen if people weren't so racist and hadn't barred her entry.

She must be part of the track team if she's in the student athlete dining hall. She probably got a scholarship—she's brilliant, yeah, and she's an even better sprinter. I wonder how long she's been here. I wonder if she's made friends.

I wonder why I still care about her.

"You like her?" Sam nods towards Mason. "You should talk to her."

"Can't."

"Come on. You're allowed to date. You're allowed to—"

"Can't," I say again. "Ex." The words get caught in my throat. "Ex-girlfriend."

Her face falls, her eyebrows knitting together as she processes this. "I thought you didn't date."

"I don't."

"Because of her," Sam says slowly.

I nod. My shameful secret is out. The gorgeous woman across the room completely destroyed me. It's been two and a half years, and I still can't tape up the battered and bruised shards of my broken heart.

"I'm going to beat her up," she declares. She puts down her soft serve and pushes up the sleeves of her sweatshirt, an enormous Newton Football thing she stole from Miles. "She's going down."

"Easy there, Cujo." I set my hand on her shoulder and press until she calms down. "I'm a big boy. I can fight my own battles."

Sam sniffs. Right there, in the middle of the cafeteria, she wraps her arms around me and burrows into my chest.

"You're a good man, Tucker Kingsley," she says, emotion clouding her voice.

"You're all right, I guess."

She laughs, looking up at me, her chin on my sternum. "So this girl… should I tell the softball team to make her life hell?"

I want to say yes. I want to give in to that selfish desire to hurt her as much as she hurt me.

But I can't sink to her level.

"Leave her alone."

She nods. "If you change your mind…"

I won't. I can't let myself sink to her level.

Mason looks up as we pass her table. Her mouth drops open at the sight of Sam and me wrapped up together. A look of hurt crosses her face before she quickly blinks it away.

We take our seats again. Miles quirks an eyebrow at the two of us. I'm not generally a touchy-feely kind of guy, and I would never make a move on my best friend's girl.

"I hate her," Sam announces to the table at large.

"You don't even know her," I remind her, taking another big bite of my sandwich. The peanut butter clogs my throat and soothes my soul in a way my spaghetti couldn't. Damn it. I should have made two.

"I know enough."

"You really don't."

"So talk to me. Tell me."

And we're back to this again. I make a face, and she

laughs. She wraps her arm around my elbow and rests her head on my shoulder.

Sam has only been a part of our social circle for a few months, but she's weaseled her way in good. We couldn't get rid of her even if we wanted to. She's good for Miles, yes, but she's good for the rest of us, too. She's brought some much-needed light into our dark house of socially awkward introverts.

"Let's go back to the house and watch the new superhero movie," she suggests.

"Can't. Homework."

Miles rolls his eyes. "It's the first week of school."

"Yeah, and I'm already behind." Especially if I have to spend two days a week in hell instead of studying.

"You're not going to get out of talking to me," she warns.

I'll take that bet. Her puppy dog eyes don't work on me.

three

. . .

Mason

I'M A CONFIDENT, capable woman, comfortable in my own skin. I can do anything I set my mind to. Except, perhaps, reunite with my ex-boyfriend.

I thought transferring to Newton would… I don't know. I didn't expect Tucker to fall into my arms at the first sight of me. But I didn't expect to spend the first semester ducking and running from him all over campus, scared of my own shadow. Transferring universities isn't for the faint of heart, and I thought I knew what I was doing when I left my safe, comfortable school for the scary and unknown of Tucker's school to try to win him back. And yet I spent the first four and a half months on campus losing my nerve every time I saw him.

King looks good. He's grown at least two inches and put on at least fifteen pounds of solid muscle since I saw him last. College has been good for him. Whereas before he was a lanky, overweight teen trying to figure out his place, he's grown into a man who knows who he is and what he wants.

And what he wants isn't me.

I can't get that blonde out of my head. The way she

wrapped herself around him. The way she rested her head on his shoulder. Playing footsie beneath the table.

He must really love her.

I never thought he would go for a blonde. Definitely not a white girl. His mothers are probably happy. I guess I didn't know him as well as I thought.

I lie in my bed and wish he were there with me. I walk through this campus, still unfamiliar to me even after a full semester, and wish he were beside me.

And now he'll be sitting next to me, four hours a day, twice a week, from now until the end of term. I wish that made me feel excited. Instead, I just feel dread.

While I've had my share of boyfriends in the two and a half years since we broke up, I don't mind being single. I have enough shitty exes in the rearview mirror that I'm not interested in starting anything new right now. Especially when the only guy I can think about is standing right in front of me.

Tucker hangs his coat on the rack beside the door. I can't think of him as my King anymore, it hurts too much. He's wearing a worn Newton Football hoodie and dark jeans that make his ass look amazing. A few flakes of snow linger on the back of his neck, bright and white against his dark skin. He bats them away with one of his enormous hands.

Everything about him is enormous in the best possible ways. He's tall and wide, which makes him a successful defensive tackle on the football field. His heart is nearly as big as he is. He is the personification of the heart eyes emoji, and I've got hearts in my eyes whenever I see him.

Even if he has a pretty blonde girlfriend now.

I've caught glimpses of him on campus and in the ASC. I didn't realize they were dating. He's always with the same group of five guys. I've seen the blonde with them a few times. I went to all of his home games last season. I've been cheering him on, even if he hates me.

I want Tucker Kingsley. I want his smiles and his laughter

and his stupid corny jokes. I want to bask in the warm glow of his affection.

But he hates me now. I've thoroughly burned that bridge. I didn't just burn it; I demolished it with dynamite. There is no bridge remaining.

We sit side by side at the reception desk and don't talk. When clients come in, he greets them with a warmly polite smile and helps them sign in. In the downtime—and there is a *lot* of downtime—he makes notes in his sociology textbook. I don't think he realizes we're in the same course. He sits towards the front on the left side by the door and I like sitting in the back, where I can see the whole classroom.

"Do you have any fun plans for your weekend?"

He grunts, which I suppose is better than silence.

"I have a track meet tomorrow."

He doesn't acknowledge me.

It's only my third meet of the season. We had two low stakes meets right before we went home for winter break. Tomorrow will be the first true test of my abilities. I have to prove they didn't make a mistake in allowing me to transfer.

I liked Georgetown. It was good for me. I was close to my parents' houses in suburban DC, surrounded by the people I knew growing up. But I never really felt at home there. Their psychology department is middle of the pack. Newton had the holy trifecta of a good coach, good academics... and King.

That he doesn't want me isn't the end of the world. I'll get over him and move on. I'll run my heart out. I'll get into a top-ranked grad school, preferably at Newton, which has always been my top choice for a Marriage and Family Therapy program. I won't look back.

Micah texts me around two o'clock. I see the wall of text he's sent me and immediately groan. My twin only writes essays like that when he's really worked up.

"I'm going to take my break now."

Tucker grunts. How charming. Why am I in love with him

again? Even when he treats me like shit on the bottom of his shoe, I can't help that sick need inside of me to catch his attention, to make him smile. He's all I've ever wanted, even when I was confused and overwhelmed.

Sitting on the bench in the hallway, I call my brother.

"What's wrong?"

"I think I fucked up."

"You didn't fuck up."

"No, I really put my foot in it this time," he says. "Mase, I'm failing."

"You're not failing. You just won your bowl game."

"No, I mean, I'm *failing*. I'm flunking out of school."

I laugh. "Mic, it's the first week of the semester. You haven't passed the drop deadline yet, you can still get out of your troublesome classes. You aren't failing."

He's quiet. "If I don't get my GPA up, I won't be eligible next season."

"It's a good thing you aren't playing next season." Micah wants to declare for the draft next month. He can do it. He's one of the top five ranked running backs in his conference. He could be selected in the second round or in the middle of the third round.

He coughs. "I might have sprained my ankle."

"Micah."

"It's just a sprain! I slipped on some black ice. I'm fine. But I can't train the way I need to right now. And if I don't train…"

My heart aches for him even as my brain spurs into motion.

"What happens if you don't declare?"

"Then I come back for fall term and play a final season." He sighs. "Provided my grades stay up. I don't know that I want to do that. I really think this could be my year, Mase."

My heart is in my throat. "What classes do you need help with?"

He laughs. "Like, all of them."

"Mic…"

"I can drop my stats class and add in another kinesiology class, but then I won't be on track to graduate," he says. And it will kill our mother if he doesn't graduate on time. If he goes into the NFL, he has a good reason not to finish his degree right away. If he doesn't… he's going to need that expensive piece of paper to get a job next spring.

We both know Micah is in school to major in football and girls. He's way more slutty than I am. He parties far more than I do. The education he's supposedly receiving is just a side benefit. He's an amazing football player, and he's destined for the next level.

"I don't know how much I can do from here," I start slowly. "I'm taking statistics this semester, too, so I can try to tutor you, but we both know it won't be that easy. Math has never been my friend."

He lets out a heavy sigh. "I know. This is on me."

"I'll help you however I can," I promise. "You need to talk to me. You and me, we're a team. We can get you through this."

"I don't know that even you can get me through it," he says, and my heart breaks at the frustration in his voice. "I'm failing, Mase. I've never failed anything before. Not one damn test."

"How did this happen?"

His laugh is bitter. "I'm not like you. School isn't easy for me."

"No, but you've always done fine before. This isn't like you."

"I was fine last semester. I was *fine*." His voice breaks. "I can't handle this, sunshine. I need help."

"I'll help you any way that I can." I'll do anything for him. He's my twin brother, my other half. If he needs help, I'll help him, because that's what you do for family.

"But you're not here. How can you help when you're all the way in—" He cuts off with a heavy sigh. "I don't know. I just don't know."

"Take a deep breath."

He does.

"Okay, so we're going to talk this out. We're going to come up with a plan," I tell him. "We'll get you a tutor if you need it. You'll drop this impossible class and sign up for something else before the deadline. We'll make this work, Mic. You've got this. We can do this."

four

. . .

Tucker

I DON'T KNOW why I'm here. The indoor track's bleachers are sparsely populated. I probably stick out like a sore thumb. I don't want to be here, and yet, I couldn't stay away. I don't know why.

That's a lie. I know why. Mason. It all comes back to her. At least I dragged Barrett with me so I don't have to be here all alone.

Barely anyone has shown up to the first track meet of the calendar year. That rankles. The stands are packed at football games even when our middle of the pack team plays poorly. They should have just as many supporters here as we do. They work ten times harder than we do on the field. And it's indoors! They aren't even sitting out in the cold and the snow! Why are more people not here?

Barrett sits beside me, no doubt texting with Diana. How they make their friendship work long distance, I'm not sure, because all of mine have fallen by the wayside. I haven't talked to my ex-best friend, Micah Prince, since the breakup. We grew up together, we were inseparable from the day we met. Now all of that has fallen by the wayside. On my few breaks at home in DC, I don't hang out with the kids I grew up with. I stick close to the house with my two moms and spend as much time with them as I can. Sometimes my brother comes home. Sometimes we go to him.

Jamal is moving on to bigger and better things. He's a rookie in the NBA, riding the bench more than anything else, but still—he made it. He's living his dream. He paid off our moms' house and cut a check for the balance of my tuition, the half my athletic scholarship doesn't cover. The same half I've had to take out loans to pay for, because my moms are cash strapped enough to worry about my school fees on top of everything else they've done for me.

I'll never make it to the NFL. That's not my dream anymore. I have one more season of football left in me. After that, I have goals, ambitions. My feet are firmly planted on the ground. I want to go to grad school and become the best damn addiction counselor there is, so other people don't have to go through what my family's been through. I may not make the kind of outrageous money that my brother could, but my life will have a purpose. I'll have a cause to work for.

Mason's race is announced on the tinny loudspeakers. I chew the inside of my cheek as she takes her place on the blocks. The 200 meter is her jam. She's got this.

The gun pops, and she's off, running, running, running her heart out. She crosses the finish line first, another woman from Newton half a stride behind her.

The blonde beside her gives her a high-five, her smile stretched wide. She looks familiar. I must have had a class with her before.

Mason is smiling, breathing hard. She takes a drink from her water bottle. Her hands on her hips highlight her lithe form, all muscle and sinew.

Barrett nudges me. "You have an admirer."

Mason is staring right at me. There's a lump in my throat I can't clear. Her eyes are wide. She lifts her hand in a stilted wave and then crosses her arms over her chest.

This was a mistake. I shouldn't be here.

"I need to go." I shoulder my bag and head for the stairs.

"Hey!" Barrett falls into step beside me. "Want to tell me what this is about?"

"Not really, no."

"Asshole."

I force a laugh. "That's not new."

"I thought we were here for the chick."

"We're not."

"Could have fooled me."

"I wanted to go to the track meet."

"And that's why we're leaving half an hour in?"

"I've got shit to do today."

He laughs, but he's not mocking me. "Yeah, okay."

I don't have the energy to make it all the way across campus to the dining hall, but there's a grab and go food station at the track team's practice facility. I badge in with my student athlete ID and grab some snacks. The selection is lacking. Chalky protein bars, popcorn, electrolyte tablets. In the warmer, I spy one lone breakfast burrito. I get to it before Barrett can.

"Are you sure you don't want to go back to the meet?" He looks at me with concern in his eyes. I don't like it.

I unwrap the burrito and take a big bite. It's lukewarm. It's not a peanut butter sandwich. I don't care.

We stand there in silence as I devour the burrito. It isn't even good. My stomach rumbles unpleasantly, protesting my less than stellar decision making. I eat the last bite and lick my fingers.

"You feeling better?" Barrett asks. There's a furrow between his brows.

"I'm fine," I tell him, which is a flat out lie. He doesn't call me on it.

"Do you want to go back to the track meet?"

Not really. I don't want to see Mason. I want absolutely nothing to do with her.

But for some reason, what comes out of my mouth is: "Sure."

He claps me on the shoulder. "It'll be good for you. Put some hair on your chest."

"Fucker." I don't have a problem with that. If anything, I have too much hair; I have to shave it off every week, and still it keeps growing right back in. Whoever my biological father was, he must have been a beast.

Barrett grins. "So we're going back?"

"I hate you."

"You love me, asshole," he says. He turns and heads back towards the indoor track arena.

"You're alright."

We're able to retake our previous seats. There is still barely anyone around. Mostly parents, it looks like. Very few students.

On the field, Blondie nudges Mason, pointing up at us. I look away, focusing on the long jump for several minutes. When Barrett coughs, I turn back to the field. Mason is still looking at me.

It's like the entire world stands still. I lose track of time. I'm lost in her eyes. Even from a distance, I know their rich chocolate brown color like the back of my hand. Her full lips curve into a smile. My traitorous heart skips a beat, and my stomach lurches. It isn't solely because of the questionable burrito.

I love her. I don't want to, but I still love her.

She's the reason I haven't dated. Nobody catches my interest like she does. Nobody makes me sit up and take notice the way she does. Not even the slip up, the indiscretion in my freshman year, can hold a candle to her.

I don't date. I don't hook up. I've slept with exactly two women in my life. The first, the only one that matters, was

Mason. The second was a drunken fumble of a hookup the week after the breakup. It was awful for both of us. I haven't exactly been hurrying back into the dating pool.

Amir, Barrett, and Greg go out and hook up occasionally, and Miles is constantly getting laid with his new girlfriend. Wes is purposefully celibate. From what I've been able to piece together, he isn't a virgin, but he has no interest in having sex with the willing co-eds who like to throw themselves at football players. He doesn't abstain for any religious reason. He's just not interested, and I can respect that.

I've only been sexually attracted to one woman in my life —Mason. Porn can get me going, but I still drift off to memories of her, of us. And there are a lot of memories. We had some good times. We were together for more than three and a half years, and once we started getting physical, neither of us were shy. I knew the soft contours of her body nearly as well as I know mine.

Up until recently, I had friends to hang out with on a Saturday night if some of the guys went out partying. Now Miles is busy with Sam, which—good for him. He deserves to be happy. Wes is more interested in his books than in watching a movie with me. And the rest of the guys flutter in and out as the mood strikes them.

I'm lonely. Sitting next to Barrett, one of my best friends, the person who knows me better than almost anyone, I've never felt more alone. I miss Mason. Even though it's been two and a half years. Even though she dumped me to go sow her wild oats. Even still. I still love her. I still want her to be in my life. I just don't want to get hurt again. I don't think I can survive another hurt like that one again.

five

. . .

Tucker

I SMELL the bright citrus of her perfume before I hear her. A glimmer of foreboding runs up my spine. My back is to the rest of the dining hall as the guys and I focus on our dinner before an epic Saturday night of sitting on the couch and playing video games.

"Hey, King," Mason's voice says quietly.

I don't turn around.

Barrett and Amir titter to themselves. Greg coughs. Miles's eyebrows go up, doubt creasing his face.

Sam sets her hand on my arm, squeezing gently. "Tucker."

I hear Mason shuffle her feet. She always does that when she's nervous.

"We should talk," she says.

"I have nothing to say to you."

"I deserve that, I do," she says. "But I would really appreciate it if you would listen."

"I'd rather not, thanks."

"King."

Still, I don't turn around. "Don't call me that. You're not my Princess anymore. I'm not your King. I'm nothing to you."

"Tucker, please." Her voice breaks. "I need to talk to you."

Amir and Miles are intrigued. Wes lowers his book.

Sam's hand moves from my forearm to my hand, where I'm clutching my fork so tightly my knuckles have turned white. Mechanically, she pries my fingers off the utensil.

"Just hear her out," she says quietly.

"I don't want to."

"We all have to do things we don't want to sometimes, Tuck," Sam says. She folds her fingers around mine. "We're here for you. I'm here for you. I love you."

Dread swells in my gut. I don't want to do this. We're done. It's over. I want nothing to do with her.

But I've never been able to say no to her.

Shoving back my chair, I turn and face Mason. Her full lips are pinched down in a frown. Her gorgeous eyes are red, bloodshot.

"Not here."

She nods. I grab my coat off the back of my chair and stalk out of the dining hall. The lobby is too crowded. I lead her outside, where the January wind is punishingly cold.

Good. I need to feel something. Anything other than apathy.

"King..."

I cross my arms over my chest. "Don't call me that."

She sighs. "Tucker..."

"I'm not hearing a lot of talking. You wanted to talk. So talk."

I'm being abrasive, a total asshole. I can't make myself care. She destroyed everything good about my life.

Mason swallows, her eyes bright. "You came to my track meet today."

"I go to events on campus."

That's a lie. I don't do anything that isn't officially mandatory. I don't go to parties. I don't go to basketball games. I stay at home with my roommates and play video games and masturbate to the memory of her.

Her face falls. "I thought you showing up meant... I don't know, maybe I'm reading too much into it."

"You are."

"But you came."

"I didn't do it for you."

Lies. Lies. Lies. I'd do anything for her, including sacrificing my own happiness to make her smile. Just for a moment. That's all I want.

She clears her throat. "Your girlfriend is pretty."

"I don't have a girlfriend." I work hard to keep all emotion out of my voice. I've never wanted a girlfriend. I just wanted her.

Her eyebrows go up. "The white girl that was all over you two minutes ago."

"That's Sam."

"And you're not...?"

I laugh. It's cold and bitter, much like the remnants of my heart after she stomped all over it. "She's dating my roommate."

She lets out a sigh of—relief? I don't know why she's relieved.

"Good. I'm glad."

"You're glad that my friend has a girlfriend?"

"I'm glad that you don't." Her chin tips up. "I was hoping that we could... I don't know."

"There is no *we*. There is no *us*."

She takes a step towards me. "But there could be."

I move back. "No, there can't."

"You really hate me that much?"

"I don't feel anything for you, Princess."

Shit. There I go, calling her by her pet name. The name that was only mine to bestow upon her. Her last name is

Prince. My last name is Kingsley. Together we're a King and a Princess. She should be a Queen—she was always the one ruling my heart. A match made in heaven.

Or in hell.

Her eyes light up at my slip up. "King..."

"I think we're done talking," I tell her.

"I miss you," she blurts.

"I don't care."

Lies. I care a whole hell of a lot.

But I can't open myself up to her again. I can't allow her to hurt me again. I might not survive it this time.

Her face falls. "So we can't..."

"There is no *we*," I repeat.

"I thought maybe we could be friends."

"We've never been friends, Mason."

Damn, even her name on my lips feels good. A warm glow spreads through me, warming my insides despite the brutal cold we're standing in.

"Maybe we should be." She takes another step towards me, her stride purposeful. I'm pushed back against the handrail. I have nowhere to go. "I've been here since August. I could use a friend."

"You don't want to be my friend."

"You're right, I don't," she says. "I'll take what I can get. We have a history, Tuck. I can't erase that. But we can start over. Two kids from DC all alone in the big city."

"Newton is hardly—"

"We grew up together," she reminds me, as if I'm not well aware. "I know you, even if you don't want to admit it."

I don't.

"We're working together. We have a class together. It would be nice if we could get along with a cessation of hostilities."

"I don't know what you're talking about."

She rolls her eyes. "Yeah, you do."

I want to pull her into my arms and kiss away her frown. I want to wrap her up in my arms and never let her go. I want the last two and a half years to have never happened.

I can't always get what I want.

"We can be friends again," she says quietly. "We should be friends again. I know what I did—"

My defenses slam back into place. "I don't want to talk about that."

"I hurt you."

That's an understatement. She devastated me. I thought we were going to spend the rest of our lives together. And instead, she wanted the freedom to fuck other guys.

"I'm sorry for that," she says for the first time ever. "I'm sorry I hurt you. I'd take it back if I could. But we would never have survived the distance."

"You don't know that." My voice cracks. "You don't know that we couldn't have survived it."

"We were too young," she says. "The distance would have poisoned everything good about us. We got to grow up a little. We weren't shackled down to—"

A sharp intake of breath. "Is that what I was to you? A shackle?"

She winces. "No. No, Tuck, you were—you were great. I was holding you back."

She really wasn't. All I ever wanted was her.

"You're a football player."

"So?"

"So I bet you're beating off girls with a stick. You're the big man on campus. Everyone wants a piece of you."

I laugh. "Mason, I've been with exactly one girl, one time since you. I don't hook up. I don't go out. I don't do anything. Nobody wants a piece of me. Nobody wants me. I'm damaged goods, sunshine. You ruined me."

Her eyes are wide, unblinking. "But—"

"You destroyed me." My breath is coming in sharp bursts

now. Adrenaline ricochets through my veins, pushing me forward. I tower over her. "You broke a piece of me I didn't think would ever break. I loved you. All I wanted was to be with you. And you threw me away. To go fuck frat guys and live the life you always wanted, shackle free. So, no, Mason, we can't be friends. I want nothing to do with you."

six

. . .

Mason

I THOUGHT I was doing the right thing. I thought I was setting him free. Instead, I condemned him to a lifetime of unhappiness.

"King..."

He flinches. "Just leave me alone. We'll work at the assessment center and we'll just... coexist."

"If... if that's what you want."

"It is." His voice breaks. Anguish twists his features.

He doesn't want this.

I nod and clear my throat. "Right. Well, have a nice life."

I take a step backwards. He takes a step towards me. Before I can so much as blink, his hands cup my cheeks, and his lips are on mine.

Electricity sends shockwaves through my veins. I move to wrap my arms around him, and he groans, tugging my body into his. He's big and solid against me. His gloved fingers tangle in my loose braid as he deepens the kiss, taking, taking. His tongue strokes into my mouth. I shudder, and it's not just from the cold.

He might hate me, he might think I'm the worst person in

the history of the world, but there's no getting around the spark between us. A part of him still wants me.

Even if he hates himself for it.

With a sharp inhalation, he releases me. He takes a step back and tucks his hands in his pockets. He's breathing hard, his dark cheeks a dull rusty color.

"Tuck…"

"I need to go."

"But—"

He hurries down the stairs. I debate calling after him. I debate chasing him, making him talk to me.

The door slams open behind me, shattering the moment. People pour out of the ASC, laughing, like my entire world didn't just implode. Tucker Kingsley may not like me, but a part of him still wants me.

Fred is waiting for me in the lobby. She frowns as I make my way back inside.

"So it went well?"

"I'm really not sure."

She sighs. "It will work out. Or it won't. Want to go get drunk?"

I laugh and thread my arm through hers. "Yes, please."

Saturday nights have a routine. My roommates and I get dressed up and go out on the town, as much as we can in a sleepy college town. Usually, that means we hit up a frat party. All night long, I watch the door, waiting for King to walk in. He's a football player, one of the best on the team. They should be dousing him in beer and showing him a good time.

I've never seen him at a frat party, not once. He used to be the life of the party. Everyone noticed when he walked in. He's a magnet for attention, for trouble. He's a hell of a good time.

Maybe transferring to the same university as my ex-boyfriend to try to win him back was a bad idea. I don't have the freedom to stretch my wings here. I've been biding my time until our paths cross again. And now they have, and now I'm getting all sorts of mixed signals from him.

He hates me. He shows up to my track meet. He tells me he wants nothing to do with me. He kisses me.

I don't think that he knows what he wants.

I want his attention. His affection. His smiles. A little piece of me is still in love with him. Maybe it's a bigger part of me than I thought.

I need to get drunk.

Back at our place in Athlete's Village, Fred, Melissa, and I get dressed for a night out. We might pregame a bit. I'm still riding the high of the kiss and the meet. I came in first in the 200-meter and second in my other two events. Not bad for my first real meet as a member of the Newton Wolfpack. I'll prove to the coaching staff that they didn't make a mistake in allowing me to transfer.

The Delta frat party is the same as it usually is. Too many people packed into too small a space. Shitty music blares from the speakers.

Fred hands me a drink. "He's not going to show up."

"He will."

"He bolted," she reminds me. "He's never come to one of these things before. Why is tonight the night?"

It just is. I can feel it in my bones.

Sullivan, one of the safeties on the football team, bobs his way over to us.

"Ladies."

"Hey, Sully," Fred says, giving him heart eyes.

He gets the hint. He blatantly checks her out, the tight, low-cut shirt and the form-fitting leggings that leave nothing to the imagination. They've been circling around each other for months. It's only a matter of time.

"You want to dance?"

"Sure." Fred pauses to check on me. "You'll be okay?"

"Go, go, dance, have fun," I urge them. "I'm fine."

Sullivan laughs and takes her by the hand, pulling her into the throng of people grinding on the makeshift dance floor. I take a sip of my drink and make my way through the party. There's a group of guys playing video games in the den. The guy on the right, with the caveman beard and man bun, looks me over with interest. I think he's one of Tuck's friends. I pause in the doorway with a group of other girls watching the show.

"Play for me," he says, thrusting the controller into another guy's chest. He lumbers to his feet and makes his way over to us.

"I need to talk to you," he says, his voice a deep, rumbly burr.

The girls titter and giggle.

The giant nods his head towards the hallway. He's tall, about as tall as King, and equally wide. Probably another defensive player. He spent most of his time in high school hanging out with the rest of the defensive squadron if he wasn't with me and Micah.

"I'm Greg," he says, offering me his hand.

Surprised, I take it. His palm is warm and calloused.

"Mason."

"You and Tucker…"

I wince. "So he's mentioned me?"

"Never. Not once." He watches me carefully, his green eyes thoughtful. "Whatever happened between you, it really messed him up. He doesn't party, doesn't hook up. He exists. He survives the day-to-day. He doesn't *live*."

"We didn't work out. It was a matter of timing."

He holds up a hand. "You don't need to explain it to me. All I'm saying is, you hurt him. And I don't know that you suddenly waltzing back into his life is good for him."

"What about what's good for me?"

"I don't care about you," he says bluntly. "I care about

him. We've spilled blood and sweat together the last two and a half years. He's a good guy. And if you're just going to screw him over—"

"I'm not."

"I don't trust you."

"I loved him. He was my everything."

He hums. "And that's why you dumped him."

"I did what I thought was right at the time." Now I wish I never had. "Is he… upset?"

"He's messed up," Greg says flatly. "You need to take a real hard look at yourself and decide what you want from him. Don't mess him around. He's a good guy. If you don't want him, let him find closure on his own. He needs it."

I don't know what I want. I just want him.

"Thank you for looking out for him." My voice breaks. "He needs someone to—"

"He's my friend," he says. His eyes soften and he clears his throat. "For what it's worth, I think he really loved you."

"I really loved him, too."

He nods. "That's it. I've said my piece. Go on, frolic, be merry."

I laugh. "Can I get you a drink?" It's the least I can do.

"I'm fine, thank you," he says. He waves me away. "Go back to the party."

He pushes past me, back to the video game room. The girls separate for him to pass through, giggling.

I used to be like them. I used to titter and giggle when a hot guy paid me attention. I used to gather outside with my friends, waiting to be beckoned in. Waiting to be selected.

Now I make my own decisions.

Draining my cup, I head back over to the keg. The guys surrounding it make room for me, pushing me to the front of the line. The frat brother in charge of the keg fills my cup for me with a wink.

"Thanks."

"Anytime, sweetheart." His eyes scrub over me. I should feel flattered. Instead I just feel dirty.

I want my King. I want the guy I used to know, the one who would bring me a cup of tea or rub my calves when I got cramps. The guy who used to love me so openly, so freely, that he couldn't imagine a time when we weren't together. The guy who built a future for us, something we could both believe in.

The guy I destroyed.

Oh, look, my cup is empty again. I wonder how that happened.

There are a bunch of guys doing shots in the kitchen. A few guys from the track team, a few basketball players. Mark nods at me and offers me a shot. It's a dark amber color, cheap, and probably disgusting.

I chug it without hesitation. It burns all the way down.

"Get it, girl," Mark says.

I hold the Dixie cup out. "More, please."

"Slow down, there's no rush," he laughs. He refills the cup.

"I know what I'm doing." I down the shot again and hold my cup out for a third pour. I know exactly what I'm doing.

seven

. . .

Tucker

MY PHONE RINGS a little past two o'clock in the morning, waking me from a dead sleep. I normally wouldn't answer. Nothing good happens after midnight. Mason's name flashes over the display, and I scramble to accept the call.

"Hello?"

"I fucked up."

"Mason?"

"I messed up. I never should have—" She hiccups. "Never should have—"

"Princess, where are you?"

"I came to the Delta party to see you. And you're not heeeeere."

She's drunk.

"You know I don't go to those types of parties."

"I want to see you."

"That's not a good idea right now, sunshine." I clench the phone in my fist so tight the case creaks. Less than twenty-four hours after I saw her, I've already kissed her and called her by the nickname that was only mine to give her. She's going to drag me back into a history I don't want to repeat. "Where are you?"

"I miss you." She sniffs. "I made a mistake."

I shove my feet into shoes and grab my coat off the floor. "No, you didn't, sweetheart."

"I did. I never should have—" She breaks off abruptly, gagging. "King, I don't feel well."

"Just hang on, Princess. I'm on my way."

The living room is empty. My roommates all turned in shortly after midnight, when we wrapped up our Star Wars mini marathon. I can hear moans and rhythmic thumping of the headboard coming from the direction of Miles's room. No surprise what he and Sam are up to.

It's bitterly cold out. I huddle into my coat, holding my phone to my ear.

"King..."

"Hang tight, Mase."

She gives a pitiful moan. "I miss you."

"I know you do."

I won't admit I miss her, too. I can't. But I do. I miss her infectious laugh and her bubbly personality. I even miss the way she used to press her freezing cold toes against my legs in the middle of the night. I miss everything about her.

The Delta house is lit with Christmas lights that stay up year round. I've been here exactly once for a party my freshman year. I didn't have a good time then. Probably won't now, either.

"Where are you, Princess?"

"I'm fine."

"You're not fine."

The crowds are thin at this time of night. Most everyone has found a partner for the evening and gone home to get their freak on. I make my way through the party.

Sullivan's eyes go wide when he sees me. "Kingsley! Didn't think I'd catch you here."

"You didn't."

"I'm pretty sure you're here."

"I'm looking for someone."

He laughs, shakes his head. "Man, aren't we all?"

I push past him and move to the kitchen. There are a group of guys doing shots at the kitchen island.

And then I see her. She's slumped over the table, her phone pressed to her ear.

"Mason."

She gives a feeble moan. "Dude, I'm not interested. Leave me alone."

"Princess..."

She looks up. Her eyes go wide. "You're here." She looks down at her phone screen. "Did you teleport?"

I huff out a laugh. "No, sunshine."

She's a little green. "I don't feel so good."

"Let's get you home, Mase."

"Okay." She gets to her feet and stumbles. I swoop forward, catching her before she can topple over outright. Dropping my shoulder, I drape her arm over my back. She's tiny. I could pick her up and carry her. "I'm so tired."

"Where's your house? Do you live in Athlete's Village?"

"I live that way." She flings her arm out and slaps me in the chest. She giggles.

"Okay, Princess. Let's get you home."

If I can't figure out where she lives, I'll just have to take her home with me. I'll set her up on the couch with a puke bucket. She's not going to feel so great in the morning.

Sullivan lets out a catcall at the sight of us. He has a girl under each arm, both pawing at his chest like he's amazing and not a mediocre safety who can't manage a tackle half the time. I flip him off and tighten my grip around her waist. She's so small. I'm afraid I'm going to snap her in half.

We stumble outside. Getting down the stairs is tricky. She leans into me, shivering.

Shit. Her coat. I don't know if she came in wearing one. I

don't know what it looks like. It's below-freezing out. She'll get hypothermia and die, and it will be all my fault.

I slip out of my jacket and drape it around her shoulders. She sighs and snuggles in, zipping it up on the second try. She's practically drowning in it. I'm a good nine inches taller than her and more than double her weight. The coat looks more like a dress.

"You good, sunshine?"

She gives me a happy smile. Her eyes are glassy. She's so far gone.

"I'm fantastic."

Wrapping my arm around her, we begin the laborious mile-and-a-half walk home. I should be cold in just a thin hoodie. Instead, I'm sweating. Simply being near her has me hot and bothered.

She snuggles into my side. "Mm. I missed you."

"I'm sure you did."

She can't pick up the sarcasm in my voice.

I hate this. I hate her. I hate that she can still make me do stupid things like run into a frat party to rescue her. I hate that I go so willingly. I hate that the sound of her voice, plaintive and pleading, can convince me to do pretty much anything she asks.

But mostly I hate that even after everything she's done, all the pain that she's caused me, I don't hate her at all.

My heart thumps at being so close to her. My skin prickles with awareness wherever she touches me. She's half out of her mind and drunk off her ass, and still I want to wrap her up in my arms and never let her go.

There's no way I'm letting her sleep on the uncomfortable couch all by herself tonight.

Helping her up the stairs, we stumble into my room. She lets out a groan that goes straight to my cock, and stumbles towards the bed. She collapses onto it and sighs in relief.

"Let's get your shoes off, Princess." She's wearing tall

boots that zip up to her knee. I drag the tiny tab down her leg and she twitches, giggling.

"That tickles."

I get the first shoe off. The second goes easier. She scrambles for the covers, pulling them up over her chest.

"You okay, girl?"

She sighs. "Love you, King."

I freeze. She can't mean that. She's drunk. She doesn't mean that.

Sighing, I toe off my shoes and lift the covers. "Budge over."

She scoots closer to the wall. I slide in beside her, and she immediately curls into me, her head on my chest. Her arm wraps around my belly.

"I do, you know," she says. "I love you."

I run my hand over her hair. "Get some sleep, Princess."

She shuffles around until she gets comfortable. I content myself by running my hand over her hair, thick and coarse. It's as familiar as the rhythmic sound of her alcohol-induced snuffles. She burrows into me.

And I let her. Because I'm a sucker for her. Anything she asks of me, I'll do it without hesitation.

I stare up at the ceiling. Her phone call woke me up from a dead sleep, but I'm wide awake now. I don't think I'll ever be able to sleep again. The rich citrus scent of her perfume wafts over me, lulling me into a false sense of security. It'll be okay. It'll work out.

Crawling into bed with my drunk ex-girlfriend isn't the single worst decision of my life. I'll probably never be able to sleep in this bed again without smelling her, remembering her. The one place I was sure she would never be has been infiltrated by her, and I can't decide if I would rather have her here or if I wish she never stepped foot on this campus. I'm caught in limbo, and I don't see a way out.

eight

. . .

Mason

I WAKE UP DISORIENTED. That's the first bad sign. I don't recognize the room I'm in. That's the second. My head is pounding and my mouth is as dry as the Sahara. And there's the holy trinity of stupid drunken decisions.

There's a man in the bed beside me. My heart skips a beat. Peeking beneath the covers at myself, I'm fully clothed, wearing leggings and a bra beneath my shirt. I'm still wearing my socks.

I let out a sigh of relief. This seems to rouse whoever's bed I crashed in.

"Mm... Mason."

A strong arm slides around my waist, tugging me back against a warm, thick body. Soft lips brush my exposed neck where my braid has fallen apart. There's a morning erection pressing into my backside.

King.

Oh, no. No, no, no. This can't be happening.

Gingerly, I disentangle our limbs. He lets out a whine of protest. He clutches at thin air, and I shove a pillow into his arms. He nuzzles into the pillow, petting it like he pet my hair last night.

"Mase."

He's still asleep. He's dreaming about me?! I don't know how to feel about this. He came to my rescue last night when I needed him most. He dropped his Saturday night plans to be by my side. I don't know how I can ever thank him for getting me home safely and securely last night. I don't remember much, but from what I can piece together, I was definitely out of it. It could have been dangerous.

My head throbs. I definitely overindulged last night. I don't usually mix beer and liquor. I know better. If nothing else, my time at Georgetown taught me how to handle my alcohol. There's a trash can on the floor beside the bed. I'm glad I didn't need it last night.

The good thing about Athlete's Village is all the houses are laid out the same. It's easy enough to find the Jack and Jill bathroom he shares with the room next door. I open the door and come face to face with a naked guy. Peeing. Completely naked.

At the sound of the door creaking open, he looks over at me and yelps. Still peeing.

He's tall and wide and so, so naked. His pasty white skin is covered in freckles. There is more flesh on display than I've ever seen at one time. I'm so stunned, I don't know what to do. I try to close the door and succeed only in jamming it against my toe. Shit. Now it's my turn to yelp. He continues to pee, now with a panicked look on his face. His aim is... not good.

There are heavy footsteps behind me. Tucker is there in an instant, his hand on my arm.

"Are you okay?" His voice is thick from sleep, hoarse and husky.

"Get out," the naked guy screeches. He's *still* peeing.

Tucker forcibly removes me from the threshold and shuts the door behind us. "Sorry, B," he calls out. He looks down at me, concern in his eyes. "How are you feeling?"

I clear my throat. "I'm fine."

"Yeah, okay." He looks me over. I'm sure I'm a hot mess. Last night's clothes wrinkled, my makeup all over my face, my hair falling out of its protective braid. I don't need a mirror to know I look *fabulous* right now.

"I should go home."

"That's probably a good idea."

His dark eyes are hard, his jaw clenched tight. None of this distracts me from the morning erection tenting the front of his sweatpants, glorious and thick. I can see the head of his dick outlined in stark relief. I wonder what he would do if I dropped to my knees right now and tasted him. I almost wish I could find out.

"It'll go away," he says, his voice as rough as gravel. "It happens in the morning."

"Right."

"Nothing to do with you."

"I didn't think it did."

"You should go."

I flinch. I was the one who suggested it, but for him to basically kick me out...

"Thanks for letting me crash here."

He grunts. He doesn't offer to help me out again. He doesn't say that's what friends are for or any other trite clichés. He doesn't make any promises he has no intention of keeping.

I clear my throat. "Um. My coat?"

"I didn't see it." He looks away. "You wore mine home."

I vaguely remember being wrapped up in his scent, enveloped in his embrace. I should have known he never would have hugged me.

"You can borrow a sweatshirt or something," he says, scrubbing a hand over the back of his neck. He goes to the dresser, digging through a pile of dark hoodies. They're all emblazoned with Newton Football or Newton Athletics. "Here."

He shoves it at me, and I swallow. Our fingers brush against each other. Sparks fly. It's not just static electricity in the air. It's something more.

I don't want him to move on. I don't want him to date anyone else. I want him all to myself, every last piece of his heart.

"Thanks."

"I want it back."

Of course he does. "I'm not a thief."

"You used to be." There's no humor in his voice, only regret. Pain.

When we were together, it was like a badge of honor to wear his hoodies. I walked through the halls of our high school with my head held high. He'd picked me. He'd wanted me.

Now, he can hardly look at me.

His hoodie is enormous. I look like I'm wearing a tent. I slip my hands into the pocket to keep from fidgeting. It's warm, and it smells like him, like cedar and sandalwood and something else uniquely him. I'm wrapped up in him. At least this way I can keep a part of him with me.

Yeah, he's definitely not getting this sweatshirt back.

"I'll see you around, King."

He flinches. "No, you won't."

"We have a class together. We work together. I'm pretty sure you don't have the power to go invisible."

My attempt at a joke falls flat. His face is carved from stone.

"You should leave," he finally says. "I don't want you here."

Damn, and doesn't that sting. He had to come right out and say it. I clear my throat to hide the tears welling in my eyes and gather my stuff. My shoes, my phone, my clutch. I'll have to go back to the frat house later for my coat. I liked that coat.

"Bye."

He grunts again. He doesn't slam the door behind me, but he isn't gentle, either.

The walk home is lonely. It's bitterly cold out. There's nobody out this early in the morning. Athlete's Village is quiet, still. I walk the four blocks over to the track and field house. All this time, we've lived so close together. Now it feels like there's a gulf between us.

It's been two and a half years. Not once have I ever drunk dialed him. I've wanted to a thousand times. But I've never let myself do it. Until now. Until that kiss.

Fuck, that kiss.

I don't know what I want from him. I don't think that he necessarily knows what he wants from me, either. I want to feel like I used to when I was with him. He says he hates me, he says I ruined his life. And then he kisses me. When I get so drunk I can barely stand, he comes to my rescue. He sleeps beside me and makes sure I don't asphyxiate in the middle of the night.

But he doesn't like me. He can't stand the sight of me.

None of my roommates are up when I get home. I trudge up the stairs to my room and collapse onto my bed. Tucker's sweatshirt surrounds me in his scent. I never want to take it off.

How do I prove to him that I've changed? I'm not the same sad, scared little girl I used to be. I've grown up. I've grown into myself. I know who I am now, what I can handle. And we're both here. We're finally in the same place again. There's no reason we can't make it work this time around.

A part of me has always loved him. Even when I dated other guys, even when I was happy with someone else, a piece of me has always missed him. He's the one who got away—the one I set free—only to inadvertently shackle him to a lifetime of misery.

But if he still loves me, why can't we make this work? Why can't we make a go of it?

Tucker and I were good together. We balance each other out. He's the yin to my yang, the peanut butter to my jelly. He's my other half.

As much as I've changed in the last two and a half years, maybe he's changed, too. He might not be the same person I remember. The same man I fell in love with all those years ago.

Micah says he hasn't talked to him. I don't like that he lost his best friend in the breakup. That's just shitty. My brother should have stayed by his side, worked through their issues to salvage their decade-long friendship.

I should have done more. I should have pushed Micah to reach out to him. I should have—

Rolling over, I punch the pillow and readjust. The thick fabric of the sweatshirt is like a cocoon of warmth.

First, we have to get on speaking terms again. He has to be able to tolerate the sight of me before we become anything more. We can start with friends. I can be his friend again. I *want* to be his friend again.

His friend who jerks him off whenever he wants? Yeah, I'm interested in that position, too. Pretty much any position he can think of, I'm willing to try.

I can't believe that he's never hooked up with anyone. He's so fucking gorgeous, it hurts to look at him. But he's not the type of guy to lie about something like that. He's not the type of guy to lie, period.

I don't know what to think. I don't know what to do. So I roll over and curl up under my blankets. Maybe a nap will bring me clarity. Maybe a nap will make the last twelve hours all a bad dream.

nine

. . .

Tucker

"ARE we going to talk about it?"

"About what?"

Barrett sets down the weights in his hand and looks at me. "You had a girl in your room."

"It's only Mason."

"Yeah, and she stayed the night."

"Nothing happened. She was drunk."

He hums. "Yeah, okay."

"I can't go there with her."

"So the girl you've been in love with forever is in your bed and you just—you don't fuck her?"

"First of all, she couldn't consent. I'm not about to—"

He rolls his eyes. "You know that's not what I'm talking about."

I lift the weights and eke out my eight reps. "She doesn't want me."

"You don't know that."

"Okay. Fine. I don't know how I feel about her." I huff and puff for breath. "My heart wants her, and my head is telling me to run far, far away."

"And your dick?"

I force out a laugh. "I know better than to listen to my dick. It just wants to get laid. I'm not about that life."

"I know, I know." He lifts a few reps and pauses with the weight curled into his chest, breathing hard. "Maybe you should, though. It hasn't steered me wrong."

"I've tried that."

"Once."

"And it was awful."

"Maybe you should try again. Evaluate a larger sample size. Maybe it was only that one chick."

I don't want to try again. Sex isn't a need for me, it's a want, and I'm more than used to repressing it. I need an emotional connection with someone before I can want to get naked with them. The only person I've ever felt close enough to in order to let my guard down is Mason.

Mama calls me demisexual. I don't need to put a label on it. I am who I am. Mom says labels are important, but living outside of them can be just as freeing. I don't know. I don't feel the need to come out like they had to. I'm just me.

I wish I knew whether I am still hung up on the past or if I'm actually in love with Mason. Sometimes it's hard to tell. I'm definitely still attracted to her. There's a pull there, a connection. I want more than just sex with her. I want a *life* with her. I want to spend all my free time with her. I want to know everything about her. I've always seen a future for us: past college, past grad school, a *real* future with marriage and babies. It should scare me. For some reason, it doesn't—it never has.

But I also have to put myself first. I have a year and a half left before I graduate. I need to get into grad school. I need to play football and keep my athletic scholarship. I don't have to have a girlfriend in order to achieve my dreams. That's a want, not a need.

Not that any random girl will do. I only want her. She's the only one I've ever wanted.

I wish I could talk to my brother about this. Jamal is great with women. He always knows just what to say, what to do. I'm not naturally suave. I'm just a big, giant loser.

My brother answers on the first ring. "Little T!"

"Hey, man," I say, ignoring the fact that I outweigh him by nearly a hundred pounds. He's tall and all lean muscle, the ideal size and shape for a basketball point guard, and I'm big and wide, the ideal shape for a defensive tackle. How our white lesbian sports-averse moms ended up adopting two black semi-pro athletes, I'll never know.

Well, Jamal is technically a real professional now. It doesn't matter that he's riding the bench. He's in the NBA. It counts.

After all these years of putting my body on the line, it's time for my brain to pull its weight. I'm going to be the best damn addiction counselor there is.

Which is another reason Mason's meltdown last night worries me. I know college kids go out. I know they drink. But this... it's not like the Mason I used to know. And I realize she's a different person now. I understand she's a grown adult and allowed to indulge in alcohol, if that's what she wants. But it doesn't sit right with me. She's hiding. Using.

I can't fix her. That's not my job, not anymore.

Jamal and I catch up. He has a game tonight in Philly, then it's back on the plane to Detroit. It feels like he's on the road more than he's home these days. Then again, he's living the life he's always dreamed of; he has to make some sacrifices, and constant travel is part and parcel for professional athletes.

I miss my big brother. We've been living apart for five years, ever since he went off to UNC on his basketball scholarship. Our relationship exists mostly through memes and random text conversations. He's my big brother, but he doesn't have time for me. It took me a long time to accept that. He's moving on to bigger and better things. He's not leaving me behind; it's just that his priorities have shifted. So have mine.

———

I don't talk to Mason all week. She sits in the back of our sociology class all by herself, where she can stare out the window and daydream. On Wednesday, I see her from across the dining hall—she's talking to her friend, the blonde woman from the track meet. We don't interact. We simply… coexist.

And then it's time for our Friday shift at the assessment center.

I don't know what to say to her. Do I say anything at all? Was Saturday night a one off? Does she go out drinking every weekend? Does she get that wasted every week?

As much as I don't want to worry about her, a piece of me is always going to care about her. Right now it's a pretty significant chunk. I want to make her smile and I want to make her laugh, yes, but I want to take care of her and make all the bad things in her life go away.

Mason gives me a polite smile when I walk into the clinic. She's already sitting at her desk, her developmental psychology book open in front of her.

I can be civil. I can be the bigger person.

"Good morning."

Her mouth drops open and her eyes go wide. "Good morning," she manages. Her throat works as she swallows. "You look nice today."

"Thank you." My beard is freshly trimmed. I'm wearing dark jeans and a hoodie, same as I do every day.

I round the desk and take my seat beside her. There's four feet between our computers. That's not nearly enough distance, and entirely too much all at once. I want to run my fingers through her hair and hold her close. I want to kiss her right here and never let her go.

We have about ten minutes of paperwork and opening duties before the first clients of the day walk in, a woman and her toddler son seeking an adult ADHD diagnosis. Mason shows them over to the kiddie corner, where we have toys and coloring books available for the kid. She crouches down and talks directly to the toddler, giving him her undivided attention. She's good with kids. I can imagine her with a minivan full of babies one day, her belly round with our child as she runs after a bushy-haired toddler with her eyes and my smile.

Woah. Hold up. We're not together. We're not anything. We're definitely nowhere close to being ready for babies.

But I can see it, and I'm not scared of it. I can see a future with her. A *life* with her.

Can I get over my pride and admit that I'm still in love with her? We've both grown in our time apart. We're different people now. I like to think that I can be a good partner to her, that we work well together. We balance each other out.

Mason glances up at me, her eyes bright. Her easygoing smile fades from her face. She swallows and stands up, brushing her hands on her leggings.

"I'll be right at the desk if you need anything," she tells the woman. She crosses the small lobby and retakes her seat. "What?"

"I didn't say anything."

"You were thinking it," she says.

I love you, I want to say.

"The nine o'clock is a no show," I say instead.

She clears her throat and shuffles the sign-in sheets. "He called right before you came in, he's running late. He'll be here by nine thirty."

The psychologists' schedule is always a little light on

Fridays. We can shift things around to accommodate his tardiness today.

"Mason…"

She raises her eyebrows expectantly. "Yeah?"

I don't know what I want to say. I just don't want our conversation to be over. I want her attention, her affection.

I clear my throat. I have no words to say.

"Tucker, what is it?"

"Forget it."

"Come on. Tell me."

"How are you doing in sociology?" I spy her textbook on the counter in front of her. It's the first thing that comes to mind. "I heard we're having a pop quiz next week."

She grimaces. "It's fine."

"We could…"

"Hm?"

"Never mind."

Her eyes narrow, a smile teasing the corner of her mouth. "Tucker Kingsley, are you asking me to study with you?"

My cock twitches in my jeans. My stomach lurches. My mouth goes dry. I hate the physical reaction to her teasing. No matter how badly she hurt me, I still want her, and I have to live with that every day.

"No?"

"I think you are." She scoots her chair closer towards mine. "I think you don't hate me nearly as much as you pretend to."

My mouth goes dry. She's at least three feet away, but the scent of her tangy and bright perfume washes over me as familiar as the back of my hand. It's calming. Soothing.

"I—" My brain turns to mush.

"I would love to study with you, if that's what you're offering," she says. Her voice is rich and husky. She looks up at me from beneath her lashes. "Tonight. Five o'clock. We can go to the ASC when our shift is over, grab dinner after."

"I'm having dinner with my roommates." It's what we do. We eat dinner together every night, rain or shine. Sam joins us for some breakfasts and most dinners. She fits in with our ragtag group of guys. She balances us out.

"You don't want to have dinner with me?" Her little pink tongue comes out to wet her lips. My jeans get tighter, remembering *other* things that tongue has done to me. Naked. "I'm a good study buddy."

I remember studying in high school with her. Her idea of studying incentives involved straddling me and removing articles of clothing as I recited the periodic table of elements. To this day, I can't think of the noble gases without getting hard.

"I don't need *that* kind of studying."

Her full lips curve into a victorious smile. "I'm talking about cracking open a few books in the dining hall. Not anything… scandalous." Her fingertips brush over her collarbone. My eyes are drawn to her clingy red sweater and down, down, down to the curve of her breasts.

My eyes dart back to hers. She's looking at me expectantly. Her smile is deadly. My stomach flips.

"It's not a good idea." I need to actually focus and learn the material, not get distracted every ten seconds by thoughts of her.

Who am I kidding? I already think of her every five seconds. Studying together or on our own, she's still going to be on my mind.

"We can be friends, King," she says quietly, her eyes locked on mine. "We can get through this awkwardness and be friends again."

"It's not awkward," I lie.

She scoots her chair closer to me. She sets her hand on my knee. Sparks of electricity travel through my veins and coalesce in my gut. My cock is definitely interested in seeing where she's going with this. Just being this close to her makes my every nerve twitch with anticipation.

"It is, and that's okay," she says. "We can get through it."

"There's nothing to get through."

"I know you won't forgive me," she starts.

"We shouldn't talk about this now." I look pointedly at the mom and her son in the kiddie corner.

"If you had it your way, we wouldn't talk about this at all."

"You're right. We wouldn't." My defenses slam back into place. It's too dangerous; I can't let my guard down around her or she'll slip right back in. I can't afford that. I won't be able to survive it this time.

"I want to be part of your life," she says quietly. "In any way you'll allow me. Let me in, King. We can do this."

ten

. . .

Mason

AT FIVE O'CLOCK on the dot, we clock out of work. Tucker goes to the rack and hands me my coat, politely chivalrous. His fingers brush mine, and I find myself leaning into the contact. My fingers zip with pinpricks of delight.

"Thanks."

He clears his throat, pulling away. He slips his arms into his coat and zips it all the way up to his throat.

"You ready for this, big guy?"

He grunts, which is better than cursing me out or cancelling our plans outright, so I'll take what I can get.

I press the button for the elevator. I'm not a small woman, I'm average height, but I feel impossibly tiny next to him. Everything about him is huge. I'm engulfed by his presence, as well as his physical size.

I love it. I've missed it. I've missed him.

He stands perfectly still. He doesn't fidget. His eyes are glued on the little buttons above the elevator doors as we click down to the fifth floor. The doors open and he thrusts his arm between them, holding them open.

"After you." His voice is as rough as gravel.

I step over the threshold, and he joins me, jabbing at the

button for the ground floor. The elevator is tiny, made even smaller by his presence. He hugs the wall, careful not to touch me.

The slowest elevator in the history of the world lurches into motion. This is the closest we've been in—years. He smells like cedar and sandalwood and something else uniquely Tucker. I can't get enough.

It's been nearly a week since I've seen him, since he kicked me out of his house. I don't know what to say to him. The silence between us is deafening. I swallow, and it sounds so loud in the quiet stillness of the metal box we're trapped in.

We tick down a floor. He's not looking at me. His arms are crossed over his broad chest, his eyes trained on his feet. I want to catch his eye, to catch his attention. Any little glimmer of attention, good or bad.

One more level. Does he miss me? Whether he hates me or not, his feelings are certainly forceful. Tucker has always loved hard. When he lets someone into his life, he wholeheartedly embraces them. It feels good to bask in the warm glow of his affection. I hadn't realized until just now how much I missed it.

The elevator lurches to a stop, the doors creaking open with a steely groan. He holds the door again, letting me pass through first.

Our walk through campus is silent. At this time of day, there's barely anyone left on campus. They've all gotten a kick start on their weekend. It's a Friday night. I should be getting ready for dinner and then a party. Settling down to study doesn't feel right.

But it means I get to spend some time with him, so I'll gladly sacrifice some partying time if it means we get to spend the evening together.

I rather thought he would head for the study rooms on the second floor. Instead, he makes his way towards the dining hall. We both badge in with our student athlete access cards. Again, he holds the door open for me.

Without a word, he makes a beeline for the sandwich bar. I follow at a more sedate pace towards the snack area. I'm not quite hungry enough for dinner yet. I'm fine with an apple and a cheese stick to tide me over for the next hour or two.

I expect him to select a big table where we have space to spread out. He surprises me again by picking a small table built for four towards the back of the dining hall.

His tray is laden with not one, not two, but three peanut butter sandwiches and a protein shake. I know he's an emotional eater, but that seems like a lot.

I can't judge him. I can't worry about him. That's not my place anymore.

He grunts and pulls out his sociology textbook. "Chapter four?"

Our course is focused on the American family. I know his family history: two white lesbian moms who adopted two black boys as toddlers, both starting out as foster placements. Throughout the years, his moms have fostered at least a dozen other kids, though none have stayed longer than a year or two. He has no contact with his biological mother—as far as I'm aware, she's still in jail, where she's been since he entered into the system when he was two years old. There's no biological father listed on his birth certificate.

I don't have that intact nuclear family unit that everyone seems to think is so ideal. My parents split up when I was a baby and have both remarried, both happily. My twin brother and I dutifully shuttled between their houses growing up. My dad has four more kids with his new wife, a kind and polite woman who is not what I would consider warm, but is a decent and effective wife and mother. My mom is busy helping to raise my stepfather's three kids, who are—fine. We're not close. They're in that awkward preteen stage where they hate the world, each other, and themselves.

I didn't go home often when I was in school in DC, and I'm even further from home now. Georgetown's campus is only a few miles away from my mom's new house, but it was usually easier to stay at school in the athlete's dorm than deal with her and the stepkids' drama. Micah is in South Carolina. My dad is busy with the babies. I don't even know where home is anymore.

I wonder how Jamal is doing. From Micah, I know Tucker's brother is in the NBA now. He's living the life. If my brother can get his shit together, next year he might be in the NFL.

Three years ago, I never would have thought my brother could be a professional football player. Half the time, I still can't believe it. All of the draft predictions think he could be selected in the first one hundred players. Maybe even in the middle of the second round. That's just insane. My little brother is a fully grown man now. He's not so little anymore.

I clear my throat. Tucker looks up at me mid-bite, his dark eyes full of guilt. He slowly lowers his sandwich back to his plate.

"Have you talked to Micah lately?"

He grunts, which I take to be a no.

"He's doing well."

He makes a noise that could politely be called questioning.

"You should call him."

He takes another enormous bite of his sandwich.

"He misses you."

Tucker snorts.

"He does. You guys were best friends. You shouldn't let something like—"

"Like you dumping me?" His voice is hard-edged and thick, bitter and full of self-loathing. He licks his lips, his eyes dark. "Yeah, that's not going to happen."

"Tucker…"

"You ask your brother why he stopped returning my calls," he snaps. "Let him tell you why."

He finishes his first sandwich with two more aggressive bites. He studies the next one carefully before he shakes his head, pushing his plate away.

"Micah said he reached out to you, that you were the one who cut things off."

He laughs. "He's always been good with revisionist history."

"What's that supposed to mean?"

"He's always been yours, Princess. He was never mine."

I want to smile at my old nickname, but the hard set of his jaw robs me of my short-lived joy.

"He was your best friend."

"Yeah. Was." He rubs at his chin, scratching through the thin layer of his beard. "That's been over for a long time, Princess."

He used my nickname again!

"Maybe you could try..."

He laughs and shakes his head. "That's done. I've closed the book on that stage of my life."

"King..."

"We should study. That's why we're here. I didn't agree to go strolling down memory lane."

"Is that really so bad?" My voice softens. "We have a lot of history. That can't all be swept away in the blink of an eye."

He pulls his plate back towards him and takes a giant bite of his second sandwich.

"King—"

"No. You don't get to call me that." He chews and swallows thickly. "That stage of our life is over, Mason. You made that abundantly clear."

"It doesn't have to be. We can—"

"Oh, so now you want me? When it's convenient for you?" His laugh is cold. Bitter. "I'm not some dildo you keep around in the nightstand for when you get lonely. You don't get to call me up after two and a half years and—"

"That's not what I'm doing."

I want him. Not just for sex. I want *him*. All I've ever wanted is him. Getting back together will fix everything.

"It's exactly what you're doing, and I'm not about that life. We can't be friends. We can't hook up again. We can't even study together." He snorts in derision and slams his textbook closed. "Face it, *babe*, there's no path for us moving forward."

"We can be friends. We can—" I stop, swallow. "You don't want to sleep with me?"

"I need to actually like the person I'm fucking," he says crudely, cruelly. "Right now that's not a possibility."

"Tucker…"

"You don't want me. You just want the idea of me."

"That's not what this is."

"Then why did you call me up on Saturday night, blitzed out of your mind?" He takes an aggressive bite of his sandwich, his eyes hard.

I crack my knuckles. "Why did you kiss me?" He doesn't answer. "You say I ruined your life, and then you kiss me, so clearly your feelings aren't so clean cut in this matter. Why. Did you. Kiss me?"

eleven

. . .

Tucker

"BECAUSE I'M STILL in love with you."

The words burst out of me before I can stop them. My breathing becomes sharp and ragged.

She blinks at me, taken aback. I can see the gears turning in the back of her mind.

"Because I'm still in love with you," I say, more calmly now. My fingers tighten on my sandwich, creating a oozing crater of peanut butter. "Because I always have been, even when I hated you."

Her throat works. "But you don't? Hate me?"

I sigh. I know when to admit defeat.

"No, I don't."

Mason rubs at her eye. "So, let me get this straight. You want nothing to do with me. You won't be friends with me. But you're in love with me?"

I take another bite of my sandwich. It's supposed to make me feel better. All it does is get lodged in my throat.

"This doesn't need to be complicated. We can make this work," she says.

Oh, the naïveté…

"There's nothing to *make work*. We'll just exist," I tell her, because that's all I can offer her.

She huffs out a breath of nervous laughter. "I don't want to exist in a world where we're not us."

"What does that mean?"

"It means that a part of me is still in love with you, too."

I drop my sandwich.

Mason bites her lip, her eyes roving over my face. "Tucker…"

"You're still in love with me?" My voice breaks. I can't believe it.

I'm angry. I'm furious. But I can't deny that this is what I've wanted to hear her say every single day for the last two and a half years. All I've ever wanted is her. She has been my whole world from the day we met when we were seven years old. I've missed her every single day we were apart.

"I am." She swallows. "And you're still in love with me."

Slowly, I nod. Something like hope blooms deep inside me.

"Baby, this isn't rocket science," she says. "We should—we deserve it to ourselves to try again."

My mouth is thick with the taste of the peanut butter. I clear my throat. It doesn't help.

"What would that… look like?"

I'm trying really hard to hold onto my anger. Faced with everything I've ever wanted… well, I've never been able to say no to her.

"That's up to you. We can take it slow, as slowly as you need." She chews on her thumbnail. "I know I hurt you. All I can say is that I did what I thought was right—for both of us. It was a long time ago."

That old familiar hurt rises up again. I rub idly at my chest. It doesn't help the itchy feeling deep inside me.

"We could have made a go of it," I tell her. "The distance wouldn't have broken us."

"It would have broken *me*," she says. Pain creases her face. "I was insecure, and I let my fears get the best of me. I couldn't stand the thought of you being here all by yourself, surrounded by all these hot girls throwing themselves at you and—"

I let out a bark of laughter. "You vastly overestimate the popularity of football players at this school."

"Girls used to throw themselves at you all the time in high school."

"Yeah, and I turned them down. Why would I be interested in some stranger when I already had the prettiest girl in school on my arm?" I scratch at my beard as I meet her eye. "I've never been interested in hooking up. I'm not about that lifestyle. You know that."

"You could have any girl you wanted."

"Yeah, and all I wanted was you."

It comes out harsher than I intended. Mason blinks and leans back.

"So clearly we have some unresolved issues…"

I snort out a breath of bitter laughter. "You think?"

"But I want to be with you," she says quietly. She swallows. "And if you still want to be with me…"

"I don't know what I want," I admit, and it might be the most honest lie I've ever told.

"Let's try it. We can try again."

"What does that mean?" I don't want to get my hopes up. I don't want to get her back in my arms only for her to disappear all over again.

"That's up to you. We'll take this as slow or as fast as you want."

I swallow. She's across the table from me. That's way too far away.

Shoving back my chair, I round the table and drop to a crouch in front of her. She bites her lip, and I reach out and tug on it.

"Only I get to bite this," I tell her seriously. "It's mine now."

"All—all yours." Her eyes are wide, unblinking, laser focused on mine.

I have to check. "You really have feelings for me?"

I need her to tell me. This isn't some trick? There isn't a camera crew lurking in the shadows ready to capture my humiliation? There aren't crowds of people gathered to laugh at my heartbreak?

"I—I think I always have," Mason says slowly. "I didn't want to. I couldn't help it. I love—"

Threading my hands through her hair, I bring my mouth to hers, parting her lips with my own. I swallow her gasp and deepen the kiss. Her hands slide up my upper arms and shoulders to lock behind my neck, holding me to her as her tongue comes out to meet mine.

Exhilaration rushes through me. It's just as good as the first time, and the last time, and every time in between.

She pulls away and rests her forehead against mine.

"Damn, Tucker," she says, licking her lips. "I guess we've still got that chemistry."

I groan. My cock twitches at those long repressed memories resurfacing to the forefront of my brain.

"Don't mention chemistry."

She runs her hand over my arm. "So we're doing this?"

I steal another kiss. "Yeah. Let's—we're doing this."

Her victorious smile steals my breath and makes my knees weak. Those same knees start to ache with the effort of crouching for so long. I make my way to my feet and take my seat again.

Mason stares at me for several long moments.

"What?"

"Nothing. I was wondering what your plans were for tonight."

"Dinner with my roommates, then watch a movie. I think

Wes wants to do another James Bond marathon this weekend."

Her soft smile makes my heart sing. Her eyes are a warm chocolate brown, bright with happiness. "Do you stay in a lot?"

"I mean, I—yeah. I don't party, really. Now that football season is over, I'm a little more lax on the bedtime and everything…" I shrug. It might be boring to other people, but it works for me.

"Do you want to come to a track party with me?"

"Tonight?"

She nods.

I blink at her. "Don't you have a meet tomorrow?" The night before a football game, we have a strict curfew to make sure we're well rested for the next day's game. Coach isn't afraid to bench us if we don't play by his rules.

"It'll be super low-key. Some of the other sprinters are doing a get together for Mark's birthday."

I don't know who Mark is. Probably one of her teammates.

I swallow my doubts. "This won't be like the frat party?"

She laughs. "Not at all. It's totally casual." She pauses. "If we're going to do this, I want you to meet my friends. They're a big part of my life here at Newton. I've found a community here."

"I—yeah, okay," I finally say, because she's right; I should get to know her friends. "Do you… would you like to have dinner with my roommates? They're awful people, but—"

She laughs. "I'm sure they're not awful."

"They are. They're rude and uncivilized and—"

Mason reaches across the table and takes my hand in hers. I lace our fingers together, some of my worries ebbing away. Just the simple touch of her hand is enough to soothe the anxiety ricocheting through my veins.

"They're your friends. Of course I want to meet them," she

says gently. "They're important to you, so they'll be important to me, too."

I strongly consider my third sandwich. "We can make this work. Can't we?"

"I think we can," Mason says, full of earnest conviction. "I really think we can."

twelve

. . .

Mason

WE SPEND the better part of an hour studying, hand in hand. We're surprisingly productive. Every once in a while, a sappy smile will take over Tucker's face and he'll just beam at me. I like seeing him happy. I'm glad I'm the one that makes him happy.

At six-thirty, Tucker clears his throat and slowly pulls his hand away. "You're sure you want to do this?"

I've never been more sure of anything in my life. Pushing back my seat, I walk around to his side of the table. He scoots his chair back, and I settle myself in his lap, wrapping my arms around his neck. His big hands come up to settle on my hips.

"I love you," I tell him again, and when the world doesn't end, I laugh for ever thinking it would. "I want to be with you in whatever way you'll let me. If you're not ready for this, we can take it slow. We can—"

His mouth slants over mine. He licks into my mouth and deepens the kiss. He tastes like the peanut butter sandwiches he's been devouring. His thick fingers thread into my hair, and he tugs ever so gently.

"I've missed you," he murmurs against my lips. "So much, Princess."

I sigh, and he kisses me again, and again, and again, until I'm panting and breathless in the middle of the dining hall. Need has me aching for him. My nipples are stiff peaks inside my bra. I shift on his lap, desperate for some friction, and his hands tighten on my hips.

"Not here," he says.

"We can skip dinner… go straight to dessert…"

Tucker laughs. He tucks a strand of hair behind my ear. "Nice try. You need to fuel up for tomorrow."

Disappointed, but knowing he's right, I slide off his lap. His hand catches mine, and he presses a chaste kiss to my knuckles.

His friends are assembled at the back of the dining hall, blatantly watching us. Well, all except for the guy on the end. He's absorbed in a thick book.

"Come on," he says, standing and shoving all his things into his backpack. He pulls out a plastic baggie and tucks away that third sandwich for later. "It's chicken parm night. You love chicken parm."

"I do." And the dining hall's rendition of it isn't bad for mass-produced school food.

He offers his hand, and I take it. We meander through the tables until we get to the front of the food line. We each grab trays. I have to let go of his hand. I feel bereft without it. Funny how I don't realize how much I need it until it's taken away from me.

I can't believe he's hungry again, but Tucker has always been a big eater. He didn't get to be his size by skipping meals. He loads his plate with chicken, pasta, and a whole lot of salad. Tonight's offering is mixed greens with marinated tomatoes, small cubes of fresh mozzarella, and a balsamic glaze that makes my heart sing. We both scan our selections into the school's nutrition app, where it calculates our macros for us. George-town didn't have anything near this fancy, only once a semester counseling about maintaining weight and calorie counting.

There are five guys already sitting at the table in the back of the dining hall, plus the blonde chick that likes to wrap herself around my man. But not for much longer. Tucker approaches the table and clears his throat.

"Um, hi."

Caveman beard—Greg, from the party—turns around and eyes us curiously. "Uh, hi? Dude, are you going to sit down?"

Tucker coughs. "Everyone, this is Mason. Mason, this is… everyone. She's going to sit with us."

The guy directly in front of us, with his back to me, pushes back his chair. I take a step back. He's tall and wide—they all are—with golden brown skin that doesn't come from a spray tan.

"Nice to meet you," he says, holding out a hand and then, realizing I can't shake, takes the tray from my hand. "I'm Amir."

"Hi."

He sets the tray down in his spot, pushing his to the empty seat across from it.

"You sit here," he says, his hands curling on the back of the chair. "That way you can sit next to each other." He winks, and some of my nervousness fades away.

Amir moves around the table and takes his new seat. With a glance at Tucker, who nods, I slip into the freshly vacated seat.

"I'm Barrett," says the guy on the end, Asian, with a ton of freckles dotting his fair skin. "I don't think we've officially met yet."

Right. The guy who peed—completely naked.

The guy on the right raises his eyebrows. "When was this?"

"We went to her track meet last week," Barrett says.

Oh, yeah. Right. He was there, too.

"We have another one tomorrow, if you guys are looking for something to do." Our stands are nearly empty. Nobody knows what indoor track and field actually does.

Barrett glances at Tucker, who nods again. "We'll be there."

I look at my—what is he? Is it too early to call him my boyfriend? I don't know. I'm not entirely sure where we stand. We're taking it slow. I'll move at a glacier's pace if it means getting to be with him again.

Tucker reaches out and wraps a tendril of my hair around his pinky. "You good with us crashing your meet?"

"You know I run my best when you're in the crowd." I set my hand on his leg. Tucker closes his eyes and takes a deep breath. "You okay, baby?"

He swallows and meets my eyes. "This isn't a dream, right? You're really here?"

I squeeze his leg. "I'm really here."

His kiss is soft, a quick brush of lips. He needs to reassure himself. He needs to process this in his own time.

Barrett gags theatrically. Tucker flips him off, and the guys laugh.

The blonde girl turns to me with a bright smile on her face. It has to be fake. Nobody is that cheerful. "Hi, I'm Sam."

"I've heard so much about you," I say neutrally.

"That's Miles," she says, pointing to the guy across from her. Right. Her boyfriend. "And that's Wes on the end."

The fair-haired guy hasn't looked up from his book. He gives a two-fingered salute at the sound of his name and turns the page.

"So you guys are a thing now," Greg says, giving me the once-over.

Tuck sets his arm on the back of my chair. "You've got a problem, man?"

"No, no problem," Greg says coolly. "It's just fast, isn't it?"

I set my hand on Tucker's thigh. I *need* to touch him. "It might seem fast to other people, but they don't know us or what we've been through."

I don't care that we've only been back in each other's lives for a week. I've been missing him for the last two and a half years. My feelings haven't gone away just because I broke up with him when I was young and dumb.

"It's been a long time coming," Tuck adds. "We're going to take it slow. I'm not rushing into anything."

Unease poisons my stomach. That doesn't sound good. I catch Barrett's eye, and he gives me a small smile. Encouraging.

I can do this. *We* can do this.

Tuck squeezes my arm and turns his attention to his meal. The guys seem to take this as him ending the conversation. Talk moves on to which James Bond movie they want to watch first. Well, Amir and Barrett talk. Miles is quiet, playing footsie with Sam under the table. He pipes in occasionally. Greg is watching me. Wes is absorbed in his book.

Tucker tips a few cubes of mozzarella cheese onto my plate.

"What's this for?"

"Mozzarella is your favorite cheese," he says. He's right. I do. My heart warms at the thought that he remembered.

He brushes his finger over my cheek, a sweet caress. "I've got you, girl."

I lean into the contact. Little glimmers of happiness run through me. I never thought we would get back to this place again. His easy affection makes my heart sing.

We have a lot to talk about. We've grown up, developed into fully grown adults. I've changed in the last two years. I'm guessing he has, too.

But I have faith. We can make this work.

He wants to take this slow. That probably means he won't want to get naked tonight. Especially if I have a meet tomorrow. He's always been very conscientious about that. Maybe tomorrow night we can properly celebrate our getting back together.

It's been too long since I've gotten laid. Those kisses earlier will keep me going for a little while longer, but they won't satiate me forever.

It's never been just sex with Tucker. It's deeper. None of the other guys I've been with have ever been able to measure up to my first love, the guy who taught me everything I know about love and being loved. I've never doubted how he felt about me, right up until the bitter end. Insecurity got the better of me. Doubt controlled me.

Not any more. We're together again. We'll be stronger for having been tested, for having gone through the past two years. If we can get through this, we can deal with anything life throws our way.

Right?

thirteen

. . .

Tucker

I DON'T KNOW what I expected from this track party. Maybe I've been watching too many 90s movies. There's alcohol, yeah, but no bong, no illicit drugs, no drunk people making out. It's just ten or twelve really fit athletes drinking and hanging out on the couch, a basketball game on the TV.

Mason all but shoves me into an armchair and then crawls into my lap. I don't think this chair is rated for my weight, much less our combined weight, but until it collapses beneath us, I can't make myself care.

She has a beer in her hand—just one, she said as she took the bottle, then offered me one—and she curls into my chest, her head on my shoulder. My hand is on her knee, drumming out a beat that only the two of us know. She's talking to her friends, laughing, having a good time. I can't focus on the conversation. I can't focus on much of anything except for the feel of her in my lap, her lithe curves and strong muscles.

I kiss her temple and tighten my arms around her. She sighs, sinking into my chest. One of her friends—the German one, I forget her name—says something and she laughs. The other woman—Melanie? Melissa?—grins and leans forward to clink their beer bottles together.

It's none of my business if she drinks the night before her race. It's none of my business if she needs to party to bleed the adrenaline off. Just because it's not the way I live my life doesn't make her way inferior.

But it does worry me.

I sip my water and zone out. Her friends are nice enough, but I'm not in the mood to chat. There's a basketball game I'm only half paying attention to. The rest of me is focused on how good Mason smells. On how good it feels to have her in my arms again. On how long I have to wait to get her naked.

I don't want to jump right back into bed. We can't blink and have things go back to the way things were. We've both changed. We've grown up. We're different people now.

At the same time, it's been two and a half years since she and I last had sex, the good, emotion-purging kind of toe-curling marathon sex that sets your heart on fire and makes your blood sing with desire. Once I get her back in my bed, I don't plan on letting her leave for a week. Maybe two. Who needs classes? Who needs food? We can just stay in bed all day and never leave.

I don't experience sexual attraction to people I don't already have an emotional bond with. I've never experienced that raw, animalistic magnetism to any other person except for Mason. When we do hook up, it's with the understanding that we have a solid foundation and a certain comfort with one another. We're on the same page in terms of our relation-ship and where it's going.

My moms were cool with my brother and me having sex under their roof. Jamal always had a rotating cast of girl-friends, never in his bed for more than a week or two before he was moving on to the next one. They'd rather we do it in the house than sneak around and get into trouble. They kept the bathroom cupboards stocked with condoms and lube and made sure we knew how to be safe. Mason's parents were so checked out of her life, they barely noticed if she didn't come home—her brother, my best friend, cared more than they did, and his issue was more that I was sticking it to his sister than that she wasn't sleeping in her bed at night.

And now we're living on our own. Yes, we both have roommates, but that's not the end of the world. We both have private bedrooms with doors that lock.

Tonight isn't the night. She has a meet tomorrow. She needs her rest.

Tomorrow night, though…

I slide my hand up from her knee to her thigh. Her quads twitch through the thin fabric of her leggings. Mason leans forward and places a light kiss to the side of my neck. Her teeth scrape over the pulse point and my cock kicks in my jeans.

"Don't start something you aren't going to finish," I warn her, my voice low and rough. She grins, tipping her face up for a sweet kiss.

"Who said I wasn't going to finish?" She scratches through my beard and I nuzzle into her like a cat getting cuddles. Her touch is electric. My veins pulse with heat, an electrical current I can't control. I don't want to control it.

"We can't. Not tonight."

She's disappointed but resigned. "Tomorrow night?"

"Tomorrow night I've got plans." I kiss her palm. "They involve you, my bed, and no clothes. How does that work for you?"

Mason grins at me, her full lips curving into a sultry smile. She presses a kiss to my lower lip, drawing it between hers. With a groan, I slide my hands up into her hair and kiss her properly. She deepens the kiss. Her hands fall to my chest, fisting the thick fabric of my hoodie.

I can't get enough of her. Two and a half years feels like fifty. It's been way, way too long.

There's a catcall from somewhere in the room. For the first time, I remember that we aren't alone.

I ease back, and she follows me, refusing to disengage. I lean back in the armchair and adjust our angles so she's sprawled over my lap. Her ass rests directly over my hard and eager cock.

"Not here," I mumble through the kiss.

She whines deep in her throat. I push her hair out of her face, my thumb drawing circles on her cheek.

"I know, sunshine, I know. We have all the time in the world. There's no need to rush."

Mason draws little circles on my chest with her fingertips. "We don't have to delay, though. There's no need to wait."

"You need to conserve your strength for tomorrow. You should rest. And what I want to do with you is definitely not restful." I trace my thumb over her bottom lip. Her mouth puckers and her tongue comes out to flick against my finger.

"We could play."

I shake my head at the hopeful note in her voice. "If you think I'm stopping before we're both spent and satisfied, woman, you're out of your damn mind. I've been waiting this long to get my hands on you. We can wait one more night."

She kisses me again, chastely, sweetly. She breaks the kiss and rests her head on my shoulder again, her arms wrapping around me.

"I love you, baby," she says, and something deep within me warms. It doesn't matter how many times she says it; I'll never get tired of hearing it.

fourteen

. . .

Mason

THERE'S a familiar rhythm to meet days. Wake up early in my empty bed, hating life. Remember it's meet day. Get a burst of adrenaline. Remember my event doesn't start until the afternoon. Power down, conserve energy. Get dressed. Head to the ASC with my roommates for first breakfast. Fuel up for the day ahead. Go to the practice facility, stretch and roll out. Get dressed in my running gear.

And then wait. And wait. And wait some more. Eat a granola bar. Wait.

Finally, around two o'clock, my race gets called. Five more minutes. I shake out the pre-race jitters and move with Fred and Melissa to the staging area.

My eyes rove over the sparsely populated bleachers. There aren't a lot of fans of indoor track and field, and even fewer people want to show up when it's nineteen degrees and sleeting outside.

In the second row, in the section directly behind the finish line, is Tucker. He catches my eye and waves, a sappy smile on his face. I'm probably wearing my own sappy smile as I wave back to him. He brought his friends. Barrett and Amir are sitting on either side of him. Wes is at the end, reading a book. Barrett nudges him, he looks up, meets my eye, and returns his attention to the book. I'm not offended. In the row behind them sit Greg, Miles, and Sam. Her smile is more like a grimace as she waves politely at me.

Fred laughs. "Looks like you've got your own personal cheering section."

"Jealous?" I roll my eyes and nudge her with my elbow. "What happened with that cute football player you were talking to? Sullivan? Didn't you have guys plans for last night?" She ended up going home with Mark of all people. I thought that was over and done with.

She huffs. "He went home from the Delta party last week with two other girls."

"Two?!"

She nods.

"I'm sorry, babe."

"Yeah, it's not fun. I'll deal with it. It's whatever." She blows out her bangs. "I can't think about him anymore. Not when we have a race to win."

Our race is officially called and we line up on our blocks.

Some people might think it's weird that I'm competing against my best friend. I think if anything, it's made our friendship stronger. We've spent months competing against one another in practice. We're always striving to improve, always trying to beat our personal best.

My eyes flick over to the stands. Tucker is sitting on the edge of his seat, worrying his bottom lip with his teeth. His eyes are glued to mine. He nods at me, and I smile, refocusing my attention on the track ahead of me.

I always run my best when he's in the crowd cheering for me.

The gun fires and then we're off. My singular focus is on the finish line, the breath in my lungs, my legs and my feet moving as quick as they can. Time stretches impossibly long and rushes past in the blink of an eye.

Before I know it, I'm crossing the finish line a breath ahead of Fred. She's panting, breathing hard, but she finds it in her to give me a high five and a hug.

Coach gives me a nod and a pat on the back. "Good job," she says, before her focus turns to the next race.

Fred and I grab water on the sidelines. Tucker is still tracking me. He doesn't look nearly as worried now. He's smiling, shaking his head at whatever Barrett is saying.

Arms settle around me, pulling me back against a hard body. I blink up at Mark and smile at him.

"Happy birthday, honey."

He tightens his arms around me. "Thanks, babe. Congrats on first place. Two weeks in a row."

"Thank you. I try." I dust off my shoulders and he laughs.

"What are you doing later tonight?"

I roll my eyes. "Nice try. I know you and Fred hooked up last night."

He grins. "You can't blame a guy for trying."

"Besides, I've got a boyfriend now."

"Oh, is that the guy you were macking on last night?"

I nod over to Tucker, who has a murderous look on his face. Not unlike the look on his face right before he tackles whatever guard is opposite him on the football field.

"Homeboy doesn't like me," he says, releasing me immediately.

"Homeboy doesn't know you. He'll like you just fine once he realizes you're the sluttiest boy this side of the Mason-Dixon Line."

Mark laughs. "What's that supposed to mean?"

"My brother is in South Carolina and he's way sluttier than you are," I say, and he grins.

"When is big brother coming to visit?"

"Little. I'm seventeen minutes older." I ignore the fact that Micah is three inches taller and about a hundred pounds heavier than me. He'll always be my little brother.

Mark grins, pulling at my braid. "I look forward to meeting him."

I chance a glance over to the stands. Tucker looks moderately less displeased. His jaw is clenched, his eyes hard. He tilts his head to whatever Amir is telling him and nods. He grinds out a few words.

My eyes locked on his, I cup my fingers together until they make a heart and hold it up to him. He swallows, letting out a heavy exhale. I blow him a kiss and he nods. He pats his chest—over his heart, I realize.

A warm glow settles over me. Even when he's being a sulky, jealous idiot, I love him. There's nothing between me and Mark—there never has been and there never will be.

Tucker and I will get through these little speed bumps. In the before, he knew all of my male friends because over the course of our three and a half years together, our friend groups naturally merged. Us having dinner with his friends and then going to a party with mine is a good start, even if we spent most of the evening making out instead of socializing.

Tonight, though, will be all about us. I'm freshly shaved everywhere that he might touch me. After the meet, I'll get dressed up in my sexiest lingerie, stuff he hasn't seen yet. I'm not the same size I used to be. I don't think he'll care much. I have a shape now that I didn't at seventeen. Then again, I could probably wear a burlap sack and he'd still want me. He's been pining after me for two and a half years. If he seriously hasn't gotten laid in the time since we broke up, he'll be desperate for it tonight.

I've been with other guys. I've dated. I've had boyfriends. I've experimented. I know more about what I like in bed, more about what I need in a partner. Sex is just one piece of it, a part of us that has always been successful. I need someone who's going to be my safe harbor, who will be there for me when my day turns to shit and everything sucks, but will also sit there and let me vent without trying to fix my problems for me. I need someone who knows when to give me space and doesn't get upset when I retreat into myself for a little while. I need someone who doesn't need their hand held every minute of the day, that's okay with a little bit of distance, but is there with snuggles and affection when we both want it.

And I need someone that respects me and my decisions. It's a bare minimum requirement. I've dated enough to know that it's not universally found, even though it should be. I have enough self respect to put myself first when it counts.

Tucker has always been good about respecting my boundaries, about acknowledging that sometimes I need a little bit of space. He doesn't get offended when I have more on my mind than when is the next time we can have sex. He doesn't pressure me into doing things I'm not interested in—which, again, is the bare minimum of human decency.

His moms welcomed me into their home. They let me stay over as often as I wanted. Micah, too. They didn't care if we had sex under their roof. They made me part of their family. They did the same with all of Jamal's two-week flings—and he had a lot of those. Tuck's brother has always been gorgeous and charming, a deadly combination for women's panties. He's also a genuinely nice guy. I miss hanging out with him.

Shit. His moms. Has he told them? It's been less than twenty-four hours. I haven't even thought about telling Micah. I probably should. The news should come from me, not from Tucker. I don't know if he'll even think about reaching out to my brother. Will their friendship magically turn back on again now that we're back together? That's shitty, if they can only be friends when we're together. I thought their friendship was strong enough to withstand anything, even our breakup.

I win my second race, but a girl from Harvard wins the third. I'm disappointed. I could have done better. I could have—

I can only control the things within my power, the voice of my old therapist warns. Someone else running faster than me is not something I can control. I can only improve, run faster, so that I can come out on top next time.

My events are done for the day, but there are still another two hours left of the meet. I jog across to the bleachers—just for a little while. I want to sit in the stands and get the full experience.

I'm such a liar.

Tucker grins at me as I approach. He meets me at the stairs, pulling me into a hug. He doesn't care that I'm sweaty and gross. He tugs me close and kisses me sweetly.

"You did great, Princess."

"I should have had that last race."

He curls my braid around his finger. "You'll get them next week. You've got this."

I wind my arms around his neck, tipping my face up for another kiss. He laughs and brushes his lips across mine, teasing, taunting.

"I missed you," he whispers, before he kisses me properly.

He used to come to all of my track meets, even the ones we had to travel to across state lines. He's always been my biggest fan, even more so than my brother.

"I'm right here," I tell him.

Tucker lets out a sigh, resting his forehead against mine. "I know. I still can't believe it."

"Believe it, baby." I kiss him again. "I'm just a girl standing in front of a boy—"

He laughs, swatting me on the butt. "Get out of here with that. You want to watch that movie? Fine, we'll watch it. You know I'm a sucker for Julia Roberts."

I grin in victory. "I have other plans for you."

His easy smile drains from his face. His eyes rove mine, searching desperately for an answer to his unasked question.

"We're doing this? It's really real?"

I trace his bottom lip with my thumb. "It's as real as we make it."

He sets out a blustery sigh. He crushes his mouth over mine, exploring, taking. My knees go a bit weak, and I sag against him. He pulls me closer and wraps his arms more securely around me.

"I love you," he says, before he kisses me again. "I think I've always loved you, even when I hated you."

"Do you hate me now?"

Tucker grins at me. "Not in the slightest."

fifteen

. . .

Tucker

EVENTUALLY, Mason has to go back down to the field. The track meet continues on, so even though her events are over, she still has to stick around. She gives me and my friends leave to head out. Although I want to spend all my time with her, she's needed on the field, and I have things to do tonight.

My sheets are freshly washed. My room is picked up. My homework is done. The guys have a vague idea as to our plans tonight—it's not like we were very subtle at the track meet or last night at dinner. Miles will be staying at Sam's place tonight. Greg is going to a party, taking Barrett with him. That leaves just Amir and Wes in the house. They're easily enough ignored. They are also mature enough to ignore any noises they hear from the direction of my room. I certainly don't plan on holding back tonight.

Shit. Condoms. I've never had to buy them before. Jamal bought me a box as a going away present before I left for college—I ended up giving them away to my roommate freshman year once it was clear I wouldn't have an opportunity to use them before they expired. I haven't needed them in the last two and a half years. Never even came close.

Barrett's door is open, but I know I can't ask him, not

without opening myself up to a lifetime of mockery. Greg is taking a pre-party nap. Amir's room is all the way downstairs. Wes is purposefully celibate—I highly doubt he keeps condoms.

I sneak down the hall to Miles's room. The door is unlocked. Good. I make a beeline for his bedside table. The drawer is ajar, a strip of condoms on clear display. I rip off two, shoving them in my pocket. After a long moment, I grab a third. Just in case.

There are footsteps behind me.

"What are you doing?"

Miles. Shit.

I hold up the lone condom. "I owe you, man. Big time."

"Buy your own." His face is hard, impassive. He looks like he's about to tackle me on the football field.

I force an easygoing grin. "I will. First thing tomorrow. I'll restock your supply."

He huffs out a laugh and relaxes, crossing his arms over his chest. "You don't need to do that. Just tell me you didn't take all of them."

"Only took enough to get me through the night. You have plenty."

He looks thoughtful. "So you and Mason… you're serious about her?"

"I'm in love with her. I've been in love with her for years. I never thought we would be able to…"

To make up. To get past all the bullshit. To be stronger together than we are apart.

Miles hums. "How does it feel?"

"Like my world makes sense again. Like I can breathe again."

There's a sense of peace that has settled over me. The itch deep inside of me has been soothed. I know our issues won't be magically resolved in the blink of an eye. I have grad school on the horizon. I don't even know her major. She might have decided psychology isn't for her.

She might not be the same woman I fell in love with all those years ago. That's a risk I have to take.

"I'm happy you're happy," he finally says. "I hope she's good for you."

"I hope she is, too."

"A lot of guys… when they get girlfriends, their concentration suffers," Miles says. "Mine did. It's hard to focus on school and football when I have Sam constantly on my mind."

"Mase and I were together for so long. We know how to be a couple. We know how to balance school and sports and each other. We've got this," I tell him.

"I believe you. I'm just saying…"

"I know. I know." I sigh. "I was happy on my own. I missed her, yeah, but I didn't feel the need to couple up with just anyone I came across. She's special. She makes me want to be better."

He snorts. "And the sex isn't half bad."

I hold up the pilfered condom again. "Thanks, man, for being so cool about this. Seriously, tomorrow I'm going out and buying a box. I should have gone out and gotten them this morning. I spaced. I haven't had to do this before."

Miles claps me on the arm. "Don't sweat it. Just don't make a habit of it."

———

Mason shows up on our doorstep at half-past six, a bag of Japanese takeout in hand.

"I brought food," she announces unnecessarily.

"Get in here." I tug her inside the threshold and pull her into my arms. She squeals and melts into me. Her cold nose brushes against mine.

"Mm. You're so warm."

"I missed you." I have to swallow back the emotions swirling within me. She's *here*. This isn't a figment of my imagination. The last two and a half years have majorly sucked without her, but she's here and wants me again. I can't wrap my brain around it.

"Missed you, too," she says, burrowing her cold forehead in my neck. She breathes in deep. "You smell good."

"It's called taking a shower."

Her lips curve into a smile as she looks up at me from beneath her lashes. "And did you think of me?"

"No." Yes. I needed to take the edge off a bit. Two and a half years is a long time to go fucking my hand. I don't want our night to end too soon.

Mason laughs. "You're such a terrible liar."

"Good thing I can't lie to you." I tip her chin up and kiss her slowly. Her arms come up around me. She's still holding the bag of food. "Do you want to eat upstairs? Or hang out down here?"

There's a cough behind me. Without turning to look, I know it's either Amir or Wes, lounging on the couch or in the armchair with a book in hand.

"Upstairs," she says immediately. She waves at someone behind me. From the laugh, I presume it's Amir. Wes would be too busy reading to pay her any attention.

Taking her by the hand, I lead her up to my room, the third door from the left. I've cleaned everything up. The bathroom I share with Barrett is spotless. I've even left the seat down for her.

She sets the food down on my desk. She rifles through her bag, coming up with a bottle of wine. "Mark got us a present. That's why I'm late. He turns twenty-one today and wanted to use his ID."

"Hm." I take the bottle, inspecting the label. I've never had wine before. Never had an interest.

"You have an opener?"

I set the bottle on the desk. "We don't need that."

She turns to me, a smile curving her full lips. "Hm?" She mimics me, her eyes bright.

"I want you one hundred percent sober and consenting when you're in my bed. No half measures." I pull her towards me by the gap between her coat's buttons. She starts forward, wrapping her arms low around my waist. "Either you want this or you don't. No in-betweens."

"I want this," she says. "I want you." She tips her face up for a kiss.

I smooth her hair back from her face. "You can still change your mind. I don't want to—"

Mason lets out a low growl. She removes her hands from around me. I feel momentarily bereft until she starts undoing the buttons on her coat. She pulls off her scarf and tosses it behind her.

"I love you," she says. "I want you. And if you don't fuck me, I swear to g—"

I pull her back into my arms. Her lithe form is so tiny against my bulk. I like the dichotomy of that. She's never cared that I'm big. Her warm brown skin is lighter than mine by a shade or two. I slip my hand into hers and marvel at her tiny palm in my larger paw.

Her free hand rises to the tab of my sweatshirt. She unzips me and slides her arms inside, so she's hugging me without the bulky fabric in her way. I lean down and kiss her slowly, thoroughly. There's no need to rush. Everything is new again. We only get one shot at a second chance.

Her tongue comes out to tangle with mine. I pull her more firmly against me. Her hands map my arms, my shoulders, my chest, exploring, memorizing.

I take a step back, and she whines deep in her throat. My hands go to the hem of her sweater, and her smile goes from disappointed to victorious. She helps me pull off her sweater and camisole until she's standing in front of me in an electric yellow bra.

My favorite color. It looks good on her. It will look even better on my floor.

Before I can make a move, her hands tug at my shirt. I let her pull it off of me, until we're standing there chest to chest, skin to skin. The lace of her bra tickles against my chest hair.

Picking her up by the waist—she's impossibly weightless—I toss her onto my bed. She bounces and squeals. Her noises subsist into a pleased moan when I join her on the bed, laying out beside her. She wraps her arms around me and pulls me on top of her. I'm careful not to crush her with my bulk—I've only gained weight since we were last together—but she tugs me closer.

"You aren't going to break me," she says quietly, brushing her thumb across my cheek. "I know what I can handle."

I bite the pad of that thumb. "Can you handle me?"

Her mouth curves into a smile. "Yeah, I think so."

I kiss her again, and again, and again, until she's panting and breathless, arching for me. Her hands explore my spine, my arms, the small of my back. She wraps her legs around my waist and bucks up against me. I'm touching as much of her as I can reach, her strong legs and the curve of her breast, her pert ass that fits so perfectly in my hand.

"Princess…"

"Take your pants off, Tucker," she says. No, demands. She's imperious in her request.

Slowly disentangling, I move off the bed. But I don't take off my pants. Instead, I work at the waistband of her leggings, drawing them down her muscular legs.

"How are you feeling? No fatigue?"

"I'm aching," she says. She props herself up on her elbows to watch me.

She's wearing matching underwear, an electric yellow

scrap of lace. Leaning forward, I place a gentle kiss to the top of her mound.

Mason's hips lift off the bed. She whines.

"Tucker…"

Before I can take off her leggings, I have to contend with her shoes. They're off in the blink of an eye. The fleece-lined pants go next until she's laying in my bed in nothing but some electric yellow underwear and a smile.

"Hang on."

She frowns. "What's wrong?"

"Nothing's wrong. I just need to take a mental picture. Memorize this moment."

She grins and poses, thrusting out her chest for me.

Memory saved for me to enjoy later, I kneel at the side of the bed. I pull her hips toward me and nuzzle her satin-smooth skin.

"Baby…"

I nose aside the scrap of lace. It's soaked through. The tip of my tongue touches her folds, and she lifts her hips, needy. Her hand slides down to the back of my head, holding me to her.

And I oblige her. She tastes a little bit sweet, a little bit salty, a little bit perfect. I run my fingers through her wetness and she sighs.

"More."

Slipping a finger inside her, I have to grunt at the feeling of her tight, wet heat clenching around me. She needs a lot of foreplay to be properly prepped, and I'm happy enough to indulge. There's only one thing I enjoy more than eating her out, and that's finally getting the chance to be inside her. I can't have one without the other.

I wrap my lips around her clit, and she groans—loudly.

"Shh, Princess. You don't want the guys to guess what's goin' on up here." I flick my tongue against her clit, meeting her eye. She groans again, more quietly now.

"They already know." Her fingers slide down her body, holding the drenched gusset of her underwear to the side for me. "It's going to get very loud in here. I refuse to apologize for that."

"As well you shouldn't. Make all the noise you want. You know I like that." I slide a second finger inside of her. "I'm just warning you, these walls are thin."

"I don't fucking care." She rides my fingers, her free hand clutching at the sheets. "Tucker…"

I give her a proper licking. "Yes, baby?"

"Close. So… close."

So I focus on giving her what she needs. Her thighs tense around my head. Her hand presses into the back of my hand with more force. Her hips work as she uses me to get off, riding my fingers, riding my face.

With a loud, long groan, she falls apart. I keep up my pace, working my fingers and my tongue against her until she collapses onto the sheets, thoroughly spent.

"King…"

"Princess?"

She gives me a lazy, sated smile. "Come hold me."

I join her on the bed, wrapping her up in my arms. "Anything you want, sunshine."

sixteen

. . .

Mason

NOTHING FEELS as good as when Tucker holds me in his arms. I bask in the afterglow, in the warm familiarity of his embrace, as my heartbeat slowly returns to normal. His hand runs over my hip, down the curve of my spine, touching all of me he can. Our legs tangle. He's still wearing his joggers, his feet covered by dingy white socks.

I tip my face up for a kiss, and he indulges me. He tastes like me, musky and rich. I pull him on top of me until I'm crushed beneath his impressive bulk. His heavy weight is like a balm that soothes my soul, exerting just enough pressure that my body feels tight and loose at the same time. My anxieties float away. I wrap my legs around his waist, bringing us into direct intimate contact. He's hard against my core. He tilts his pelvis into mine, grinding slowly.

I familiarize myself with his new body. There's a scar on his shoulder I don't recognize. Another on the inside of his forearm, jagged and thick. His legs are thick and strong. There's something about his broad chest that calls to me. I run my hand over his belly. I have a visible six pack, which is more a function of my low body fat percentage and the amount of time I spend running than any real ab workouts—I much prefer his natural, soft belly to another set of perfect abs.

Tucker grinds into me, but he doesn't make any attempt to take off my bra and underwear, doesn't try to hurry us along. That's something I've always enjoyed about him: he takes his time, he savors the moment. He ducks his head and nuzzles my neck, sucking gently on the pressure point. His teeth scrape over my sensitive skin and I'm just—I'm done. I need him—right now.

"Pants. Take your pants off." With my feet, I try to move his waistband south. He chuckles softly into my neck and scoots back. His eyes meet mine, and he swallows thickly. His pants inch down, revealing more of his smooth brown skin.

He's hard, thick. My mouth waters at the sight of him. I didn't know how good I had it until it was gone. He kicks away his sweatpants, and his cock bobs up against his thick belly. A healthy dose of hair covers his chest, about two or three days' worth of growth, pointing down in a line that leads directly to his cock. He's freshly manscaped.

"King…"

He fists his cock. "We don't have to do this."

Oh, hell no. I sit up and reach behind me to take off my bra. He growls, releasing his cock to press me back against his pillows. Dragging down the cups, he drags his teeth across my nipple before he sucks the tip into his mouth, sucking in earnest. My head falls back against the pile of pillows.

It's exquisite torture.

He pinches my other nipple, rolling it between his fingertips. He plays me like a violin, beautiful and perfect.

"King."

He releases my nipple with a pop, rubbing his bearded cheek across the sensitive nub. "Yes?"

"I think you should fuck me."

He grins at me, devious and defiant. "Oh, I should?"

"Yeah. Right the fuck now."

"As my lady commands." He moves away, grabbing the condom on his bedside table. He sheathes himself and gives a few rough strokes. "Last chance to back out. I don't want to pressure you."

I sit up and unhook my bra, tossing it aside. "Do you not want this? Is that why you keep asking for a status check?"

He fidgets, playing with the tip of his cock. "I want you to be sure."

My hand on his cheek forces him to meet my eyes. "I'm sure. I'm positive. But are you?"

"I don't do this. I don't hook up," he says. "It means something to me. To share this with you, of all people. I just —I want—" He lets out a gusty breath. "It *means* something."

I swallow. "It means something to me, too."

As much as I want to get laid, I want him to be okay with this more. I never want him to regret being with me. He's never been interested in casual sex. Even when we were together in the before, we were on the same page: two young kids drunk on love and hormones. It took ages to convince him to get naked. We were together for nearly a year before he would allow us to get to the next level. He moves at a glacial pace. It's never bothered me before. It shouldn't bother me now.

Slowly, I slide my hand down his broad, heavy chest. I scratch my fingers through the hair there and he whines deep in his throat. Bending down, I scrape my teeth across his nipple, puckered and tight.

His hands fall to my hips, his grip tight as he maneuvers me back against the pillows. He stretches out beside me, half on top of me. His cock twitches against my hip.

"I love you, Tucker. The good, the bad, and the ugly. I love all of you." I lay my hand on his cheek. "We're not taking this step lightly."

He seems to see whatever he's looking for in my eyes. He

shifts above me, his cock positioned at my entrance. On a controlled exhale, he slowly pushes inside of me.

My whole world shifts thirteen degrees to the left. Tucker lets out a grunt and sinks further into me. He drops forward, propping himself up on his hands. I tilt my hips up, rocking into him. His groan echoes in the quiet room.

"Princess, you need to give me a minute here."

I cup the back of his neck. "Everything okay?"

"I've spent the last two and a half years fucking my fist and thinking of you, but it doesn't compare to the real thing. I need—I can't—"

His fists curl into the sheets on either side of my shoulders. In contrast, his kiss is soft, sweet. I try to deepen the kiss; he won't let me. He runs a hand down my side, as if he's memorizing the feel of my skin pressed to his.

Slowly, impossibly slowly, he sinks deeper inside of me, until he's buried balls deep within me. My whole body is alight with glorious anticipation. His presence engulfs me in a cocoon of love and warmth.

"Princess, you feel so good." His grip tightens on my hips. "I might not be able to make this last very long. I promise I'm going to take care of you, even if it ends too soon."

I slide my hand from his neck to his cheek, brushing over his lip with the pad of my thumb. "I don't care how long this lasts. I've got you forever."

His mouth slants over mine again. He licks into my mouth, deepening the kiss. My fingers dig into his meaty shoulders, pressing his chest to mine. He rocks his hips, withdrawing and sliding back in, again and again and again, until I'm breathless and a little dizzy and so, so full.

Tucker raises up off of me. He works a hand between us so he can play with my nipples again. He bends his head to take one in his mouth, scraping his teeth lightly over the sensitive bud. I clench around him, and he groans. The hum reverberates through me.

His thrusts pick up in both speed and force. He slides his hand down my belly to my clit. The feel of his rough, calloused thumb against me nearly makes my eyes roll to the back of my head.

"Baby…"

"I know, Princess, I know." His voice is thick, rumbling through me.

He grabs the headboard for more leverage. I rise up onto my elbows to stay close to him, working my hips and riding his cock. His thumb increases in both frequency and pressure against me as his hips slam into mine.

That elastic band inside of me grows taut. It's like every nerve ending is on fire, all at once, and only he can smother the flames. The room feels like it's tilting, or spinning. My breath comes in fast pants, like I'm running my personal best for my fastest sprint ever. I can't regulate my breathing. My skin feels elastic and pliable.

"King…"

"Hang on, girl. I've got you."

"Kiss me." I tug him to me. He drops down, his belly brushing mine. Pinpricks of delight ricochet through me. I wrap my arms around his neck and kiss him. His rhythm falters.

"Mase."

"Yeah?"

He chokes out a laugh. "I really fucking love you right now."

Emotions rise up from deep within me, threatening to overwhelm me. I love him. I want to be with him. So why is doubt creeping into the back of my mind? I didn't make the decision to hop into bed with him lightly. It's an important step, one we can't undo. Sex changes things. How can it not?

"I love you, too," I say, right before he does this swivel thing with his hips that has me seeing stars. "King—"

"I've got you, sunshine." He does it again. My inner walls spasm, tense. "Let go. Don't fight it."

He focuses on my pleasure. His thumb on my clit. His mouth on my neck. He knows what I need and he lets me take it from him.

Relief hits me like a truck. There's no dainty trembling here; I devolve into full body convulsions, riding the waves of pleasure. He grounds me through it, supporting me, until I collapse, limp with pleasure. He's still hard inside of me. He bends over me and takes what he needs. The cords in the side of his neck stand out in stark relief. His whole body goes tense as his orgasm hits. His groan rattles through me.

Tucker collapses on top of me. The heavy weight of him sends my senses into overdrive. He meets me for a sweet, tender kiss.

"I love you, Mason," he says. He brushes a strand of hair out of my face. "So much. I wish I could express what this means to me, us being us again."

I swallow my hesitations.

"Love you, too." I wrap my arms around him and kiss him thoroughly.

He slides out of me. Immediately, I feel the loss of contact. He rolls off of me, tying off the condom. He grabs a tissue and begins to mop me up.

"Let me go clean up," I tell him, stopping his movements. He nods, chewing on his lip. "Be right back."

In the sanctity of the bathroom, I'm quick to freshen up. I brace my hands on the sink and stare at myself in the mirror.

It's just sex. Sex with my boyfriend, the guy I love. The guy who's been there for me through thick and thin, the guy who loved me even when I broke his heart. The guy I want more than anything. The reason I transferred universities and moved here in the first place.

I can do this. This is going to fix me.

Still naked, I open the bathroom door. Tucker is laying in

his bed, his legs splayed. He's wearing a pair of boxer briefs and nothing else, all of his gorgeous brown skin on display.

"Come here, Princess," he says, patting the space beside him.

Instead, I go over to his desk. "I brought food. We should eat it before it gets cold."

He gets off the bed and comes to stand behind me. He wraps his arms around me and tugs me back against his sweaty chest. "I don't care about the food." He nuzzles my neck. "How are you feeling? No regrets?"

I turn in the protective circle of his arms.

"None," I lie.

His kiss is so tender it brings tears to my eyes. He frowns. "What's wrong?"

"Nothing's wrong," I tell him. "I'm just so happy."

seventeen

. . .

Tucker

WE EAT IN MY BED, sitting cross-legged and laughing as we share a few sushi rolls, a noodle dish, two different kinds of dumplings, and a carton of soup. She even remembered to get a double serving of edamame, my favorite, and there's a bento box with chicken in it in case I need more protein to tide me over.

She thought of everything.

I can't stop touching her. A hand on her knee, my fingers in her hair. The curve of her hips makes my pulse go thready. When we're both ready for a round two, I show her my devotion. As much as I enjoy the sex for the pleasure of it, the physicality of it, it's made all the more better because it's with her.

I'm still waiting for that inevitable moment when I wake up and realize it's all a dream. Until then, I'm going to enjoy it for what it is—super satisfying, soul-soothing sex with the woman of my dreams.

Being with Mason makes my whole world make sense. I don't care that it's only been twenty-four hours that we've been on speaking terms. I know there are things we need to talk about. We're moving fast. We're making up for lost time.

I need to tell my moms. I need to tell Jamal. I need to shout it from the rooftops. She loves me. She wants me. She could have her pick of all the guys in the world, and she picked *me*.

We have a lot of things we need to talk about. I want to know nothing about what she's been up to the last two years. I want to know everything. Does she date? Does she go to frat parties and get drunk every weekend? Does she hug on guys like Mark after track meets?

I realize my reaction to our breakup was… extreme. Most people would have moved on by now. Most people wouldn't become a celibate recluse and retreat into themselves. My moms tried to get me into therapy. I went to two sessions before I realized that talking about her just made me miss her more. I wasn't ready. I don't think I'd ever have been ready. I was mired in the past.

And then she crashed back into my life. I feel at peace again. Stable. I can't make her promise me we'll be together forever. I don't know that two years from now or ten we'll still be the same people.

But for now, I'm going to love her for as long as she'll let me.

Round two is slower. We take our time. She likes when I rub my beard against her neck. She likes the feel of it against the sensitive skin of her inner thighs even more. She touches me with reverence, like she's memorizing the feel of my skin pressed to hers.

My skin vibrates with need for her. I arch my back, thrusting balls deep inside of her. Mason sighs and moans, clenching around me. The headboard thumps against the wall with the force of my thrusts. I don't care. I can't care. My singular focus is on the feel of her surrounding me, on getting her off again, and again, and again, until she's spent and exhausted.

It's more than just the physicality of it. Sure, I like to get off. Sure, I love to be inside of her. But for me it's more about the connection we share when we're connected so intimately. I feel at ease when I'm with her, like I can be wholly myself. She knows everything about me, the good, the bad, and the ugly.

She used to know everything about me. I don't know that she does anymore.

Mason's fists curl in the sheets as she lifts her hips to meet mine. Her moans increase in both pitch and frequency. She's getting close. I work a hand between us to rub at her clit the way I know she needs, firm and unyielding.

She falls to pieces. Her hands scrabble at the sheets, searching for purchase, as her inner walls squeeze me in a vise grip. She pulls me down onto her for a soul-searing kiss, more tongue and teeth than anything else.

The orgasm builds deep in my gut and runs up my spine. I follow her over the edge with a shout that she muffles with a kiss.

"Shhh," she says, running her thumb over my bottom lip. I bite that thumb, and she giggles.

"I love you." There's a lump in my throat I can't clear. I'm so overcome by my feelings, I don't know how to survive it. If I can survive it.

"I love you, too," she says, her smile sweet, but her eyes are sad.

I collapse onto the bed beside her. I should go clean up. I should help her clean up. I should do something. Say something.

She curls up beside me, her head on my chest as we both work to regulate our breathing. For being a big guy, I'm in pretty decent shape, but the last two hours have made it clear I need to spend a few more days on cardio and a little less time lifting weights. Well, let's not go crazy. Just adding the cardio should make a difference.

Eventually, she shifts. Mason turns away and wordlessly

heads to the bathroom to clean up. I tie off the second condom and wipe up with the washcloth strategically waiting on my bedside table.

Something is up with her. I wish I knew what it was. Is it that we're rushing into this? I hope not. I hope it's just something else bothering her, like track drama or a demanding coach or something with her friends.

She's withdrawn into herself again when she comes out of the bathroom.

"We should talk," I say, offering her my hand. She doesn't take it.

"I'm exhausted." She yawns and stretches. I'm momentarily distracted by the swell of her chest as her lungs expand and contract. "Can I stay the night?"

"Of course, Princess." I force myself into motion. I straighten the sheets and pull the blankets over the bed.

She comes up behind me. She wraps her arms around me, her head on my back.

"I'm so happy we're doing this," she says to my back.

But she doesn't sound happy. She sounds miserable.

I force myself to clear my throat, clear the moment. "Do you want a t-shirt to sleep in?"

"Ooh, yes, please."

Slowly, I disentangle her arms from around me. I grab an old shirt from freshman year and hand it to her. It's comically large on her. The fabric hangs nearly to her knees and down to her elbows. She doesn't care. She hugs herself with a wistful smile on her face.

"Come on, baby," I tell her, offering my hand again. "Let's go to bed."

This time she takes it.

We crawl onto the mattress, and I pull the covers over her. She scoots over until she's wrapped around me, her head on my chest.

"Do you have any plans for tomorrow?"

My calendar is wide open. "I need to get a lift in, probably in the afternoon. The guys and I usually go around two."

"How about we stay all day in bed and only leave to go get food?" She grins up at me, her eyes tired. "I like the way that sounds."

"As long as we also go to the pharmacy, I'm good with that plan."

"What's at the pharmacy?"

I chuckle quietly. "A new box of condoms. I only have one left."

Her swallow is loud in the quiet room. "Oh."

"You should have seen me sneaking around the house to steal them." I shake my head. "It's the only thing I really should do, like, ASAP. Everything else on my to-do list can wait a few days."

"You don't keep them on hand?"

"I don't need them. I don't use them." I run my hand over her upper arm, memorizing the feel of her. She's all lithe muscle, solid, compact. "I never came close to wanting to use them. It just wasn't on my radar."

She snorts. "Right."

"What's that supposed to mean?"

"Nothing. I'm tired."

"No, Mason. Tell me."

She rolls away, her back to me. She curls up into a little ball. "I don't want to talk about this right now."

"Well, I do."

"Well, we can't always get what we want."

I have no idea where this sudden coldness is coming from. I run my hand over her arm and she flinches, pulling away from me.

"Mason."

"Go to sleep, Tucker."

"I can't. Not if you're upset with me. I don't know what just happened."

She whirls around to face me. "Really? Never, not once did you hook up with another girl?"

My throat feels tight. "I told you. I've only slept with one other woman. It was right after... after... after *it*—and it was awful. I felt miserable after. I didn't go to parties. I didn't hang out. I was that guy who stayed in every Saturday night and played video games alone in my dorm room, because I was so numb I didn't know how to function. And then by the time I figured out how to live my life again, it was ingrained as habit. I like staying in. I don't like parties. They're loud and the music is shitty and I never know what to say to people when I don't want to drink. So I hang out with my roommates. They're good guys. And after a football game, I'm usually too tired and bruised to want to do anything."

I take a deep breath. She's still looking at me with that hard expression on her face.

"So, no, I don't hook up. I don't go out trawling for easy pussy. I've been in love with you since I was fourteen, Mason. That doesn't just go away. You broke something deep within me. It doesn't just get fixed in the blink of an eye. I'm not magically healed. It's going to take work. We're both going to have to put in the work to get back to where we were. But, baby, I believe we can do it. We can get there again."

Her eyes are bright. "Okay."

"Okay?"

"I'm sorry I snapped. I'm just—I—" She hugs her chest. "It's been an emotional twenty-four hours. I believe you. I want to be with you. The past is the past. We have to move forward. We can't keep looking back."

"I want you, Mason, as much as you'll give me." I reach out my hand and I'm gratified when she takes it. "I don't want to casually date. I don't want to hook up. I want to be *with* you. This is the real thing, sunshine. No half measures."

She unwinds. "No half measures."

I brush my thumb across her cheek, and she leans into the contact.

"I freaked," she admits, and I chuckle out a breath of laughter.

"I can tell."

"You're right, we should talk," she says. "Not right now. Not tonight. But soon. We should make sure we're on the same page with where this is heading."

"Agreed."

I meet her for a soft, sweet kiss. I pour all of my emotion into it. Her arms wind around my neck, pulling me close.

"Let's get some sleep, Princess," I finally tell her. I brush some loose hair back into her protective braid. "It's been a long day."

She settles in my arms. She lets me curl around her, my arm around her waist. Our legs tangle in the sheets.

"I do love you, King," she says as I turn out the lights. "I know sometimes I get scared, but I—"

"I know. I do, too." I run my hand over her arm, and she sighs.

"Good night."

"Sweet dreams, Princess."

eighteen

. . .

Tucker

MY PHONE VIBRATES with a text from a number I never thought I'd see again. Micah Prince. It's made even worse by the fact that I'm wrapped up in bed with his sister. His very naked, very sexy sister.

My friendship with the Prince twins began in the second grade, about a week after I moved to Elmwood Elementary. My brother and I were waiting for the school bus to take us home. I was already big and tall for my age. Some of the fifth graders were picking on me, saying I was too big and dumb to function, that I must have been held back a few years.

Before Jamal could say anything to defend me like a big brother was supposed to, Micah came flying in out of nowhere and kicked the meanest bully right between the legs. Mason was right behind him like a feral cat, hitting and scratching anyone she could get her hands on. Before we knew what was happening, the situation devolved into a full on brawl. Nine year old Jamal had a fifth grader in a head-lock. Micah and Mason gave as good as they got.

And I just stood there, struck dumb, as these two strangers I'd never talked to before attempted to beat down three bigger, stronger, older bullies.

The bus monitor eventually pulled them apart, holding Micah aloft by the collar of his shirt and Mason by her pigtails. (It was a different time back then.) They were both spitting mad, nearly frothing at the mouth like the feral children they were.

When the monitor moved on, herding the bullies down the hall, he brushed off his shirt and held out his hand.

"Hi, I'm Micah," he said. He hooked a thumb over his shoulder. "This is my sister, Mason. Yes, we're twins, and no, we're not identical."

I said nothing. Jamal nudged me. I still didn't talk.

"He's Tuck," my big brother said for me. He pushed me forward. I stumbled and fell down.

And then the prettiest girl I'd ever seen was crouching down and offering me her hand. I took it and my whole world fell apart. I was smitten.

All this to say, I've known the Princes for close to two-thirds of my life. Micah and I were inseparable. He was the one who convinced me to ask Mason out when we were fourteen. He was our biggest supporter. He didn't get squeamish when we kissed, or when I couldn't hang out with him because I was spending time with her, or when our relationship started getting more serious. He covered for us with their parents when we wanted some alone time—naked—at my house. He was my best friend.

And then right before I left for college, she texted me to tell me it was better if we didn't go to college "with strings holding us back from being who we're meant to be." She didn't answer my calls. Neither did he.

I stopped calling after that first miserable week on campus. I got drunk and went to a frat party and slept with a random girl I met that night. I don't know her name. I don't remember anything about her, aside from the fact that she wasn't Mason. It didn't feel right. I never should have gone through with it. But I did, and I had to live with the consequences.

I called Micah that night, drunk out of my mind. Confessed all of my sins. He never responded to my two o'clock in the morning voicemail. He never responded to the dozens of texts I sent him over the course of that first semester. Eventually I stopped trying. Our teams never met on the football field. He slipped out of my life in the blink of an eye. When Mason ended things, I lost my two best friends in one fell swoop.

So it's super shitty that he's only texting me now that we're back together. I haven't told my moms yet. I haven't told Jamal yet. The only people who know are the people at school.

The text is simple. *Hey man, what's up?* I shake my head and drop my phone back onto my nightstand. I'm so not in the mood to deal with him right now. I have a pretty, nearly naked girl in my bed, one condom left, and nothing to do for the next several hours.

Mason makes a cute little snuffling noise. She's waking up. I run my hand over her arm, gentle, soothing, and she leans back, searching for me. Wrapping my arm securely around her waist, I drop a kiss to her shoulder and tug her back into me.

"Go back to sleep," she whines, tossing and turning her head on the pillow. "It's too early."

"It's ten."

Her body goes tense. "It's ten?!"

"Yes?"

She's wide awake in the blink of an eye. "Shit. Shit!"

"What's wrong?"

"I have a study group for my abnormal psych class at eleven at the library." She flies into motion, rolling over me and off the bed.

"You have an hour."

"I need to go home and shower. I smell like sex."

"You can shower here."

"And what, wear yesterday's clothes?"

I didn't think about that. "Yes?"

"I don't have my books, I don't have my backpack, I—"

"Princess." I set my hands on her shoulders. "Breathe, okay? We have an hour. Forty-five minutes before you need to walk over there."

"Don't tell me to calm down, Tucker." Her eyes flash, and she ducks out of my grasp, grabbing her leggings.

"I'm not. I'm only saying, take a breath. We don't need to panic. There's plenty of time for you to take a shower, gather your things, and make it to the library by eleven."

She sits on my desk chair to pull on her pants.

"I know. I *know*."

"What do you have planned for the rest of your day?"

Mason sighs, scrubbing a hand over her face. "I need to study. I have a quiz in my statistics class on Tuesday."

"Okay, great. I have a lift with the guys, and then I need to run some errands. Do you want to have dinner tonight?"

She swallows. It shouldn't be a big decision. That it's giving her pause is making me nervous.

"Maybe another night. I should spend some time with my roommates."

I force a smile. "Sounds like a good plan. Can I see you one night this week? We can grab dinner or something."

"Yeah, sure. Tomorrow works for me." She pulls her pants on, then takes off my t-shirt. She hunts on the floor for her bra.

"Mase."

Her sigh is aggravated. "What?"

"Are we okay?"

"Why wouldn't we be?"

"I don't know. That's why I'm asking. Because last night was pretty fucking spectacular, and then things got weird, and I want to make sure we're on the same page."

Her smile is entirely too peppy to be real. "We're great, babe."

nineteen

. . .

Tucker

WHAT I THOUGHT WOULD BE a straightforward
conversation turns out to be a landmine.

"Hi, Mom. Hi, Mama," I say, waving to the videochat
screen.

My mom rolls her eyes. "What's wrong?"

"Nothing's wrong. Why would you automatically assume
that something is wrong?"

"Boy, I changed your diapers. I know when something is
bothering you."

I bite my lip. "So, I have good news and bad news."

Mama sighs. "That sounds promising."

"I have a girlfriend," I blurt. "I'm dating someone."

Mom slaps the table, making the camera shake. "About
damn time. I'm happy for you, kid."

"What's her name?" Mama asks.

"That's the thing. It's Mason."

Mom blinks at me. "As in…"

"As in, Mason Prince. Yeah." I rub the back of my neck as
heat rises to my cheeks. "She transferred here last semester.
We recently reconnected, and we're… yeah."

They're both quiet. For a moment, I think the video chat might have frozen.

Then Mama coughs. "Well, I'm happy if you're happy, Tuck."

"I am. I will be. I just…"

Mom sighs. "What did she do?"

"It's just weird. She's being weird."

"Maybe because you haven't talked to her in the last two and a half years," Mama snarks. "How well do you really know this girl?"

"I know her." I know her as well as I know myself.

At least, that used to be the case.

"I used to know her," I amend. "Last night was great, but then it got a little… weird. And this morning she was off."

"Was it the sex? Did that freak her out?" Mom asks.

"I don't know. I don't think so. She was totally into it at the time. It was after that she started flipping out."

Mama's eyes narrow. "Flipping out how?"

"She picked a fight over something innocuous that I said, and I—I don't know what triggered it. We were good. We were great. And then we were fighting and—"

"The female mind is a mystery even to us women," Mom says. "Maybe she just needed to process. How long have you really been together?"

"A day and a half. It happened Friday afternoon. We didn't…"

Mama laughs. "Consummate?"

"Yeah. Until last night." Heat rises to my cheeks.

"And did she… enjoy herself?" Mom raises her eyebrows pointedly.

"Multiple times." I bite my lip to hide my pleased smile.

She grins. "Attaboy!"

"Thank you?"

"So it wasn't the several orgasms that freaked her out," Mama says dryly. "What else could it have been?"

I chew my lip. "I think it bothers her that I didn't date when we were split up. That I didn't… experiment."

"You weren't interested in it," Mom says gently. "You tried. It didn't work for you. There's no shame in that, kiddo. You have to own who you are."

"I am. I do." The word demisexual haunts me. There's so much more to me than a label that may or may not apply to me. I don't want to dig too deeply to find out whether I am or not. It doesn't matter to me. It shouldn't matter to me.

"If she can't accept that about you, then maybe you have to consider that she isn't the right one for you."

"But I love her."

Mama sighs. "Sometimes love isn't enough."

I swallow. I just got her back. I don't want to give her up again so soon.

"It'll work out," Mom tells me. "Either you figure it out or you don't. There's no need to rush a decision."

"Yeah. Yeah. You're right."

"Of course I'm right. I'm your mother," she says. "Are you eating enough?"

"Yeah. I'm about to head to the ASC for a pre-workout snack."

Mama peers intently at the screen. "Did you do something different with your beard?"

"I trimmed it. It was time."

"I like it," she says. She hits Mom lightly on the arm. "Our baby boy is all grown up now. He has a beard and a girlfriend."

Mom laughs and wraps an arm around her. "He's been a grown up for a while now."

"No, he's still our baby."

I groan. "Stop being weird."

"We're not being weird. You're being weird." Mom makes a face at me. "Call your brother. He hasn't heard from you in a week."

"We're playing phone tag. I called him on Thursday." He left me a voicemail on Friday, while I was in class. He had two games back to back. He actually got some playing time last night. He got three two-pointers and one Hail Mary three-pointer at the end of the first half. Not bad for a rusty rookie riding the bench.

"Well, call him back," Mom says. "He should hear your news."

"I will. Today."

Mama clears her throat. "We'll let you get back to your day. Go get something to eat, do your workout. Get on with your day."

"Love you."

Mom blows me a kiss. "Love you more, baby."

I disconnect the call and close my laptop, setting it beside me on my bed. I close my eyes and take a deep breath.

Mason is probably just processing the newness of our relationship. It's a lot to throw at her. We went from not even speaking to back in bed in less than twenty-four hours. She has feelings for me; she wants to be with me. I have to trust her, trust that this behavior is simply temporary as she works through everything. I'll get the old Mason back any moment now.

I can't call Jamal now—I'm so not in the mood to deal with his teasing me over this—but I can respond to that text message.

I never deleted Micah's number. I couldn't bring myself to get rid of his contact. I didn't want to accept that it was over.

Not much, how about you?

There. I did it. I texted him back.

I stare at the contact screen. My last messages to him show up earlier in the conversation thread. Desperate pleas for him to call me back. Memes and jokes I thought he would like. A cry for attention. A cry for affection.

Those three grey dots immediately jump at the bottom of the screen.

I'm good, Micah writes right away. *Coming to visit in two weeks.*

You're coming to Newton?

Gotta see the sunshine's new digs.

So he doesn't know.

Or maybe he does. I don't know. I can't tell.

Micah texts again. *No response to that? Have you seen her?*

Yeah.

And how was that?

You should talk to your sister.

I do.

Not recently?

Did something happen?

You should talk to her.

Dude. What the fuck.

Talk to Mason.

Why are you being so weird about this?

Because I fucked your sister last night, I type out. No. That's needlessly antagonistic. I erase the text.

It's not my news to share.

There's news?? Does this mean what I think it means?

I don't know.

Are you back together??

What kind of sorcery is this?

You should really talk to your sister.

Dude.

I stare at my phone for several long minutes.

We haven't talked in the last two and a half years. Why now?

Because I'm coming to visit. Just booked the ticket.

Great.

I don't know how to react to this. I lay my phone down on my chest and stare at the ceiling.

I miss my best friend. If Mason was my world, Micah was

my moon. He balanced me out. We worked together, we worked out together, we did everything together. He was my best friend from the very first day we met.

That's why it hurt so much when he dropped me after the breakup. I didn't realize her dumping me meant he would, too. I lost my two closest friends in one fell swoop, in the course of dissolving the relationship I thought would last forever.

Maybe she was insecure. Maybe she couldn't have handled it. I know myself: I wasn't about to cheat on her with all of the college girls hanging out at football parties. I was devoted solely to her.

We're dating, I finally text him. *We're together again.*

He types something, then erases it. When he finally sends the message, I have to blink.

Fucking finally!

So you're happy?

I'm fucking ecstatic, Micah writes. *Glad you two finally pulled your heads out of your asses.*

Thank you?

It'll be just like old times. The three musketeers. We're going to party our faces off next week.

twenty

. . .

Mason

MY STUDY GROUP meets in the psychology library, a small offshoot of the humanities and social sciences libraries. It's a small meeting room with six desks and tables, a few computers, and some shelves of textbooks and reference books. There's also a printer where we can print twenty free pages a day. It's become my home away from home, a quiet little sanctuary where I can escape the hubbub of the track team house or the ASC and surround myself with other like-minded people.

I show up to study group at 10:58. I'm freshly showered and wearing clean clothes, which is not the case for all of my study buddies. One girl is clearly hungover, pounding Gatorade like her life depends on it. A guy is wearing sweatpants and a wrinkled t-shirt that smells like he slept in it. We're a mess.

We crack open our abnormal psychology textbooks and crank out two chapters' worth of review. It's slow going. Jack has an anecdote about every single case. Dvora constantly thinks she might need to be diagnosed with whatever new disorder we're reviewing. And Rachael? She chomps on her gum so loudly, I might strangle her.

I don't have time to think about Tucker. My body aches with the pleasant soreness that comes after a night of vigorous sex. I missed sex. I missed sex with him.

But I can't think about him. If I think about him, I'm going to doubt myself, and if I start doubting myself, I'm going to spiral into a web of anxiety I don't think I can pull myself out of.

Are we making the right decision?

He keeps repeating that he loves me, like he's afraid I'm going to forget. He seems to need constant reassurance that I feel the same. I do.

I think I do.

It was so much easier to date in high school. The rules were clear: hold hands in the hallway, make out at lunch, go to each other's sporting events. Wear his sweatshirt to warn all the other guys to back off, to let all the other girls know he was off limits. We'd go to parties on Friday nights and hang out with the other football players and cheerleaders. We'd go to the movies on Saturday nights and then to the diner for a milkshake and French fries before sneaking home minutes before curfew.

There was a routine. It made sense.

Dating in college is... different. Neither of us have paying jobs—we can't, not while being student athletes and keeping up with our insane practice and competition schedule. All of our meals take place in the dining hall. Sure, there are parties every night, but I don't think Tucker is the type of guy who goes out drinking and living it up. He said it himself: he hangs out with his roommates and plays video games.

I don't know that I want to become a reclusive shut-in with him. I like my friends. I like going to parties. And, yes, I like drinking. Last weekend was an aberration. Normally, I know where to draw the line. While I might get drunk, I don't get blitzed. It was a blip. It won't happen again.

Everything about Georgetown was a mistake. I made too

many mistakes there. Coming to Newton was supposed to give me a fresh start, and for the most part, it did. I made new friends. I surrounded myself with better influences. I'm taking classes I enjoy, learning things I'm interested in. I'm going to take the GRE and get into grad school.

And now I have a boyfriend again. It should thrill me. I should be ecstatic. This is what I wanted, Tucker back in my life.

Instead I just feel hollow.

Micah sends me a wall of text, which means he's worked up and anxious like he was last week when he thought he'd fail out of school. I don't have the bandwidth to deal with him right now. He sends a second text in quick succession, so I pick up my phone to skim.

Why didn't you tell me your plan worked?? I had to hear it from him.

Tucker told Micah? Tucker and Micah are talking again?? On the walk back to Athlete's Village, I call my brother. He answers on the first ring.

"Is it true?"

"Yeah. It's true." There's a lump in my throat I can't clear. "Mic, I'm having second thoughts."

"This is what you wanted. Everything is going according to the plan," Micah reminds me. "We were texting for a while. It took him forever to confirm it. Kept saying I needed to talk to you. So, I'm talking to you."

"We're back together," I tell him, and that aching pressure on my chest increases exponentially. "We consummated it last night. It's officially official."

"Gross, Mase."

"Well, what sort of details do you want?"

"Does he still have feelings for you? Is he happy?"

"He's over the moon. Needier than I remember." Or maybe he's only needy now because I devastated him so thoroughly. "He's... good."

"I can't believe it took so long," he says. "I thought for sure you'd have this over and done with by now."

"Me, too."

I've slept with other people, guys whose names I don't remember with one hundred percent clarity. I've had two other boyfriends. I've experimented. I put myself out there. I tried again.

And he just curled up into the fetal position and hid away from the world. I feel bad that what should have been a straightforward breakup devastated him so much. What did he expect was going to happen? We dated all through high school, but we were moving to different cities for a minimum of four years. High school relationships don't last through college and beyond. We were needlessly tying ourselves down. It was better to set each other free and spread our wings.

I flew. He fell out of the nest. He would still be there if I hadn't forced him to address his feelings.

I want to be with Tucker. I just want him to be the man I need. And that might not necessarily be the man that he is. I can't ask him to change for me, and I can't force him to be someone he's not. He needs to live his best life.

Even if that means his best life isn't with me.

I just don't see how we get past this. He doesn't party. He doesn't go out on Saturday nights. He stays at home—and there's nothing wrong with that. I just don't want to stay shut in all the time. I want to go out. I want to see my friends and celebrate a fucking awesome track meet and enjoy a birthday party without being made to feel like I'm inferior to want to socialize.

And it's not that he's said anything. I don't think he will. But it's either spend time with my friends or time with him, and I don't know which one to choose. I don't want to be forced to choose.

Fred is lying on the couch when I get home. She gives me a none too subtle once-over.

"Late night?"

"Girl. You don't even know." I laugh. I've already been home, showered, left, and now I'm coming back. I feel worn down and hungover—and I didn't even drink last night.

"So the sex—it was good?"

Heat rises to my cheeks. "Yeah, it was… it was perfect."

"Good. I'm glad. You deserve to be happy. You deserve to get laid."

I laugh again. "Somehow I see that happening quite a bit. You won't like it when we're over here."

"Oh? Is he loud?"

"No, it's me. I'm the loud one."

She waves a hand. "I can barely hear you. Your vibrator is louder than you are."

"That's because I'm trying to keep quiet."

"You should love yourself often and enthusiastically," Fred says with her German pragmatism.

"I do."

"I know," she laughs. "I can hear the buzzing."

My mouth drops open, and I gape at her for a second before I laugh. I grab the pillow off the end of the couch and toss it in her face.

"I hate you," I tell her.

"You love me," she counters. She sits up and stretches. "I'm hungry. ASC?"

"It's a plan."

twenty-one

. . .

Mason

THE ASC IS CROWDED. All of the student athletes are fully dressed and showered, unlike the people in my study group. I'm guessing at least half of them have already gotten their workouts in, and the other half have them scheduled for later in the day. At some point today, I need to stretch and do a little bit of yoga. The day after a meet is always a recovery day for me. My body aches with the pleasant soreness of a job well done.

"There's a new pilates class at four," Fred comments as we make our way through the snaking food line. "We should try it."

"Yeah, maybe."

She raises her eyebrows. "You have plans with loverboy today?"

"Not as far as I know." I need some space. Some time to process everything. I like him, I love him, but I can't be all up in his business every moment of the day.

She nods to the far side of the dining hall. "Because he's watching you."

I turn, and sure enough, Tucker is with his roommates at the end of the room. He meets my eye and smiles so radiantly my cheeks hurt from the mere act of looking at him. I force a smile and wave.

"Yeah, we're definitely not going over there," I tell her under my breath, and Fred laughs.

"We totally are."

"Girl. Please."

"He's your boy toy. I want to meet him."

"You met him at Mark's party."

She rolls her eyes. "You mean, the two of you made out at Mark's party. I didn't talk to him. That's why I went home with Mark."

"Nobody forced you to sleep with him." I'm so curious, though. "How was it?"

She considers, piling salad onto her plate. "Enthusiastic. He's like a puppy. He went down on me for, like, ever."

"Would you repeat?"

"Maybe. If we were both bored and had nothing else to do." She shrugs. "It wasn't bad. Maybe next week after the away meet."

We have a meet against Providence College. We leave late Thursday afternoon for the drive down, have a quick practice Friday morning, and then Saturday is go time. There will probably be a low-key party in the hotel, a lot of horny athletes burning off adrenaline. We'll drive back on Sunday mid-morning and go back to our everyday lives.

Tucker is still watching us. I grit my teeth and paste a smile onto my face. Fred and I make our way over to them. He's sitting with three other guys. The one at the end has his book again. Wes, I think his name is. Barrett and Amir are sitting across from him. There's no sight of Greg or Miles.

"Hey, baby," he says, getting out of his seat. He kisses me on the cheek and takes my tray out of my hands, setting it beside his. "I didn't think I'd get to see you again today."

"Surprise?" I say weakly. "You remember Fred, right?"

He grins at her. "Nice to see you again."

"Likewise." She eyes the rest of the guys. "You're okay if we join you guys?"

"The more, the merrier," Amir says, looking her over with blatant interest.

Fred sets her tray down in the seat directly opposite him. The better to bat her eyelashes at him, no doubt.

"How was your study session?" Tucker asks as we take our seats.

"It was… productive. I talked to Micah on the way back. He said he talked to you."

His cheeks go pink. "Yeah. It was—yeah."

"It went well?"

"I think so?" He rubs the back of his neck. "I talked to my moms. They say hi."

"Tell them hi back."

"I will."

I take a bite of my lunch. The noodles are greasy and oily and so, so good. The potstickers are steamed, which makes them health food. Right?

Tucker's working on a plate of cucumber salad and has a side dish of edamame. I would have thought he got his fill last night. There's no sight of a peanut butter sandwich anywhere, which I guess is a success.

"Do you have anything planned for the rest of your day?"

"We're going to take a pilates class at four."

"We are?" Fred asks. I raise my eyebrows at her. "Right. Yeah. We are."

"Pilates is a tough workout," Barrett says. I look him over. I never thought he would be the type of guy who did pilates. "My best friend makes me go to classes with her sometimes. It's intense."

"I like it. Low impact. It's a good recovery workout."

"Maybe I should try it," Tucker says slowly. "I like the idea of low impact."

"We can all go after our lift," Barrett says.

Oh, no. That was not the goal. I don't want to take a cadre of football players to class with me.

But I can't tell them not to come, not without making this into a big thing. They're free to join any workout class the ASC offers. I don't want to fight with Tucker. So if he wants to join us, if he wants to put himself through an hour of torture at the hands of the pilates instructor, I can't stop him.

"Sounds like a plan," Amir says. He and Fred make doe eyes at one another.

Wes grunts and turns a page in his book. I think that means he agrees.

We make small talk through lunch. The weather is nice. The dining hall has surprisingly decent food. The guys miss having a football game every week, but they enjoyed going to the track meet yesterday; they'll have to come to a few more.

It's… pleasant. Tucker finishes his meal and sets his hand on my leg. His touch sends a warmth that spreads through me from the inside out. It's not sexual and it's not possessive: it simply is.

He drops a kiss to the top of my head and stands to clear both of our trays.

"He's cute," Fred says in a stage whisper.

Barrett laughs. Amir gives me a knowing glance.

"Yeah, he is." I watch his ass as he moves through the crowd of people at the tray return. He has a good butt. His shoulders are strong, his arms like cannons. He is a glorious amalgamation of muscle and strength.

Fred clears her throat. "So, yoga? We'll see you later for pilates?"

Barrett grins. "Sounds good."

An hour later, Fred stretches out on her yoga mat and gives me a pointed look. "Girl, you need to spill."

"Spill what?"

She looks confused. "Did I say it right? I need details."

I laugh. "Yeah, you said it right. It's just that there's no details to give."

"I call bullshit. You guys are together now. Why are you being so weird around him?"

"I'm not."

She rolls her eyes. "Right, this is just the guy you've been obsessing over since the day you transferred. You've finally got him right where you want him. And now you're a skittish little kitten around him."

"It's just weird. We need to talk and clear the air, and I just don't have the energy to deal with that right now."

She nods and relaxes into downward dog. "You should. You'll feel better."

"It'll feel worse in the immediacy. It won't be fun." I stretch my sore hamstrings. "But eventually, yeah, it'll make us stronger. It's just that I don't want to do it right now."

"So instead he's going to attach to you like a koala."

"Yeah." I exhale slowly. "He's been very… needy the last few days. Like he's afraid he'll blink, and I'll disappear."

I'm not going anywhere. I want to be with him, I do. But I also value my space. I need some alone time to process every-thing. Fred is right; I've been thinking about him from the minute I got my transfer acceptance. Never in my wildest dreams did I think we'd get here so quickly.

We retreat into silence for a good forty-five minutes, following a workout video we play on Fred's tablet. It feels good to stretch out. My whole body is tense.

At three forty-five, we pack up and head to the pilates studio next door. It's half full with other student athletes, people who have nothing better to do with their Sunday afternoon than work out. There are a handful of other guys in the room. Tucker, Barrett, Amir, and Wes are by far the biggest. I've never seen Wes without his book. His eyes are a light green, bright and clear.

Tucker is wearing baggy gym shorts and a t-shirt with the

sleeves cut off, highlighting the cut of his shoulders and his muscular arms. His feet are encased in dingy white socks.

"You ready for this, babe?" he asks, grinning over at me.

"Yeah. Totally." I attempt an enthusiastic thumbs up. It falls flat. His brow furrows. I clear my throat. "Let's grab rings."

We set up on yoga mats with our pilates rings and weights. I settle on my back and try to focus on my breathing.

Tucker wants to chat. He sits cross-legged beside me and watches me breathe.

"What?"

"Nothing." He shakes his head and turns to the front of the room. "I'm just glad I get to see you."

My heart melts a little bit. He's trying.

This is all a *me* problem. I'm the one itching to pick a fight. It's just that everything he says triggers some kind of involuntary anger response in me. I want to be with him. I want him to love me. So why am I acting like this? I honestly don't know. It's like there's an itch inside of me that I can't scratch. I can't make everything magically be okay.

The instructor begins the class with some light breathing exercises. I can hear Tucker beside me. It's like there's a neon highlighter yellow sign pointing right at him. Look at me! Notice me!

I can't not notice him.

We move on to some light ab work. I chance a glance beside me. Tucker's keeping up with the class. So is Fred. Amir is cursing under his breath. From what I can tell, Barrett and Wes are doing just fine.

It's an intense workout, there's no doubt about that. My abs are on fire as we do leg lift after leg lift after leg lift. We set the ring between our thighs and squeeze and do more leg raises. It doesn't matter that I'm in the best shape of my life; this is hard.

Tucker is huffing and puffing, but he manages to keep

pace with the rest of us. One of the other guys—I think he's a baseball player—collapses onto his yoga mat with a defeated groan.

My man stretches his hand out towards me. The tips of his fingers brush against mine. I link my pinky around his thick index finger. Tucker gives me a tired smile, breathing hard, as he does a million bicycle crunches.

The instructor moves us through the class. It's been ages since I've done a pilates class. Normally, I stick to yoga or a dynamic stretching routine on my recovery days. I kind of miss it. I'll have to make sure to schedule this class for next week after the away meet.

We add in weights for an arm workout. My triceps burn as we do a million tricep kickbacks. I meet Tuck's eyes in the mirror and he winks at me. He's using baby five pound weights, same as me, and sweat pours down his face and dampens his shirt. I know he's fit. I know he can lift. But it's slightly gratifying to know that my big, strong boyfriend is having just as much difficulty with this workout as I am.

Fred's face is pink, the only indicator that she's working hard. Her twin French braids are perfectly neat, not a hair out of place. My hair is falling out of its ponytail and sticking to my face. Sweat pools in my sports bra and at the base of my spine.

The burn feels good. My muscles are deliciously relaxed. Blood rushes in my ears as my heart pounds at a thousand beats per minute.

We head into a cool down. It's a lot of stretching, a few poses borrowed from a yoga repertoire. My body feels loose and pliant. I can do anything. I collapse onto my mat and take a deep breath.

After class is officially over, Tucker turns to me and gives me a tired smile. "That was great, baby. Thank you for suggesting it." He offers a hand and helps me to my feet.

"Any time," I say, a bit weakly. I don't know how to tell him I didn't suggest it; he did.

He leans down for a kiss, and I duck out of his grasp.

"I'm all sweaty."

"I don't care." His hand catches mine, and he slides his sweaty fingers between mine, his face so incredibly earnest it makes my teeth clench. "Come here and kiss me, babe."

Like I'm under his spell, I tilt my face up for a kiss. He parts my lips with his tongue and licks into my mouth. His hands settle on my hips, squeezing gently, as if to reassure himself that I'm physically there. He doesn't tug me into him. There's a solid foot between our bodies.

Our friends start to gather in a half circle around us. Wes looks exhausted, his eyes weary, sweat dripping down his plain white t-shirt. Amir and Barrett are also sweaty messes, though they look considerably more enthusiastic about the last hour than he does.

"I need to come back next week," Amir declares, wiping his face with the hem of his t-shirt. He flashes his big brown belly, hairy and sweaty. He doesn't seem to care. "You guys do this every week?"

"It was our first class," Fred says. She looks immaculate, the only sign of her exertion her beet red cheeks.

"We'll be back," I promise the guys. Even Wes looks intrigued at the idea of doing this again, his mouth quirking up into a half smile.

"We'll have to make it a regular thing," Tucker says, all in and enthusiastic. Because that's the way he is: when he commits, he goes all in. He doesn't do things in half measures. There's no in-between with him.

twenty-two

. . .

Tucker

SOMETHING IS OFF WITH MASON. I don't know what it is, but I know when something is bothering her. She's not telling me something.

My roommates and I spend a few hours hanging out, catching up on a few episodes of Wheel of Fortune and Jeopardy! that Wes recorded. Normally, the six of us gather on Sunday evenings and watch the week's episodes. With half of us having plans tonight, that might not happen.

It's a rare night that Sam isn't with us. She's having a girls' night with her roommates, Miles informs us as he hands me my bowl of popcorn. We're having a guys' night in. When we make it through all of the week's episodes, Wes opens his book and Greg pulls out the video games, and we make it a party.

My phone doesn't ring. I debate texting her, texting Micah, texting Jamal. My brother has a night off in Detroit—he's probably out getting laid with a devastatingly pretty woman who will warm his bed for a night or two before he moves on to the next one. Micah hasn't been a part of my life for two and a half years; I don't know if I know who he is anymore.

He's a top ranked NFL draft prospect. He probably isn't the laid-back guy I remember.

Mason hasn't posted on social media in the last forty-eight hours, but she's replied to a few comments other people have left. She talks a lot with Fredericka, Melissa, and Mark.

I only kept my social media profile because the athletic department requires it. My profile is almost entirely highlights and clips from football games. There's a video of me deadlifting my personal best that I particularly enjoy. Otherwise, I don't post. I use the account to stalk Mason more than anything else.

Observe. Keep watch over. I don't stalk. Her profile is public; she never removed me as a friend.

I know she's had boyfriends. There are pictures of her kissing an Asian guy wearing a Georgetown tennis shirt. Photos with a group of good-looking guys with their shirts off. They all have six-pack abs and virtually no body fat.

It's hard not to feel insecure. Why would she want me when she can get with a guy like that? She can have any guy she wants.

She wants me, a voice says in the back of my head. It sounds a lot like my mom. She wouldn't be with me if she didn't want me.

I just wish I knew what was going on with her.

I go to sleep in my empty bed and think of her. In the morning, I go to class and think of her. She's in my sociology class. She smiles at me and takes her usual seat in the back of the room. I know I won't focus back there, so I don't sit with her; I take my normal spot in the front of the room. The entire time, I think about her. Her smile was wan. Did she get enough rest last night? Did she think of me, too? What on earth is going on with her?

She passes by my desk on her way out. "See you tonight?" she asks, giving me a weak smile.

"Sounds good. Dinner?"

"It's a date," she says.

My stomach churns. A date. I should take her out on a date. What do college kids do for dates? Miles and Sam go to a lot of frat parties—she's in a sorority, so it's a big part of her life, and he doesn't mind the parties. Greg, Amir, and Barrett might casually date, but that usually involves hooking up with the same girl for a week or two before they move on. There isn't a lot of money in the budget for a night out on the town.

I'm not interested in going to a frat party. I don't drink. I never have; when both of your grandfathers die slowly of alcoholism and your mom is a recovering addict, it doesn't make you want to take up drinking or recreational drugs. I don't care if Mason drinks; I just don't want to do it myself.

An idea strikes me on the walk through campus. I'm going to need some help from the boys to pull this off.

———

The table is set. The candles are lit. I sit at the same table where we declared our love for one another and wait. And wait. We never set a time. I don't know when she'll get here. Maybe she'll—

Mason walks into the dining hall with her friend Fred and stops short. Her hand goes to her mouth.

I clear my throat and stand as she approaches. "My lady."

Her eyes are bright. "What is all this?"

"We're having our second first date," I tell her. I usher her into her seat.

The table is set with a red checkered cloth. Two tapered candles are lit in the center of the table. Her plate is already made, chicken piccata on a pillow of mashed potatoes and a mixed greens salad with pomegranate seeds. She loves pomegranate.

"You went all out."

I tug at my tie. I'm wearing my game day suit, all dressed up for the occasion.

"Anything for you, Princess."

She settles across from me. Her eyes are bright as she takes everything in.

"Thank you for doing this."

"I'd take you out if I could. You deserve the world."

"I love this." She pokes a pomegranate aril out of her salad and sucks on it. "This is perfect."

"I know it doesn't come close to our first date, but—"

Our first date together was the Winter Formal, our freshman year of high school. I sweated through my under-shirt, shirt, and suit jacket, I was so nervous. It was the first date I'd ever been on, with the only girl I'd ever even thought about dating. We went to the dance with a group of eight or nine other couples. It was like a mini prom. We all gathered at someone's house for an hour of photos, we took a limo to dinner and then the dance, and we shared our first kiss on the dance floor. Micah got into a fistfight with another guy, and the three of us left the dance early. We ended up going to the diner for milkshakes and French fries in our formal attire, her brother an awkwardly comfortable third wheel.

"It's perfect," Mason says firmly.

I clear my throat. "How was your day? You ready for your stats quiz tomorrow?"

She makes a face. "No, not really. I should probably spend a few hours studying."

"Miles is a stats whiz. He's great at all math, really. He tutored Sam last semester. Want to see if he has any pointers?"

"I think I'm good. I just need to concentrate on reviewing for a little bit and I should be okay. Thank you, though."

"How was your abnormal psych class?" We're in two different sections of the same course, taught by two different professors. I have mine tomorrow.

"It was good. We have a paper due next week. I'm going to work on it while we're at the away meet this weekend."

Good. She brought it up naturally.

"Did you want me to go?"

"To my meet?" Her brow creases. "It's an away meet."

"I used to go to all of your away meets in high school." Even the ones outside of the immediate area. Micah and I used to bribe Jamal into driving us across state lines. We'd split a few pizzas during the meet, then he'd drive us home and the three of us would go out to celebrate or commiserate about the outcome of the meet. Sometimes Micah would bring a girl along. For the most part, he had a girl on his arm on Saturday nights, but he wasn't the type to have a steady girlfriend. He liked the casual dating hell that I hated.

Mason rolls her eyes, a small smile twisting her lips. "You don't have to come to Rhode Island this weekend. I'll see you when I get back."

"And before?"

"What?"

"Can I see you before you leave?"

She drags the tines of her forks through her mashed potatoes. "There are three more nights between now and Thursday morning."

"I know. That's why I'd like to see you."

"You mean have sex."

I set down my fork and meet her eyes. "Mason, if that's where the night takes us, so be it. If we spend the next month abstaining, nothing would change for me. I still want to be with you. I want to spend time with you. Hell, we can sit on your couch and watch chick flicks while you paint your toenails, and I'd still want to spend time with you. *I like you.* Being with you makes me happy."

She swallows. "You have all these big feelings. I don't always know how to react to them."

Of course I have big feelings. I'm a big guy, and I'm in

love with her. Even when I hated her, I loved her. My feelings for her have never been easy.

"I'm still me. I haven't changed."

"No, but I have." She looks away. "I'm not the same little girl I used to be. I'm a whole different person now."

"And I want to learn who you are now." I reach across the table and am gratified when she lets me take hold of her hand. I lace our fingers together. "You said we can take this slow, so let's take this slow. Let's date. We'll spend time together. We'll get to know one another again. There's no rush, sunshine. It's just you and me."

Her fingers tighten around mine. "And if I said—if I wanted to try abstaining…"

"We don't need to have sex every night for this to be a mutually satisfying relationship," I tell her. "If that's what you want—"

"I don't know what I want."

"Okay. So we'll start with that." I bring her hand to my lips, kissing the back of her knuckles. "All I want is to be with you. I want to do stupid boring shit like talk about our day and study in the library and eat meals together. I want to wake up beside you and fall asleep with you in my arms, even if we don't have sex. I just want to be with you."

She swallows again. "I—I want that, too."

"We don't have to make this complicated."

Mason takes a bite of her chicken, her eyes locked on mine. "How was your day?"

"It was good. I got a good lift in this afternoon." We have another six weeks before spring ball starts up, so I'm enjoying my freedom while it lasts. Once we have practice every day again, I'll have almost no free time for anything that isn't school, football, or sleep. "My abs are still sore from pilates class yesterday. I'm going to have to try that again."

She huffs out a laugh. "Yeah, it's pretty intense. I like it, though."

"Me, too. Barrett called Diana last night to crow about the workout."

"Is that his girlfriend?"

"His best friend. She goes to USC on a soccer scholarship. They've been friends for years. Nearly as long as you and I have known each other."

She cracks a smile. "You were such a cute little kid."

"You were feral."

Mason laughs. "I was not!"

"Spitting and scratching every big kid on the playground who was mean to me and Jamal."

She grins. Her eyes shine with amusement. "They deserved it. They should have known better than to mess with you."

"They learned quick." I squeeze her fingers. "Thank you for that. I don't think I've ever said how much it meant to me. To both of us."

"I'd do anything for you, King," she says quietly.

twenty-three

. . .

Mason

HIS EYES GROW WIDE, and he swallows. His fingers spasm around mine. He doesn't know what to say, how to react. He shoves an enormous bite of chicken into his mouth.

I shake my head and smile, because at the end of the day, he's still my King, the big guy with the big feelings who eats when he gets upset, who eats when he's happy, who eats when he doesn't know what to do.

I focus my attention on my meal. He made me dinner—from the dining hall, sure, but he took the time to think about what I would enjoy the most. He put thought into our evening together.

"Do you have a lot of homework tonight?"

He shrugs. "Nothing crazy."

"Do you want to maybe hang out a bit?"

His smile stretches from ear to ear. "Yeah, baby, I'd like that."

"We can watch *Notting Hill*," I suggest, just to watch him squirm.

But he doesn't squirm. "I haven't seen that movie in forever."

"You'll watch chick flicks with me?"

"Girl, I'd watch paint dry as long as I got to do it with you." He laughs, shaking his head. "Besides, you know I have a thing for Julia Roberts."

"This is true."

"Do you want to come over? My roommates and I usually watch Wheel of Fortune and Jeopardy! before we go our separate ways." He chews on his lip. "No pressure. If you would rather go to your place…"

"Your place sounds good," I tell him. "I haven't watched Jeopardy! in forever."

"Wes is, like, obsessed," he admits. "It's the only time he puts down his book."

"Yeah, what's up with that? He doesn't talk."

He shrugs. "He's a decent guy who's had a tough life. I cope with my feelings by eating everything in sight. He copes by retreating into himself and reading books. He talks, he just needs to really feel comfortable around people to open up to them."

"And he's opened up to you?"

"We've lived together for a year and a half. We've played three seasons together. You can't do that and not become friends." He lifts his shoulders again. "We spend a lot of time together. He's antisocial as fuck and doesn't care who knows it."

"We should set him up with someone. What kind of girl is he interested in?"

"None of them."

"He's gay? Or ace?"

"Neither. He doesn't date." He shrugs. "He doesn't talk about it. He's more than happy to spend every Saturday night in his armchair with a book."

"Hm…"

"Now, if you insist on matchmaking, I know Amir has a thing for your friend Fred," he says slowly, and a smile spreads across my face.

"Yeah, I think I can make that happen."

Tucker shakes his head. "Eat your dinner, baby."

We make small talk through dinner. His brother is in the NBA—riding the bench, but in the professional league nonetheless. Micah is weeks away from declaring for the draft. My mom is doing well. My dad is up to his eyeballs in babies. His mom recently got a new job as a senior partner in a major lobbyist firm, fighting for improvements to the foster care system. His mama's dental office is expanding; she had to bring on two new partners in the last three years.

It's easy, being with him. He's restful company. I don't have to pretend to be anyone else; I can simply be myself with him.

When we finish our dinner, he clears our table and disappears into the snaking food line. He comes back a few minutes later with protein brownies topped with soft serve and chocolate sauce. A healthy sundae.

"For you," he says, setting one down in front of me. He drops a kiss to the top of my head.

"Thank you. You really went all out."

Tucker lifts his shoulders in a self-conscious shrug. "I'd do anything for you, too, Princess."

I don't know what to say to that. I can dish it out, but I can't take it back.

We finish our dessert in a silence that's more awkward than usual. When we're done, he clears the table before I can. He stuffs the tablecloth and the candles into his backpack. Next to his suit and tie, I feel conspicuously underdressed in my leggings and sweatshirt.

He offers me his hand, and I take it. He slides his fingers into mine, and I have to swallow at the intensity in his eyes.

"Love you, baby," he says, before he drops a chaste kiss to my cheek.

We're doing this all backwards. We've said *I love you*, we've consummated the relationship, and now we're having our first date. Do we really need to adhere to some arbitrary guideline about how our relationship is supposed to evolve? Our feelings aren't clear cut. Our history isn't perfect. I can't erase our past.

He talks about his developmental psychology class and the group project they're working on. He chatters the entire walk back to Athlete's Village. I make the appropriate noises to indicate that I'm listening, but my mind is elsewhere, floating away into the ether.

The football house is warm and bright when we arrive. Tucker hangs up his coat and then takes mine, hanging it on the same hook.

"Come on in and see the guys," he says, leading me into the open living room.

Wes is sitting in an armchair by the corner, a book in his hand. Amir is sitting across from him in another armchair. The sofa is occupied by Sam and Miles, canoodling together, and Barrett, who looks distinctly perturbed at the sight of them.

Tucker sits in one of the other armchairs, pulling me down into his lap.

"You're late," Greg says, appearing over us, and I jump.

"You're early," Tucker tells him.

Greg thrusts an enormous bowl at me. Popcorn. Yum.

"Nice to see you again," he says. His guard is up.

I haven't forgotten the warning he gave me at the party.

"You, too." I relax into Tucker's lap. He slings his arm around me, and I cuddle into him.

Greg passes out popcorn bowls to everyone else— everyone gets their own, except for Miles and Sam, who share. He takes the only empty armchair and nods to Wes, who closes his book and picks up the remote.

The Wheel of Fortune theme song plays and they all chant together: *Wheel. Of. Fortune!*

Tucker presses a kiss to my temple and tightens his arm around me.

We all call out guesses as more and more letters are revealed. Wes is quiet, his eyes intent on the screen. When he speaks, his voice is rich and thick, confident. He usually gets the clue right, too.

Sam and Miles spend more of their time making out than watching the TV. The only one who seems to care is Barrett, who has to sit next to them. Sam moans. He hugs the other end of the couch.

Resting my head on Tucker's chest, I inhale his familiar woodsy scent. The persistent thump of his heart under my cheek is like a lullaby. I could sit here wrapped up in him forever.

When we finish the episode, Wes turns to tonight's episode of Jeopardy! Again, the guys call out the answers. Wes gets most of them right, too.

"Come on," Tuck says, nudging me, when I haven't said anything for a full half hour. "I know you know these answers."

I force a smile for him. "Just getting the lay of the land. I don't want to presume—"

"Presume away," he says. He wraps his pinky around a strand from my ponytail and presses his forehead to my temple. He breathes in deep.

"Are you sniffing me?"

"You smell good," he says. He drops a kiss to my forehead and leans back in the armchair. His hand shifts higher on my thigh.

When the episode ends, I look around the room curiously. What happens now? Do we sit here and watch cable TV together like we're eighty?

Miles clears his throat and stands. Sam clings to him with doe eyes.

"Good night," he says.

"Use protection," Greg tells them, and Miles' face goes beet red.

"Thank you, we will," Sam tells him seriously.

Tucker snickers quietly into my ear. "Want to head upstairs?"

My pulse goes thready. "You want to…?"

"We can turn on *Notting Hill*," he says, his eyes bright.

I slip off his lap.

"You're leaving us, too?" Barrett says, his eyebrows raised.

"We'll catch up with y'all later," Tucker tells him. He claps Greg on the shoulder as he passes by.

"Don't forget the condoms!" Greg yells after us, as we start up the stairs.

twenty-four

. . .

Tucker

I'VE BARELY CLOSED the door after us when Mason is in my arms. She laughs and winds her arms around my neck, bringing our bodies together.

"I'm not really in the mood to watch a movie," she admits. Her hand trails down my chest, over my belly, and brushes against my cock. She presses the heel of her palm into my crotch and slowly strokes.

All of my blood rushes south. "And what are you in the mood for?"

She tips her face up for a kiss. "You. Naked."

My cock jerks in my suit pants. "That can be arranged."

"You don't want a month of celibacy?" Her smile is wry, but her eyes are sharp.

"If that's what you need, I'm happy to go along with that plan," I tell her honestly. "I'd much rather spend the next month fucking you into next Tuesday."

Her warm brown cheeks turn a dusky pink. "Yeah?"

My mouth descends hungrily upon hers. She opens for me, pulling my body flush against hers. Our tongues meet and my entire body shakes. I need her like an addict needs a fix, like I can't breathe without her in my lungs, like I can't function without her in my heart.

Maneuvering her across the room, we tumble into the bed. Her fingers pull at my tie and tug it loose. I work her sweat-shirt up over her head. Her hair is a static-y mess, sticking up everywhere. She pushes me back against the mattress and climbs on top of me, straddling my hips. Mason slowly undoes the top three buttons on my shirt, her slim fingers exploring the exposed triangle of my chest. Her hips grind into mine, searching for friction.

"King," she says, panting against my lips. "Please tell me you went to the pharmacy."

"We're fully stocked and ready to go." I pull her hips into mine, arching up into her. I can feel the heat of her through her leggings, burning me through our clothes.

She returns her attention to my shirt. I pull hers over her head until she's straddling me in just a thin beige cotton bra. Her nipples are pebbled beneath the cups, dusky rosebuds just begging to be sucked. I run my thumb over one, and she groans, throwing her head back.

"I forgot... how good you are... at this," she says, breathing hard. Her hands scramble for my belt. Leather whistles through the loops and the metal buckle clinks as she works her hand into my pants. Her small fist closes around my cock, and it's my turn to groan.

My veins pulse with electricity. My entire body cries out for her, to make her mine.

We've always been good at this. Sex with Mason is never boring. We never had to sneak around or hide what we were doing. We were given freedom to experiment and learn what worked for us.

Her hand tightens around my cock, stroking me from root to tip. She maps the ridges and veins with delicate fingers, her thumb sliding over the sensitive head.

"Baby…"

"Shh," she says, squeezing me more firmly, the way I need her to. "You don't want everyone to hear us." She echoes my words from Saturday night.

Right now, I don't care if the entire campus can hear us. I pull her down onto me and kiss her, my tongue licking into her mouth and taking, taking, taking what I need. She lets out a gasp of surprise that turns to a moan when I cup her pert ass over her thin leggings. I slide my hands beneath the fabric barrier and am met with the smooth skin of her bare butt. She always favored thin thongs with barely there straps—no panty lines. I like to see that some things haven't changed.

I pull the fabric down her hips. She releases me to help me, rolling off of me for a moment to kick away the stretchy leggings. At the same time, she peels off her soaked thong. I make quick work of her bra. She's fully naked, and I'm mostly clothed, my cock out and springing up towards my belly.

"Off," she says, tugging at my open pants. In short order, my clothes are tossed on the floor until we're naked together, skin pressed to skin. I roll her underneath me, and she arches up, wrapping her legs around my waist. Her wet, hot pussy pulses against my cock. She groans and tilts her pelvis into mine.

"Princess—"

"I need your cock, Tucker." I try to move down her body, and she pulls on my shoulders to keep me exactly where I am. "Now."

Working my hand between our bodies, I rub gently at her clit. She shudders and lets her head fall back against the pillow. I slip one finger inside of her, and her body clutches at me with a vise grip.

"Not now," I tell her. "More prep." With my thumb on her clit, I work my finger in and out of her a few times. She's so tight. Her muscles are coiled tight, tense. "Relax, baby."

"This is me relaxed." Her fingertips dig into my shoulders. "There. Right there."

I press the pad of my finger against that spot on her inner wall, the place that makes her eyes roll back in her head. Her legs slip from around my waist, spreading open on the mattress, as she rides the high. Her hips work, arching up to meet me.

Nuzzling my bearded cheek against her pebbled nipple, she gasps and tightens around my fingers.

"King..."

"I've got you, Mase." I close my lips around her nipple and tug. She moans—loudly—and an animalistic sense of satisfaction runs through me at the idea that I'm the one making her make these noises that my roommates can definitely hear. Hell, our neighbors can probably hear her three doors down.

She falls apart, and slowly, I help her put the pieces back together, my fingers pumping slowly inside of her. She gives me a lazy, sated smile, wrapping her arms around my neck and bringing her lips to mine for a lazy, sated kiss.

"How are you feeling?"

"Fucking amazing," she says, letting out a happy sigh. She scrapes her teeth over my shoulder.

I roll off of her, and she lets out a whine. Sitting on the edge of the bed, I reach for the unopened box of condoms— ribbed, for her pleasure. She sets her legs on either side of mine and wraps her arms around me, her head pillowed on my back.

Her hands don't meet around my middle. I should feel embarrassed about that, a voice says in the back of my head, and I immediately dismiss it. Mason is tiny. I'm big. It works for us. She's never complained or cared about my size.

Slowly, she slides her hand across my belly to my cock. She strokes me a few times, her tight little fist touching me exactly the way I need it. I wrap my hand around hers and together we touch me with strong, even strokes. Precum beads on the tip of my cock, and she coats her fingers in the sticky wetness, spreading it over my length.

"Is this what you've been doing the last two years?" she murmurs quietly to my back. Her other hand slips between my legs to cup my balls, her touch feather-light as she plays with the sensitive seam running up the middle. My cock jerks in our combined fists. "Do you touch yourself and think of me?"

"It was never as good as this."

She presses a kiss to my shoulder blade.

Slowly she withdraws. I mourn the loss of contact immediately. She reaches for the unopened box, ripping the top off and pulling out the strip of foil squares.

"I want you to fuck me," she declares. No, *demands*. She hands me the square and gets onto her hands and knees, her pert ass in the air.

"Mason..."

"Come on, Tuck. Just fuck me." She sounds more exasperated than turned on. That doesn't sit right with me.

"Baby, hold on a second. Look at me."

She turns over, and her eyes go directly to my cock. She runs her hand over my length again. Her pretty tongue comes out to wet her lips, and my cock jerks.

She looks up at me from beneath her lashes. "Would you like me to suck your cock, baby?"

Yes. No. Not when she's being evasive. Yes. I don't know.

She leans forward, and her little tongue darts out to lap at the precum beading on the tip. I groan and her fist tightens around me, stroking at a pace so tortuously slow I might explode. She sucks the head into her mouth and hums. My brain gives up and walks away. I forget what I was going to say. I forget everything except for the feel of her mouth on my cock.

"Princess..."

She takes more of me into her mouth, sucking and licking as her hand strokes the parts of me that won't fit. Her free hand cups my balls, weighing them in her hand, as her fingers reach behind to press against my perineum.

I take a step back, pulling my cock out of her mouth. A trail of precum and saliva connects us.

She squeezes my cock. "Tucker."

I pick up the discarded condom and roll it down my length, giving myself a few firm strokes. "You want this from behind?" My voice is hoarse. She wants to be fucked, so I'll fuck her, but we're getting to the bottom of this later.

Mason scrambles back onto her hands and knees again. Without preamble, I step up and slot the tip of my cock against her entrance. She arches her back, pushing back against me.

I slide in slowly, each inch more intense than the last. She hangs her head and groans, the sound echoing in the quiet room. My heart pounds. This is too much.

Her mood is too up and down. I can't read her. But I know her body. I know the sound of her sighs and the clenching of her pussy. I know that when she slides her hand between her legs, she's close, and when she plays with her nipples, she needs more interaction.

I wrap my arm around her torso, heaving her upright. Her back leans against my chest as I pound into her from behind, supporting our combined weights. The bed thumps against the wall. My whole world zeroes in on this, on us, on making the most beautiful girl in the world come all over my cock.

She gasps and clutches at my arm. "Tuck."

I slide my hand over her breasts, over her pebbled nipples, and brush against her clit with the pad of my fingers. She clenches around me.

So I do it again, this time more vigorously, until she shatters in my arms. She's boneless, breathing hard, as I fuck into her with ruthless abandon.

"Down." She's gasping, clenching around me.

She drops back onto her elbows and spreads her knees impossibly farther. I can get even deeper now.

There's a certain kind of clarity that only comes balls deep in a beautiful woman screaming for my cock. I can do anything. I *will* do anything for her. All I want to do is live in this moment, to capture it for all of posterity, to never let it go.

The orgasm starts at the base of my spine almost before I'm ready for it. My balls draw up, tight and aching. Sweat slicks our skin. My hands tighten on her hips as I slam into her once, twice, three more times before it crashes into me. It consumes me.

My heart pounds in my ears. There's a faint buzzing somewhere in the background. Everything is kind of fuzzy. My knees buckle and I collapse onto the mattress, pulling her down onto me.

"Mm." Mason meets me for a sweaty, sated kiss. I reach for her and she rolls over beside me, a solid two feet away.

"Come here."

She laughs. "I can't move."

We lay sprawled out for several minutes. I wish I could touch her. I wish I could hold her.

She struggles to sit up, her face carefully, intentionally blank.

"Don't get up." Rolling across the bed to get to her, I wrap my arms around her and hold her to me like a koala afraid to let go of its tree branch.

"Tucker, I need to clean up."

I sigh. "That's where we went wrong."

"What's that supposed to mean?" She squirms free and swings her legs over the side of the mattress.

"Last time we had sex, we were fine, and then you went to the bathroom, and all of a sudden we weren't fine anymore."

I catch her hand in mine. "So don't get up. Let's stay in our perfect little sex bubble."

"We're fine," she tells me. She rolls away and heads to the bathroom, shutting the door firmly behind her.

But we aren't fine.

twenty-five

. . .

Tucker

SHE'S distant when she comes back. Put together in a way that I can't penetrate.

"Let's go to bed," she says, crawling back onto the mattress.

"Okay." It's still early. I'm usually up for another three hours. But if it means I get to fall asleep with her in my arms...

"I have a class at nine."

I clear my throat. "We have a lift at eight. I usually head out around seven thirty."

She smiles. It looks forced. "Perfect. That will give me enough time to shower and get ready."

It feels so clinical. Mechanical. Like we're slipping into this automatic routine, boring and predictable. Are we already so entrenched in our ways?

"I'm going to take a shower," I announce.

She blinks. "Now?"

"Yeah. I'm all sweaty. Do you... would you like to join me?"

She swallows. "Your roommates won't mind?"

"Mase, we're not going to fuck in the shower. We'll lock Barrett's door. He won't walk in on us. It's a shower."

"Yeah, I can… we can…"

"I'm not pressuring you into doing anything you don't want to do," I tell her, more harshly than I want to. "Join me, don't join me, I need a shower before I go to bed."

She flinches. "Tucker."

I'm done. I'm not avoiding this any longer. Still naked, I make my way into the bathroom and lock Barrett's door, though he's usually pretty good about not barging in while I'm in there. I start the water and pull an extra towel out—just in case.

I'm in the shower for less than thirty seconds when Mason pushes aside the curtain.

"Can I still join you?"

"Always, baby." I hold out my hand, and she steps into the tub. Her hair is pulled up into a haphazard bun. She shivers, and I move aside so she can get the benefit of the hot water.

"Are we ever going to talk about it?"

She turns her head away. "Talk about what?"

"Whatever is bothering you."

"I'm fine."

I roll my eyes. "Okay, so already we're at the avoidance stage. That's brilliant, Mason."

"What's that supposed to mean?"

"It means talk to me. Tell me what got you upset. Was it something I did?" My finger on her chin tips her head back, so I can look her in the eye. "Are you not having a good time?"

"I'm enjoying myself."

"Yeah, and that's why you're wound so tight, you can hardly look at me."

"I have a lot on my mind."

"So let me share some of the load." I have to fight back the urge to kiss her. It won't make the situation any better. "We're supposed to be in this together."

She snorts. "What's this?"

"A relationship? Life?" I honestly don't know how to answer her. "If we're supposed to be a couple, that means—"

"Maybe we shouldn't," she blurts. Her eyes go wide and she covers her mouth. "I didn't mean that."

My blood runs cold. Or maybe that's the lack of hot water. "Yeah, you did. You wouldn't have said it otherwise."

She's been telling me all along that she wants this. She's the one who pursued me. And now?

"I'm just stressed," she says.

"Mase—"

"It's been a long day."

There's a lump in my throat I can't clear. "If you don't want to do this…"

"Do what?"

"Us. If you don't want to be together—"

"I do. I do," she says. She reaches for me, wrapping her arms low around my waist. "My head is just a mess right now. I want to be with you."

"Except you don't."

"Maybe we should revisit that month of celibacy thing." She chews her lip. "I thought I was okay. I thought I was ready. But maybe we're taking this too fast. We weren't even talking a week ago. This is all—it's all so fast."

I run my thumb over her cheek. "Whatever you need, babe. I just want to be with you. Whatever you'll allow, all I want is you."

As much as I'm not looking forward to a month or more abstaining, I know I can handle it. I've handled the situation for the last two and a half years. A month or so until she gets comfortable with me again? With us? That's a sacrifice I'm more than willing to make.

I pour some soap into my hand and run it over her shoulders. She bites her lip and stares up at me guilelessly.

"I love you, Tucker," she says, like she has to convince herself. "I want to be with you."

"You have me, baby. Take what you need. I'm yours."

I duck down and kiss her cheek. It doesn't feel like an affirmation; it feels like the end.

We shower in silence. She doesn't offer to soap me up. She doesn't touch me. She curls in on herself, draws herself into whatever cacophony is going on in her mind. I'm not privy to it.

I'm not sure if I want to be.

We towel off in silence. I hand her a t-shirt to wear, and we dress in silence.

"I need to study for a bit," she says.

"That's fine. I have a book I want to finish."

"Oh? What are you reading?"

I show her the title. It's something I borrowed off Wes. He likes gritty suspense stories with ultra-masculine buttoned up heroes who drink bitter black coffee because they hate themselves and refuse to let anyone into their lives. I'm good with mysteries, but the heart-racing suspense novels typically wind me up too much. This is a paranormal afro-futuristic cyber-crime series set in Nairobi. It's the fourth book in the series and I. am. hooked.

I change the sheets—they're a sweaty mess—and Mason helps me make the bed, like we're an established couple with set routines. I crawl into bed with my book, and she sits cross-legged beside me with her laptop and her statistics notebook. I set my hand on her bare knee, exposed by the hem of my t-shirt.

She looks over at me, a lazy smile on her face. "Hm?"

"Nothing. I just wanted to touch you."

Her smile softens. She leans over and kisses me. Soft, sweet. Tender. Before she can pull away, I slide my hand into her hair, memorizing the sharp citrus scent of her skin mixed with my soap, a perfect blend of me and her.

"Tuck…"

"Study," I tell her, setting my hand on her knee again. "You have a quiz tomorrow."

Two and a half hours pass almost without us realizing it. I reach a good stopping point in my book because if I don't stop now, I'll stay up until three o'clock in the morning reading, and nobody wants that. She feels confident in her preparation for the quiz.

We turn out the lights, and Mason squirms closer to me. She sets her head on my chest and wraps her arm around me.

"I don't know what I was saying earlier," she says into the darkness.

"Mase…"

She rolls over to face me. "No. I don't know. That's what I'm saying. I thought I was sure, but now I'm not sure of anything. All I know is I love you and I want to be with you. The rest of me? I'm freaking the fuck out, Tucker."

I run my hand over her arm. "What's making you freak out?"

"Nothing. Everything. I don't know." She sighs. "I had a plan. It was working. And you came in and were you, and now I don't know anymore."

"I don't want to derail your plans."

"But you did, in the best way possible. I'm happy when I'm with you." She sniffs. "I only want to be happy with you."

"I'll do my best to make that happen."

"That's the thing. There's nothing you can do. I can't ask you to regulate my emotions. That's an impossible ask. I have to do the work."

"Okay, but we can work on it together." I run my hand over her arm again. "You can tell me when you're not happy. We can talk. We don't hide away from our feelings: we have to address them head on."

I hear her swallow. "Like you never moving on?"

My mouth goes dry as I'm forced to confront it. "I wasn't ready. I wasn't pining, not exactly. I just wasn't ready. I tried the therapy thing, and it just made me miss you more. I tried getting with someone else and it made me feel worse. So I stopped trying. I got stuck in the past. It was easier that way."

She's quiet for a minute. "Does it bother you that I dated other guys?"

"Sometimes," I admit. "But then I remember that I'm with you now and they aren't, and they're probably the ones jealous and pining, and I get to hold you in my arms. So, no. What happened when we were apart doesn't bother me. It got us to where we are now."

She makes a noise of contentment. "That's very grown up of you."

I sniff. "I'm very mature. I'm almost twenty-one."

Mason laughs, and even though we're laying there in the dark, my whole world lights up. I'll do anything to make her laugh.

"I really do love you, Tuck," she says into the darkness. "I want to be with you. I want this to work."

"It will," I tell her with a confidence I'm not entirely sure is real anymore. "Or it won't, and we'll know, and we'll both be able to move past it."

"Will you?"

"I don't know. I hope so. If it's over, if we try, and it doesn't work out this time, then I hope I'm able to. I don't want to be stuck." I tighten my arm around her. "All I can do is give it my best try. That's all I can promise you right now. And that has to be enough."

"It is," she says, curling into my chest. "It has to be."

twenty-six

. . .

Tucker

ON TUESDAYS, Mason has a half hour break between her classes. We spend the time making out in the hallway, in full view of everyone and anyone who walks by, before her alarm goes off and she slips into the classroom seconds before class starts. On Wednesday, we eat dinner with my roommates. Nobody comments on any potentially loud noises they heard on Monday, and everyone is perfectly polite. She's quiet, but then again, she's usually quiet in a big group of people she doesn't know well. I walk her home, her hand in mine, and I kiss her goodbye on the porch for a solid forty-five minutes. We go home to our separate beds and our separate plans.

Thursday she leaves for Rhode Island. It's a quick drive, but the process of carting over a hundred student athletes, support staff, and coaches on two big coach buses is a laborious one. I meet her in the parking lot of the track and field practice facility with a bottle of orange Gatorade—her favorite—and a chocolate and coconut protein bar—also her favorite—in a gift bag with a few special things. She jumps off the bus and into my arms, kissing me in full view of the track team.

Wolf whistles and catcalls sound off from the other

runners. She doesn't care. She lifts her middle finger at them and kisses me back, again and again and again, until I'm dizzy and breathless.

"You're here," she squeals, hugging me again.

"I came to see you off. I'm sorry that I can't be at your meet on Saturday."

There's simply no easy way for me to travel across state lines. There's no straight bus or train route. I don't have a car, nor does anyone that I know. I have to support her from afar.

She clutches the gift bag to her chest. "You made this for me?"

I rub the back of my neck. "It's only a few odds and ends."

A book of crossword puzzles and a sparkly purple pen. A slap bracelet. Some chewing gum. And a small stuffed monkey, because she loves monkeys.

"Baby, thank you." She gives me a sweet kiss. "I love it."

"I love you." My hands tighten on her hips. "You're the best part of my life, Mase. I want to make you happy. That's all I want to do."

"You do. You are." Her eyes are mysteriously bright, and she sniffs a few times. "I love you, too, King."

I brush my gloved thumb across her cheek. "Run fast at the meet. You're going to crush them."

Her tender smile turns cocky. "You know I will."

I kiss her again, once more for luck. Or for me, because I need it, too.

"Get on the bus. I'll see you Sunday." I swat her gently on the ass. "I'll miss you."

"Miss you more." She kisses me one last time and then pulls away. She boards the bus and waves at me from the window, where she's hanging over Fred. Her friend squeals and grabs at the goody bag.

I wait until the bus pulls out of the parking lot, and then I go back to my everyday life.

———

The assessment center feels empty without Mason there beside me. I don't like it. My bed feels cold and empty without her in it. She's only been back in my life for a week, and already I feel the absence of her presence as acutely as I did in the first weeks after the breakup.

But we haven't broken up. We're simply going through a rough patch. Growing pains. We'll get better at this. She'll figure out whatever is bothering her, and we'll go back to having awesome earth shattering sex a few times a week and everything will be fine. It'll be great. We'll go back to being us again.

Friday night comes, and I stay home with my roommates. Amir, Barrett, and I watch a movie and play video games while Wes sits in his armchair and reads. Afterwards, I go upstairs and jerk off thinking of her. This time I'm not some sad, pathetic loser pining over a girl I can't have: I'm thinking about my girlfriend, the woman who loves me, with whom I'm in a serious committed relationship.

As much as I'd rather sit around in my underwear and think of her some more, on Saturday morning, Barrett drags me to the gym, and we get in a good lift. I hit the treadmill for some cardio and wonder what she's up to. She has her race today. I wonder if she still has a pair of lucky socks she wears for every meet in the season. If she likes her Newton team-mates more than her Georgetown friends. If she's thinking about me.

I almost can't remember what I did before her, except that some things are crystal clear. I moped. I pined. I was trapped in a limbo of pain, powerless to the force of my misery.

I stayed at home. I hung out with my roommates. I played video games and watched movies with the guys. I kept tabs on her social media. I had no life, and I liked it that way.

Somehow I missed that she transferred to Newton last fall.

Somehow, I missed that her entire life changed. She was so close to me—only four blocks away! We ate dinner at the same dining hall and never saw each other. We existed in the same bubble of school and the athletic department and never crossed paths.

Well, she might have seen me. She certainly wasn't surprised to see me at the assessment center orientation. Maybe she planned it, as a way for us to reconnect over a neutral topic. Maybe she spent last semester gathering her courage to approach me. Maybe I should give her the benefit of the doubt.

Barrett stops at the end of my treadmill. "You're thinking about her again."

"Always." I wipe my forehead with my shirt. "Is it that obvious?"

"You really love her," he states.

"It's like the last two and a half years, I was existing, but I wasn't living. I was going through the motions. Everything was in black and white. She makes my whole world turn technicolor."

He shakes his head. "Sometimes I want that."

"What? A relationship?"

"Yeah. And then I realize I like being on my own, I like having my own schedule, and I like not having to answer to anyone about how I spend my time." Barrett laughs. "Maybe when I'm out of college and have a real job."

"You don't know what you're missing."

He rolls his eyes. "Consistent sex with the same person every night?"

"It's so much more than that," I tell him. "It's knowing there is someone who loves and respects you, who supports you, who is there when you need a shoulder to lean on. She's the person I want to talk to at the end of a long day. When I wake up, I look forward to seeing her, and she's the last thing I think about when I go to sleep. Talking to her makes my whole day better. Actually seeing her, spending time with her?" I shake my head. "It's great. Even when we fight, even when we have issues, my life is better because she's in it."

"You've only been together a week. Aren't you taking it a little fast?"

I give this the courtesy of serious thought. "I don't know how much of it is our past and how much is our present. I just know that being with her makes me happy."

He claps me on the shoulder. "I'm happy you're happy, man. You deserve to be happy."

"So do you."

"Yeah, but I'm happier being on my own," he says.

"If you change your mind, Mase has a ton of hot friends."

He considers. "That Melissa chick is kind of cute. Maybe…"

"Want me to set something up?"

Barrett is like a brother to me; if he wants a date with one of Mason's friends, the least I can do is try to arrange something.

"We'll talk about it later," he says. "I'm heading to the sauna."

Hopping off the treadmill, I join him and some of the other guys in the sauna. Sullivan, one of our safeties, is there with a bunch of freshmen and sophomores, regaling them with stories of his greatest achievements, which usually involve dropping the ball or missing a tackle at a crucial moment. He doesn't share this with them.

Barrett and I exchange a look and head to the back corner of the sauna, where Wes is sitting with a book.

"Hey."

He grunts. There are too many people here for him to be comfortable. He would probably prefer if Barrett and I left, too.

Sullivan crows on for another twenty excruciating

minutes. Finally, he leaves, taking his cadre of underclassmen with him. The three of us spread out a little.

"Any plans for tonight?"

Wes grunts, which I take to be no.

"There's a Delta party I might hit up," Barrett says, then sighs. "I don't know. I'm over the whole partying thing. It gets old, fast."

"That's why I don't do it," I tell him. "It's not fun being the only sober person in a group of people drunk off their ass. And they're always drunk."

He acknowledges this. "I don't know. Sometimes I feel like we're wasting our youth, staying in every Saturday night. And then, I remember I would rather stay in and hang out with you guys than try to be someone I'm not."

"Life's too short to be miserable," Wes says, not looking up from his book. "Be yourself. Accept who you are. You'll be happier for it."

twenty-seven

. . .

Mason

THE MEET GOES WELL. The after party is even better. Mark and Bryce buy enough alcohol for fifty people, despite the fact that there are only twenty people crammed into this hotel room. Melissa, Fred, and I are dressed to the nines in actual jeans and low cut tops that show off our small boobs. That's the downside to being a sprinter in excellent shape: small boobs.

"Your boobs are totally bigger than mine!" Melissa tells me. She grabs one of mine and one of Fred's to compare.

Okay, so maybe we've had a little too much to drink.

"Hey! Only Tucker gets to grab my boobs!"

She honks. "You and loverboy sure seemed chummy at dinner the other night."

I laugh. "Not my fault you didn't want to join us."

"Yeah, maybe never," she says. "The only football player I talk to is Sullivan, and that's more because I see him sneaking out of Fred's room than any other reason."

"Hey, that's over," Fred says. "Sully and I haven't hooked up in weeks."

"He's a dick," I inform them.

"With three legs," Melissa says.

Fred sighs. "Yeah, that was kind of nice. He knew how to use it."

"Better than…?" I nod towards Mark, who's wrapped up in a pretty blonde long-distance runner. I think she's a sophomore.

"Oh, yeah. There's a difference between skill and enthusiasm." Fred bites her lip. "What if we combined them? Find a guy with a giant dick who knows how to get me off and doesn't mind going down on me for, like, an hour?"

I grin.

"Oh, shut up," Melissa says, smashing her hand into my face. "Stop looking so smug."

"I'm getting laid tomorrow night," I declare. Whether Tucker knows this yet or not, I don't care. So what if having sex only makes me more confused? So what if I start doubting myself every time we hop into bed? It feels good, and he knows how to get me off—more than that, he *wants* to get me off. He cares about my pleasure as much as he does his own, if not more so.

I should tell him.

It takes three tries for the Face ID to recognize me. I go to my call log and click on the most recent name. He called me last night before bed, and I fell asleep to the pleasant hum of his voice in my ear. I woke up to a sweet voicemail and a dirty text, wishing me luck today.

I have the best boyfriend in the whole world. He should know that.

He answers on the third ring. The room is dark. There's rustling as he shifts and turns on his bedside lamp.

"King!"

"Hey, Mase."

Oh, no. He sounds tired. Did I wake him up? I've lost track of what time it is. I take another sip of my drink.

"I miss youuuuuu."

He chuckles, rubbing at his eyes. "I miss you, too, baby."

"I killed it in my race today."

"Congratulations. I knew you could do it."

"When I get home, we're going to fuck," I inform him. "I wish you were here right now."

Tucker raises an eyebrow. "Have you been drinking?"

"Just a little party with everyone." I turn the camera so he can see the party. Mark is full on making out with the blonde now. Bryce is wrapped up in some guy I think might do long jump. "You should be here. Why aren't you here?"

"Because you're in Rhode Island, baby."

"You always used to come to my meets."

He sighs. "We agreed that I wouldn't come to this one. Remember?"

Oh. Oh yeah. I forgot.

"I still miss you."

"I'll see you tomorrow," he tells me. "I'll meet you when the bus comes in."

"King! You're going to come pick me up?"

"Of course, baby," he says. His voice softens. "I'm looking forward to seeing you."

"You mean fucking."

Fred and Melissa start snickering. I shush them. Can't they see I'm on a phone call?

"If that's what you want," he says. He doesn't sound happy. Tucker pinches the bridge of his nose. "Are you okay, girl?"

"I'm great. I just miss you."

"I'll see you tomorrow," he says again. "Don't get into trouble, Mase."

"Who? Me?"

"Yeah, you," he says. He forces a laugh. "You're trouble, sunshine. You always have been."

"I love you, King."

The girls laugh outright now. I flap a hand at them to get them to shut up.

Tucker sighs. "Love you, too, Mase. Go get some sleep. Drink some water."

———

Morning dawns way too early. I throw off Fred's arm from around my middle—she likes to cuddle when she's been drinking—and slowly take stock of the situation. My head is pounding. My mouth is as dry as the Sahara. Everything hurts.

I'm never drinking again.

Cautiously, I try to piece together the evening. I remember going to Mark and Bryce's room around ten for the party. People kept showing up. My cup was never empty, Melissa made sure of that. We started off with tequila. It's never a good night when we start with tequila.

After that came the rum. Bryce kept cutting it with Diet Coke, even though I hate Diet Coke—the aspartame gives me a headache. At some point we ordered a mountain of pizzas. There were at least twenty people there, and everyone ate their fill. I wonder who paid. I probably owe them money.

There's a vague memory of calling Tucker on video chat. He was shirtless, tucked up in his bed like a good little boy. He's going to meet me at the bus, I remember, and then the nausea comes back in full force.

He's going to meet me at the bus.

I hobble to the bathroom and lean against the cool tile of the shower. The hot water helps make my world make sense again. I am never drinking again. It only gets me into trouble.

Fred knocks on the door. "Let me in. I need to pee."

"It's open."

We live together, and we share a bathroom. We work out together. There's nothing she has that I haven't seen before.

The door opens and some of the steam escapes. I mourn the loss of warm air as she pads into the bathroom.

"You good, girl?"

Fred groans. "Did I make out with that pole vaulting guy?"

"Only for, like, five minutes, before we pulled you off of him. He was certainly… enthusiastic. It looked like you were five seconds away from vaulting on his pole."

"Shit. How am I supposed to look him in the eye now?" She flushes.

"Since when have you cared?"

"Since he's on the fucking team."

"You hooked up with Mark last week," I point out.

She snorts. "Mark is like the team bicycle. Everyone's been with him at least once. Except for you."

"Nope. Never, not once," I smile smugly to myself. I don't need him. I've got a man of my own.

A pasty white hand sneaks into the shower curtain and turns the water from nearly boiling to freezing. I shriek and jump away from the stream of ice pellets masquerading as water.

"What the fuck, Fred?"

She laughs. "Enjoy your shower."

Muttering under my breath, I fix the temperature and resume my shower. We have team breakfast in an hour and then we hit the road. I should probably try to study a little on the bus ride home since I'm missing my abnormal psychology study group. I'm sure the precious few hours remaining in my weekend will be taken up by Tucker, Tucker, and more Tucker.

I miss him. I get to see him in five hours. That will have to be enough.

Fred is packing. She laughs at the sight of me, shivering in my towel, and ducks into the bathroom for a shower of her own. Briefly, I debate retribution. Eventually I decide against it. I don't want to sink to her level.

My phone has half a dozen texts. One is a wall of text from

my brother—I ignore that for the bus ride, when I'm sure I'll need a distraction from fifty horny athletes bored out of their minds.

The other texts are from Tucker. They're all marked for shortly after two o'clock in the morning, a time when I would have sworn he would be asleep.

Are you okay?

Baby, talk to me.

What's going on?

Mason.

You're really worrying me.

Have a good sleep, baby.

I remember calling him shortly after midnight. We video-chatted for a bit. My call log tells another story—a ten second call, followed by a three minute and twelve second call around one thirty. Another call right before two, this one declined.

Shit. What did I do?

twenty-eight

. . .

Tucker

MY FIST STRIKES the bag with a satisfying thwack. Barrett doesn't flinch. He simply holds the punching bag steady and lets me have another go. Thwack. Thwack thwack.

"We should talk about it," he says.

"There's nothing to talk about." I wipe the sweat off my face and prepare for another bout.

"All I'm saying is—"

"Well, stop."

"Dude."

I strike the bag. Again, and again, and again, until my hands ache and my arms shake and all I can feel is the adrenaline coursing through my veins.

She drinks. She's a partier. She's the type of person who goes out and gets drunk every weekend.

And I don't know if I can be with a person like that.

"Maybe with some perspective, it won't seem that bad."

"I don't." Thwack. "Need." Thwack. "Perspective." Thwack thwack.

"Come on, man. Let's—"

"I'd rather not."

Barrett rolls his eyes. "Clearly."

He holds the bag steady as I work out all of my frustration. I don't need perspective. I need a girlfriend who is on the same page as I am. Someone whose life fits into mine. And I don't know that someone who goes to parties every weekend and drinks their face off is the right person for me.

She's Mason. She's the girl I'm in love with.

But she might not be the right girl for me. And so I hit the bag a few more times, again and again and again, because I can't scream at the universe and I can't cry and I can't do anything. I don't want to change her. I don't want to force her to be someone she's not. But I also can't surround myself with negative influences.

Both of my grandfathers died of alcoholism. It's how my moms met, in a support group for children of alcoholics, a fact she's well aware of. My mom is a recovering addict—pills, something she got hooked on after a surgery twelve years ago. She's been clean for ten and a half years. It's something she still struggles with every damn day.

Family history alone makes it easy enough for me to abstain. For a guy my size, it would take so many drinks for me to get drunk, it almost isn't worth it. On top of that, I don't like the taste of alcohol. I'm still underage until June. I have no reason to drink. I try not to surround myself with people who are into that lifestyle. No judgment on them for liking it—it's just not for me.

I know some of the guys in the house drink. Barrett nearly bought out the liquor store when he turned twenty-one last summer and fully stocked our liquor cabinet for years to come. After one night of consumption for the hell of it, the bottles have rarely been touched. Most of them are still sealed. Greg has been known to have a few beers at a frat party; he always stops before he gets wasted. Amir will have one or two drinks to be sociable, but he isn't interested in the partying scene. Miles goes to frat parties now that he's dating Sam, so who knows what he's been up to in recent months.

And Wes doesn't leave his armchair, so if he's drinking alone in his room, that's news to me.

I've been to two frat parties in my life: one was the mistake I made freshman year, and the other was to pick up Mason. Football parties are far more tame in comparison. No booze, no pot, nothing that would get us kicked off the team. I don't usually go to those, either. I don't particularly like socializing. I would much rather sit on the couch with the guys and watch a movie or play video games than make small talk with guys trying to take my place in the starting lineup.

"It'll be okay," Barrett says. He grunts when I hit the bag with a particularly hard thwack. "Or maybe it won't. Fuck if I know."

"What if it was Diana?"

He blinks at the mention of his best friend. "What about her?"

"If you and Di were together—" He flushes red and I make a mental note to reexamine that later. "If you and Diana were a couple, but she had a hobby that put you at risk—"

"Mason isn't putting you at risk," he tells me. "What is she doing? Loving you too much?"

"She drinks."

"So?"

"No, I don't mean she goes out once in a while. She's gone out twice in three weeks and got blackout drunk, and we were together that third weekend, so I can only guess what she would have done if we didn't have plans." Thwack. Thwack thwack. "And I can't be around someone like that. I can't live my life with someone who—"

"Someone who indulges in something that is perfectly legal," he reminds me.

"She's not twenty-one yet."

"She will be soon enough."

"In May."

"So what's four months? Is that going to magically change the way you think about it?"

"No. I don't expect her to abstain altogether. That's not what I'm saying." I sigh and wipe my face again. "The blackout drunk is what worries me. How much of this is because she wants to, and how much is because she can't control herself? Or how much is she trying to run away from problems? I want to be an addiction counselor, and I can't even talk to my own girlfriend about this shit."

"Twice in three weeks is cause for concern," he admits. "Maybe she's not doing it on purpose, maybe she doesn't know her own tolerance levels, but yeah—maybe you have a reason to be concerned. But fucking talk to her about it."

"Yeah. You're right."

Barrett laughs. "Of course I'm right."

———

The bus pulls into the parking lot shortly after two. I stuff my hands into my coat pockets and wait. And wait. And wait.

Mason is one of the last people off the bus. She bounds over to me and slings her arms around my middle.

"King!"

"Hey, Princess." I kiss her cheek. "Did you have a good drive?"

She frowns. "Would have been better if you were with us. Melissa slept the whole time, and Fred was doing homework. It felt like it lasted forever."

I force a laugh. "I've had bus rides like that." It's part and parcel of being a student athlete: they can't all be home games, sometimes we have to travel. "Ready to go?"

She nods, biting her lip. "Are you okay? You seem off."

"I'm fine," I lie, because I'm not ready to confront the truth. "I thought maybe we could go for a walk through town today."

"Oh, do you have errands to run?"

"No. I just want to spend time with you." I reach for her duffel bag and sling it over my shoulder. "If you want to go home and take a nap, I'm cool with that, too. I thought maybe some time together awake and vertical might help."

She smirks. "You don't want to get horizontal?"

"I mean, yeah, but if we're spending the next month abstaining, that's probably not a good idea."

"So we are? We're not...?"

I cup her cheek. "I'm following your lead here, Princess. You said you're freaking out. I'm trying to give you what you need. If sex is confusing you, we don't need to do it for a while. You should be comfortable. I never want to pressure you into doing something you don't want to do."

She chews her lip. Gently, I tug it from between her teeth.

"What did I say? Only I get to bite this."

She flushes. "King..."

I kiss her gently, sweetly. I pour all of my love for her into this kiss, this one perfect moment.

"I love you," she says softly, then burrows her face into my chest.

I cup the back of her head as her cheek presses against my heart.

"Love you, too, Princess."

But I don't feel warmed by the innocent display of affection. Instead, I feel cold. Empty.

I take her hand and we head towards Athlete's Village with the rest of the crowd. She rests her head on my upper arm as we walk.

She chatters about her weekend. She got some good study time in on the drive home. Mark puked on the bus and stunk up the place. Her races went well—she came in first in one and second in the two others. She has team dinner tomorrow night and nothing else on the horizon.

"Oh, and Micah will be here next weekend," she adds as an afterthought.

My stomach tightens at the mention of her brother, the guy who used to be my best friend. I haven't heard from him since our one text conversation.

"It'll be good to see him," I say neutrally.

"He misses you," she tells me.

Is that why he hasn't contacted me once in the last two and a half years? Is that why he dropped me the second she did? If that's the way he treats his friends, maybe I don't want to be his. I'm fine with the guys in the house.

It will be weird having him on campus. Mason and I are still so new. And they clearly have remained close over the years—they're siblings, of course they're close. I'm oddly nervous for him to meet the guys. For him to judge the life I've built without him, without her.

I get the same nervous antsy anticipation whenever Jamal or my moms come to visit, however infrequently that may be. They're usually good for one or two visits a year. For the most part, they give me the space to live my own life outside of our family unit, something that I've appreciated more and more as time goes on. I need to figure out who I am and what I stand for. My family is there if I need them.

Mason's house is four blocks away from mine. I follow her into the little yellow house. It's laid out the same as mine. All the houses in Athlete's Village follow one of three floor plans. They have six bedrooms, three bathrooms, a small kitchen, and a living room. There's a small laundry room on the lower level, my favorite feature—it majorly sucked when our washer stopped working last fall and it took them six weeks to fix it.

Her room is at the back of the house, overlooking the small yard. She shares a Jack and Jill bathroom with Fred. Melissa and another sprinter are across the hall.

She opens the door and I blink back my surprise. Her

room at her mom's house was a dark blue and covered in posters. Her dad's house featured a room that was bubble gum pink. This is… different. She has the same boring white walls we all do. Twinkly lights hang from the ceiling, looping around the room. The walls are plastered with pictures.

There's a section of photos from high school, people I recognize as being on her track team or in the newspaper club. There are pictures that have to be from Georgetown— the logo is featured on her chest in a number of them. There are pictures from Newton. Fred, Melissa, and Mark are prominently featured. Over her desk are photos of her and Micah and their mess of step-siblings.

And then there's the wall devoted to me. Pictures of us, hand in hand. Wrapped up in each other. Kissing. There are quite a few pictures of us kissing. Our first date, that terrible winter formal. Three years of homecoming dances. Junior prom. Date nights. Senior prom. Graduation. That last idyllic summer, beach trips and days at the community pool. It's a wall of us.

I'm at a loss for words. It doesn't look like these are newly printed photos, that she just put them up last week. They've been on her wall for awhile. She's been staring at pictures of us for who knows how long.

"Mase…"

She looks at me over her shoulder, totally oblivious. "What's up?"

She might still be processing what we are now, but it's clear she's been pining for me just as long as I've been pining for her. When I shut down, she lit up. We were both coping in our own ways.

"Nothing." I drop her bag on her bed and press a kiss to the top of her head. "I'm great."

twenty-nine

...

Mason

I'M NOT sure what I expected when I jokingly suggested it, but Tucker agreeing to a month of celibacy was not on my list. He seems perfectly fine with abstaining for a month or longer.

Aren't guys supposed to want sex all the time? Isn't he supposed to be all over me after going without for the last two and a half years? Either he's not as okay with this as he says he is, or he's getting some on the side. I know sex is important to him, that it's a meaningful experience for him, but I just can't wrap my brain around the fact that he would rather not have sex with me than have sex with me right now.

So I call Micah.

"What did he do? I'll beat him up," my twin tells me.

"He didn't do anything."

"He upset you."

"I upset myself." Maybe calling my brother for reassurance was a bad idea. I can't recall a single time he's actually been helpful to me in the last twenty years. "He won't have sex with me."

I can hear Micah gag. "Gross, Mase."

"Well, that's my problem. I was freaking out and said something I shouldn't have, and he's taking sex off the table."

"So you mean he's actually listening to you and trying to make you feel better?" Micah scoffs. "Yeah, I can see how you might freak out about that."

"Mic…"

"No, no, this gets better," he says. "Because having sex is upsetting you, he takes sex off the table, and now you're upset?"

"Well, when you put it like that…"

"Just because you've had shitty luck with assholes in the past doesn't mean he's like those guys," Micah says. "He's a decent guy. Take him at his word. He loves you and respects your boundaries. Stop freaking out and let the poor bastard love you."

I clear my throat. "You're kind of the worst."

He laughs. "You love me, bitch."

"You're okay."

We talk a bit about Dad and the babies—there are so many babies. Every time I turn around, his wife is pregnant again. Mom and the step-siblings are fighting again—surprise, surprise, they're bratty preteens, I'm not sure what else she was expecting.

It's good to catch up with my brother. For so many years, he's been my rock, my constant. At all of the crucial moments in my life, either he or Tucker has been there for me, if not both of them. They get along so well together.

They used to. I don't know if they will now. He's changed. He's more stoic, more reserved. Micah's never met a party he didn't like. They've both grown over the years.

My phone vibrates with a text. Tucker is on his way over for our date—we're going to have dinner at the ASC again, just the two of us, then come back to my place for a movie. If everything goes according to plan, there might be some casual making out—horizontally, in my bed. Maybe even naked.

I can respect that he doesn't want to have sex. As much as

I want to get laid, I don't think I'm ready for the emotional overload that comes with sex with him. I want easy, casual, no strings attached sex with the man that I love. That shouldn't be contradictory. It should be easy for us to navigate after what we've accomplished together.

And he's not built for that. Our relationship isn't built for that.

So we'll wait. We'll get more comfortable with one another. I'll get over this weird hangup I seem to have developed overnight, and we'll get back to how it used to be. I love him. I'm in love with him. I want to be with him. It's only natural that we have sex. Right? Right. Him taking it off the table can't last long.

Tucker greets me at the door with a chaste kiss. He hands me a small bouquet of sunflowers—my favorite flowers. He remembered.

"Come on in," I tell him, beckoning him inside. He chews the inside of his cheek as he steps over the threshold.

"You look great, Princess," he says, and I beam. I'm only wearing leggings and a boxy Newton Track and Field t-shirt, the same clothes I've been wearing all day.

"Thanks, babe." I put the flowers in a cup of water and set them on the kitchen counter. Now all of my roommates will know that I have the type of boyfriend who brings me flowers. Tonight I'll take them up to my room, where I can admire them for the next week or so. "You ready to go?"

He catches my hand at the door and draws me in for a kiss that leaves me gasping. "Yeah, now I am." He swats me lightly on the ass and grabs my coat off the hook. He holds it open for me to step into. "How was your day?"

Hand in hand, we make small talk on the way to the ASC. He holds the door open for me and then retakes my hand. We swipe through and make our way through the dining hall lines. He opts for turkey meatloaf. I have my sights set on the tilapia.

We eat dinner and talk about our day. We have a paper due next week for our sociology class; we make plans to hit the library together on Wednesday before my track practice and after his football meeting. It might be the only time we get together this week. Thursday night he has a video chat scheduled with Jamal, who's never been my biggest fan, and then Friday afternoon my brother will arrive. We'll have to make the most of our limited time together.

Tucker takes my hand in his and slowly runs his thumb over my knuckles.

"What?"

"Nothing," he says, with a secret little smile curving his gorgeous mouth. He squeezes my fingers. "I'm glad we're doing this. I wish I could take you on a real date, the way you deserve."

"This is a real date," I remind him. "It works for us."

He presses a kiss to my palm. "Want to get out of here?"

"Thought you'd never ask."

He grabs both trays and returns them before I can get up and do it. He drops a kiss to my temple on the way back. He offers me his hand, and I slip mine into his.

Being with Tucker is easy. I don't have to pretend to be someone I'm not. He knows me—at least, he knows who I used to be. We have a history. That doesn't get erased simply because it's been a while since we've been together. If anything, it's made us stronger. We're not picking up where we left off, not exactly; we're building something new, using existing pieces of the puzzle.

I don't get nervous butterflies in my belly when I'm with him. I don't freeze up and lose my mind. I'm the best version of myself when he's around. He makes me want to be a better person, full stop.

Melissa is on the couch with some guy I don't recognize. They're touching but pretending they're not, like we don't notice his hand high on her thigh or her hand inches from the very obvious boner tenting his joggers.

"Hey, girl," she says.

I grab my sunflowers. "We're going upstairs. Don't have sex on the couch."

"We're not—I'm not—"

"I don't care. Not on the couch, please. Do it in your room or the shower like the rest of us."

Tucker snorts out a laugh. I take his hand and lead him up to my room.

I didn't even think about the pictures the other day. He looked like he didn't know what to think of them, of us. I like the memories. I didn't lock them away; I celebrated the good times and mourned the bad. I remembered him, the good, the bad, and the ugly.

He kicks off his shoes and takes a careful seat on the edge of my bed. I push ineffectually at his shoulder, and he laughs, pretending I'm actually moving him, until I have him in the position I want: laying on my bed, his front pressed to my back, his arm wrapped around my middle. I lay my head back on his shoulder and sigh.

"You okay, sunshine?" He drops a kiss to my shoulder.

"I'm perfect." I snuggle closer, and he tightens his arm around me. I'm enveloped in a cocoon of his warm embrace.

Turning on *Notting Hill* is the best idea I've had since I approached him in the dining hall that night he kissed me. We watch the movie we've both seen nearly a thousand times, reciting lines of dialogue to each other. His hand roves over my hip, my ribcage, my thigh, touching, touching.

He doesn't try to get into my pants. He doesn't try to grope me. He simply touches me, holds me, as we watch my favorite movie. Occasionally, he kisses my shoulder or my temple.

"How are you doing?" I crane my head back to look at him.

"I'm great. You okay?"

Slowly I shuffle in the bed, so we're facing each other. I lay my hand on his bearded cheek and kiss him softly.

Tucker pulls back. "Nope. Nuh-uh. Not happening."

I frown. "I'm not—"

"You're trying to seduce me," he says. His eyes are bright with mischief. "You think turning on Julia Roberts and batting your eyelashes will change my mind. We're not having sex tonight, Princess. Not until you work through whatever is bothering you."

"I'm not trying to seduce you," I protest weakly. "It was just a kiss."

He runs his hand through my hair, his enormous hand cupping the back of my head, cradling my skull. "It always starts with just a kiss, and then it always turns into more. You know I'm defenseless around you, baby."

thirty

. . .

Tucker

HER EYES ARE BRIGHT. "I kind of like that about you."

I kiss her slowly. "No sex."

Mason pouts. "Some casual making out?"

"Clothes on."

She trails her fingers down my chest. "I was really hoping I could give you a blowjob."

My cock gets interested in this conversation real quick.

"No."

She frowns. "King…"

"Baby, I would die for your mouth on me again," I confess. My cock thickens in my pants as if it's actually going to happen. I have bad news for the both of us. "Sex is freaking you out. That means we're not having sex until your head is on straight again. I don't care how long it takes. You're worth the wait."

Her finger traces over my lips. I kiss her thumb. "How did I get so lucky to find you again?"

"Just fate, I guess." I roll over, tucking her beneath me, and kiss her properly. She squirms beneath me, trying to wrap her legs around me. My hands on her hips keep her pinned under me. I tackle grown men weighing more than I do every day. I can handle a sprightly little thing like her.

We make out for—I lose track of time. All I can think about is her mouth on mine, her body pressed against mine. Her hands stroke my arms, my shoulders, digging into the tender muscles there. I hiss, and she breaks the kiss.

"You okay?"

"Bruise." I missed a tackle and ended up on my back at the wrong angle. After practice, I spent some time with the team massage therapist, but it's still sore.

Mason frowns up at me. "Let me see?"

"You just want me to take my shirt off."

She blushes. "I mean, that's a side benefit. I'll take mine off if you do."

"Clothes are staying on."

She arches her hips into mine, where I'm hard and aching for her. I can always go home and jerk off. I won't let her—

Her hand trails down my chest to the front of my jeans. She cups me through the fabric.

"If you won't let me give you a blowjob, can I at least touch you?"

I frown. She pouts.

"That doesn't seem fair. You get to touch me, and I can't touch you?"

Mason smirks at me. "Your rules. Or we can both get naked and touch each other."

I want to. I want to do bad. But I also don't want her to freak out on me again. I want all of her, not some withdrawn shell of a person that can't communicate what's wrong.

She pops the button on my jeans. Her nimble fingers work my zipper.

"Mase..."

"I want to touch you. Let me touch you." She grabs my cock through my boxers and I shudder at the heel of her palm pressing against me. "I'm not freaking out. We're not having sex, I get that. I respect that. But I want you. I want you to feel good."

She rubs her thumb over the sensitive head and I groan, covering her mouth with mine. She licks into my mouth as her hand delves beneath the flimsy layer of fabric separating us. Her warm palm wraps around my length. Pleasure ricochets through my veins.

"We shouldn't…"

"Come on, babe," she says with a laugh. "It's just a handjob."

"It's not *just a handjob* to me, Mason." I tuck away my angry cock and zip up my pants. "It means something to me because we're doing it together. Us. We're doing this because we love each other, not because we're so desperate to get our rocks off that anyone will do. I only want to do this with you. You're not just anyone. You're important to me."

She chews the inside of her cheek. "You're important to me, too."

"I said we should keep our clothes on, and I meant it," I tell her gently. I brush a strand of hair out of her face. "Sex complicates things. We need to be on the same page for this to work."

She swallows thickly. "I'm sorry."

"There's nothing to apologize for."

"I'm ruining this. I'm making you wait—"

"That's what you're not getting, sunshine. You're worth waiting for."

She sniffs. "Will you…"

"What?"

"Will you hold me?"

I sigh. "Of course, baby." I collapse beside her on the bed and pull her into my arms. She rests her head on my chest and curls into me.

"I want to get my head on straight," she says quietly. "I'm trying."

"I know you are. I'm not pushing you. You'll be ready in your own time."

"I really do want to suck your cock. I like having you in my mouth."

My traitorous cock twitches against her, and I know she can feel it. "I like that, too. Maybe another time."

She swallows. "Will you stay with me?"

"There's nowhere else I'd rather be."

thirty-one

. . .

Mason

MICAH LOOKS DISGUSTINGLY good for having flown on a plane and taken two bus rides to get to me.

"Come here, sunshine," my brother says, before he wraps me in a hug.

I haven't seen him since last August, when he and my dad helped me move into Athlete's Village. He spent his winter break on campus, preparing for his bowl game, and then I had a cold for the main event and stayed home babysitting my dad's kids instead of infecting everyone.

When I was at Georgetown, I tried to go down to South Carolina for at least one or two football games a year, and he always came home for a track meet or two. I always have a meet over spring break, so it's not like I have a surplus of time to spend with him. We both train for most of the summer. College athletics are year-round regardless of when the sport is actually played.

"Missed you," I say to the crook of his neck.

"Missed you more." He tugs my ponytail like he's done since we were in diapers.

Micah is my other half, my twin. We have a mess of half siblings and step siblings, but nobody else grew up in those houses with us. Nobody else lived that life with me. He knows me as well as I know myself.

"Let me see you," he says. He makes a twirling motion with his finger, and obediently, I twirl. "Damn, girl, you look good. Have you gained weight?"

"Three whole pounds." It's hard to maintain weight during the season. It's even harder to add muscle.

"It's paying off. You're going to smoke them tomorrow."

"You know it."

He offers his hand for a high-five. We do it, and then he grabs me by the wrist and forces me into a headlock, giving me a noogie.

"Mic!"

My brother laughs. "You should have seen that coming a mile away."

"Excuse me for thinking you were finally grown up."

He shakes his head. "You know better than that. Where's the boy?"

"I don't know what you're talking about."

Micah rolls his eyes. "So he still won't have sex with you. Good."

I frown, remembering the... discussion we had on Monday night. The light kisses on the cheek he gave me on Wednesday for our study session. I didn't see him at all yesterday. I miss the poor bastard.

"No, he's not."

He throws his arm over my shoulders. "You'll change his mind soon enough."

"Yeah, I hope so."

Sex is supposed to feel good. It's supposed to be relaxing. Who cares about love when sex is on the line?

Except that while it feels good in the moment, after the fact I don't feel good about myself. That's what Tucker is trying to avoid. I know he's right; I just don't know how to fix it. I'm not broken. I don't need therapy. I'm just... me.

"I'm starving," Micah announces. "Take me to your nearest food place."

"There aren't a lot of options." There's a reason I take all of my meals in the ASC: it's because all of the other dining halls suck.

"I don't care. Feed me."

I roll my eyes at his dramatics. He picks up his duffle bag and slings it over his shoulder. After a moment, he pulls my backpack off my shoulder and throws it over his, too.

"You don't have to carry my bag."

He laughs. "Yeah, I do, Princess."

"No. You don't get to call me that."

"Priiiiiincess." He chases after me, wrapping both arms around me in a bear hug. "You like it when he calls you that."

"Yeah, because it's his name for me. Not yours." I shove him away. "Only he gets to call me that."

"All right, all right."

We laugh and joke on our way to the ASC. It's good to see him. I didn't realize how much I missed his light-hearted earnestness until confronted with it again. Using one of my coveted few guest passes, I badge him into the dining hall, and we stow our things at a table. It's still early; there aren't a lot of people eating at this time of day.

The back table where the football team sits is occupied only by Greg, with the man bun and caveman beard. His back is to me as he hunches over his plate, a thick textbook open in front of him.

Micah loads his plate with two chicken breasts, steamed veggies, and a whole grain roll. He's still on the pre-combine eating plan, trying to gain a few pounds of lean muscle. I opt for the Thai green curry with brown rice. Knowing him, he'll probably try to steal a few bites and end up eating half of mine in addition to his.

"So this is Newton," he hums, taking a look around.

"I like it."

"Yeah, and how much of that is the people here?"

"That's not fair. I've made friends here," I point out. "You're not allowed to sleep with Fred or Melissa or the other girls I live with. Anyone else is up for fair game, but you have to go back to their place."

He rolls his eyes. "I'm here to see you, not hook up. I'm sleeping on your floor whether you like it or not."

"The couch is perfectly serviceable."

Micah laughs. "Yeah, I slept on that thing when we moved you in. It's as hard as a rock. I'll take my chances with the floor."

A shadow looms over us. "This guy bothering you?" Barrett booms, puffed up with big guy bravado, staring down at us with a hard look in his eye. Amir and Wes are flanking him, a book tucked against his tray.

I laugh. "Stand down, guys. This is my brother."

Barrett blinks.

"You don't look alike," Amir says distrustfully.

"We're twins," Micah says.

He looks more like our Korean-American side of the family, tan-skinned with high cheekbones and monolids, whereas I look more like our Black family members, darker brown with a high forehead and prominent nose and mouth. That's the beauty of genetics: you never know what you're going to get.

Tucker appears on the other side of the table. "Mic. Hey." He sets his tray down on the table.

Micah gets the hint. He pushes his chair back and claps Tucker into a manly hug.

"Hey, man," my brother says. "How's it going?"

"Oh, you know. Same old."

Amir frowns. "You know this guy?"

"Micah Prince. Mason's brother," Tuck says. "He goes to school in—North Carolina? South Carolina? I can never remember."

Of course he knows. We all went on a recruiting trip together.

"South Carolina. Patterson."

Amir nods, his jaw tight. "Right."

Wes grunts.

"No, I don't think so," Barrett says. "We'll leave you guys to your reunion."

Tucker picks up his tray.

"Sit with us," Micah tells him. "I haven't seen you in two and a half years, and you run away at the first sight of me?"

Tucker's shoulders are tense. "I was giving you guys some alone time."

"This whole weekend is alone time," I tell him, trying to break some of the ice between them. I tug on Tuck's hand. "Hang out with us."

He drops into the chair. After a moment, he leans over and drops a kiss to my cheek, pressing his forehead to my temple.

"Hey, sunshine," he tells me quietly. He runs his thumb over my cheek. "I missed you the last few days."

"Same. Fuck school. Who needs classes? Let's just spend all our time together naked."

He chuckles quietly. "Don't tempt me, Princess." He kisses me softly. I wrap my arm around him and pull him into me, trying to deepen the kiss. He won't let me. He keeps it chaste and sweet. "You're going to kill me one of these days, sweetheart."

Micah coughs. "Okay, okay, I get it, you're in love and all that bullshit."

Tucker goes red. I set my hand on his thigh, and the muscles jump beneath my touch.

"Shut up. Like you've never been in love before."

"Nah, I don't date," my brother says with a drawl he picked up in South Carolina. "I fuck."

I roll my eyes. "Yeah, yeah, you don't want to be tied

down. All girls want to do is trap you. I get it. You've been listening to Mom's bullshit again."

My mom is convinced that Micah's conquests are secretly poking holes in the condoms to try to score a huge payday. First of all, my brother is still a broke college student. He doesn't have a job. He lives in a gross student apartment and doesn't clean his bathroom. He's no shining star.

On top of that, if he somehow did manage to impregnate some poor woman, it's not like he's going to abandon his child. He's the type to be an active, involved parent. I've seen him with our dad's new kids: this guy loves babies, and babies love him.

Our parents got married when our mom was four months pregnant with us. They split up before we were two, though the divorce wasn't finalized for another four years. She tried to trap him, and it backfired. So now she thinks all women are out to do the same thing.

Micah will be a good catch—a year from now, once he declares, gets drafted, and is playing in the NFL. He's relatively charming, usually polite, and doesn't have any STDs that he knows of, and I know he gets checked every week during the football season when they check for PEDs. Only one of his exes has ever slashed my tires or keyed my car, and she thought it was weird for brothers and sisters to hang out together in a group of friends, so clearly she was more twisted than either of us realized.

Tucker coughs. He reaches for his food, and all three of us take in the two giant peanut butter sandwiches on his plate beside his meal. We all know what that means.

"You okay, baby?" I stroke his thigh.

"I'm great," he says around a mouthful of peanut butter.

Micah leans forward. "You can talk to us. What's wrong?"

He stuffs more of his sandwich into his face. "Mm-hm."

"We'll be here when you need us," I tell him quietly.

thirty-two

. . .

Tucker

THE PEANUT BUTTER turns to paste in my mouth and clogs my throat. It's a delicious burn.

I can't do this. I can't sit across from him and pretend like nothing is wrong. He dumped me. He abandoned me. At a time when I desperately needed a friend, my best friend, he was nowhere to be found.

And now we're supposed to *party our faces off*, which I'm guessing is code for "drink a shit ton of alcohol and act like idiots."

Mason's hand on my leg anchors me to this plane. Her fingers dig into my thigh as I finish my first sandwich.

It doesn't help. I don't feel better. But I don't feel worse. I start in on my actual dinner, saving my second sandwich for when I'll need it. Because between the two Prince siblings, I'm going to need it.

I clear my throat. "What do you have planned for the weekend?"

"Party tonight, obvs," he says. "Go to sleep early. Track meet. Mason beats those stupid UNH idiots to a pulp. And then more partying. I get on a plane at four o'clock on Sunday. We have a lot of ground to cover."

She turns to me. "We were going to go to a low-key track thing tonight and a Delta party tomorrow night." She swallows, chewing her cheek. "Do you want to come with us?"

No. Not at all.

"Yeah, sure," I tell her. She's nearly as surprised as I am.

"You aren't hanging out with the guys?"

"I'd much rather spend time with you."

Not a lie. I would simply prefer that our time together wasn't at a party.

She beams at me. "Great."

We eat in quiet silence. The chicken curry is good. I prefer the Thai style curries to the Indian curries they have more frequently.

"This is awkward, right?" Micah says. "It's not just me?"

Mason forces a laugh. It's clearly fake. "No, it's not."

Yeah, it is. I'm the source of the awkwardness, the big pink elephant in the room. The Prince twins dumped me, and I fell apart. Now Mason and I are back together, but Micah and I aren't friends, not anymore.

I don't know that I want to be his friend if the terms are conditional on my dating his sister. I love Mason; I want to be with her. But that shouldn't impact my relationship with Micah. I thought our friendship was strong enough to withstand her and me crumbling to pieces. It turns out I was wrong.

Micah clears his throat. "So tell me who's going to be at this party. Do I get to meet the infamous Mark?"

She glances at me, her brow furrowed. I remember the way Mark wrapped his arms around her at that first meet I went to. I know she's dated other guys. Did she and Mark have a thing?

No. I don't care. I can't care. She's not with him now; she's with me, and she's not about to cheat on me, so I can't go down that path. It only leads to heartbreak and misery.

Mason clears her throat. "Yeah, Mark will be there. So will Bryce."

"Fucking Bryce! Man, that dude cracks me up." Micah wipes at his eyes. "And Fredericka?"

"If you call her that, she will stab you in the foot," she warns. "I'll even tell her which is your bad ankle."

"Okay, okay, don't tease Fred. Melissa is still a hot mess?"

"Always. She doesn't know how to stop at one drink. She always ends up hungover on race day."

"Rookie mistake," he says, shaking his head. "I showed up hungover on game day once—once!—and Coach reamed me a new one. Played like shit. Felt like shit. Never made that mistake again."

Our coaching staff has us on strict curfew on game nights. Guys who get caught partying the night before a game don't get benched—they get kicked off the team entirely. It's not worth it.

Mason sets her hand on my thigh again. "You okay, baby? You're quiet."

I force a smile. "I'm good."

"You want to get out of here?" Her voice softens. "Maybe save your sandwich for later?"

My jaw clenches. "I'm not a child, Mason. You don't have to treat me like one."

Her eyes flash. "That's not what I'm doing."

Yeah, it is. My frustration boils over. "I'm coping. I'm surviving. What do you want from me?"

"I want you to thrive. I want you to not need your coping mechanisms," she says loudly. Too loudly. People at other tables look over at us, eager for drama. "I want you to tell me what's bothering you."

"Nothing. I'm fine." I push back my chair. "I need some air."

I grab my coat and my sandwich and get the fuck out of there. The cold January air seeps into my bones and chills me from the inside out. I take a bite of my sandwich. Everything sucks. Everything is awful.

He's here. He's here and he's acting like absolutely nothing is wrong.

Mason and I can pick up where we left off, but he and I can't. We're not dating. We can't kiss and make up. I take another bite. Peanut butter soothes my soul in a way that nothing else can. It makes everything better. Nothing is insurmountable with a peanut butter sandwich in my hand.

Oh, no.

Am I using my peanut butter sandwich the same way other people use alcohol? I stare at the remains of the sandwich in my hand. It's so good. It tastes delicious. It has never treated me poorly, always been there for me when I needed it most.

I've always been an emotional eater. I eat when I'm happy. I eat when I'm sad. I eat when I'm stressed. That's nothing new. There are far more destructive vices I could have: alcohol, drugs, gambling, meaningless sex…

Shit.

I want to be an addiction counselor so that nobody else has to struggle like my mom and my grandfathers had to. And I seem to have inadvertently developed an addiction of my own. My coping mechanism isn't helping me anymore: now it's having a detrimental impact on me. What am I going to do? Call up a clinic and say I have an addiction to peanut butter sandwiches? I can't just stop eating altogether: I can't go on a feeding tube and skip meals for the rest of my life. How do I cut food out of my diet? How do I walk the line between emotional eating and healthy, sustainable eating?

There are footsteps behind me. I cram the rest of my sandwich into my mouth. Farewell, dear friend. You have treated me well.

"Tuck."

It's Micah. I hunch my shoulders as I chew, intent on

getting the fuck out of there. He can't see me: I'm invisible. If I will it into being, it'll happen, right?

"Tucker." He's jogging now, trying to keep pace with me. "Tucker Kingsley."

"Fuck off."

"Come on, man." A hand lands on my arm. I throw it off. The fucker does it again.

"I suggest you don't touch me unless you want to lose that hand. I'm pretty sure you're going to need it if you're going to be drafted."

"Tucker. Don't be like this."

"Like what?"

"Like a dick," he yells. "You're being a dick."

"Leave me the fuck alone."

"You know I can't do that."

I whirl to face him. "And why the fuck not?"

"Because my sister is in love with you, asshole. That means we're stuck together, whether we want to be or not." He crosses his arms over his chest. "Jesus fuck, it's cold. How the fuck do you people deal with this every day?"

We're stuck together. He doesn't want to be my friend. He doesn't want anything to do with me. He's putting up with me for Mason's sake.

"How long?"

Micah blinks. "What?"

"How long have you been simply tolerating my presence? For how long have you only put up with me because of her? Were we ever really friends?"

"That's not what I meant," he backtracks.

"You were my best friend," I tell him. "It was the three of us, one cohesive unit. And then she dumped me, and you dumped me, and I was all alone. The two of you had each other. I had nobody."

"Tuck…"

"You chose her, and you dumped me just like she did."

"I couldn't pick sides!" he yells. "She's my sister! What the fuck was I supposed to say? It was a high school relationship. We were all moving to separate colleges. Of course we lost touch. Of course you guys broke up."

"We're together again. How fortuitous that you come crawling back into my life now." I cross my arms over my chest and stare him down. "Fuck you. Go back to South Carolina."

"Are you serious right now?" He's laughing, the asshole. "Get over yourself. I'm not here for you."

"Yeah, you've made that pretty fucking clear."

"Mason wouldn't want us to fight."

"Don't talk to me about what she wants." My voice is low and hoarse, a warning. "Don't you talk about her."

"Who the fuck do you think she talked to about it? She couldn't talk to you," he snaps. "I'm the one whose shoulder she cried on for weeks. She didn't want to break up with you, asshole."

"And yet she did it anyway."

He throws his hands up in the air. "And now you guys are back together, so what the fuck does it matter?"

"It matters," I tell him lowly. "It fucking matters to me."

"I'm sorry, okay," he yells. "I'm sorry I stood by my sister when she needed me."

"I needed you, too!"

My pulse pounds dully in my ears.

"I needed you, too," I repeat, more quietly now. "Everything was new and scary, and I needed my best friend just as much as I needed my girlfriend. And instead, both of you were gone in the blink of an eye. You left me hanging. You couldn't shoot me a text to say you didn't want to talk to me anymore?"

"Jesus," he says, wrapping his arms around his chest. "It's fucking cold out here."

My blood is boiling. I have peanut butter on my favorite

black gloves. The guy I thought was my best friend hates me now. It's all cool. Nothing's wrong. Everything's fine.

"There you guys are," Mason says. She jogs over to us. "Fuck, it's cold." She slips her hand into mine and I automatically squeeze, lacing our fingers together. "You okay, baby?"

"I'm fine."

"Glad you were able to find him," she says to Micah. "Sorry I took so long, Fred wanted to chat about tonight."

What's her end game here, make me fall back in love with her and then destroy me all over again? She can. She has a power over me I've never been able to deny. I'd do anything for her—and she knows it.

Once upon a time, I never would have thought that the girl I loved could do something so sinister. Now? I'm wondering if I ever really knew her at all. I certainly don't now.

thirty-three

. . .

Tucker

THE HOUSE IS ALREADY PACKED by the time we arrive. I'm still processing. I don't know what to think. Mason hangs up our coats and hugs Mark. I will probably never like him, but I can pretend with the best of 'em.

Micah offers me a cup of beer.

"No, thanks."

"Come on, man. It's an apology." He pushes the cup towards me again.

I push his hand away. "I don't drink."

He gapes at me. "What?"

"I don't drink. No thanks."

"Like, you only have one or two?"

"Like, at all. I'm not interested."

He shakes his head. "Damn. You have changed."

"I really haven't." I grab a bottle of water from the cooler. That's the good thing about student athletes, there are always bottles of water around. I didn't drink in high school, either, but that was more due to lack of opportunities than a lack of desire. "I'm still me. I don't need to drink to have a good time."

He pours a second beer and takes a sip.

I'm not an addict. I don't feel an urge to drink when I'm around alcohol. Mostly I just feel bored. Drunk people aren't exactly the most fun to be around. They're not funny. I have no desire to hook up with someone I'm not involved with. I'm even less inclined to get with someone that's been drinking.

It's easy enough to abstain: I have no interest.

Mason joins us, and he hands one of the cups to her. She takes it with a smile and frowns at me. "You don't want one?"

"I'm good, thanks."

We stand awkwardly in a circle. I don't know what to say —to either of them.

How long ago did he decide he wanted to stop being my friend?

How much of my life is a lie?

I have this inexplicable urge to call my moms. Jamal. Someone who knows me, someone who knows the past. My friends are great, but they won't understand. The Prince twins were my whole world. "Best friend" doesn't adequately explain the depth of our decade-plus friendship. "Girlfriend" doesn't adequately explain how much I love her.

Barrett would be sympathetic for a minute and then tell me to get over myself. Amir would tell me to break up with her. Wes would grunt and say that's what I deserved for deciding to hook up with someone in the first place. Greg and Miles? I don't even know what they would say.

Mason and I need to have a hard conversation. Several of them. But we can't do that with her brother chaperoning us like an awkward third-wheel. We have to get to the bottom of this sex hang-up she has. I only want her to feel good with me. That she doesn't enjoy herself after sex is a no go for me. She needs to do some hard thinking about what's making her not feel good with me. I don't like that she treats sex so callously. Not when it means so much to me.

And then there's her drinking. I don't care if she has one

or two on a night out. What concerns me is the constant need to go out and drink every weekend. Getting flat out drunk every time. What's wrong with staying sober? What's wrong with having a few drinks and *not* getting drunk?

I'm not ready to lay down an ultimatum. We need to talk about it first. We haven't even addressed this yet. But I can't keep surrounding myself with people who drink heavily every weekend. It's not good for me.

And I don't know that she'll pick me over drinking with her friends. I don't know that I can ask her to decide.

Mason slides her arms around my waist and rests her head on my shoulder. "You seem tense, King."

"I'm fine." I wrap my arms around her and breathe in the familiar citrus scent of her shampoo. "A lot on my mind."

She frowns. "You can talk to me."

Except that I can't.

I force a smile and run my thumb across her cheek. "I will."

When I'm ready. Maybe never.

She rises onto her tiptoes for a kiss. I can't say no. I let her kiss me, sweet and chaste.

Mason studies me, her eyes worried. "You don't seem like yourself tonight."

"I'm fine," I lie again.

"King…"

I kiss her temple. "Let's just enjoy the party. You've got a big day tomorrow."

She's adding an extra event to her repertoire after one of the other girls tore her hamstring. She's out for the foreseeable future, maybe the rest of the season, so Mason is slotting in to her spot in the relay. It's right up her alley. She's going to smash it. As much as it sucks that the other girl is injured, sometimes that's what it takes to get ahead: one opportunity, one chance to prove her mettle.

She sinks back against me, her back to my front, and

draws my arm around her. I'm happy enough to stand here with her and let her monopolize the conversation with her friends. Micah bobs nearby, talking excitedly with Bryce about something to do with a manga series he's been obsessed with for the last ten years.

It's nice to see that some things haven't changed.

I drink my water and hold Mason, and the party continues on around us. Is this what I was missing the last two and a half years? Somehow I don't think football parties are as well behaved as the track team. Sure, there might be more video games—I don't think any of the guys on the team have ever passed up a game of Madden, even the pretty boy quarterbacks and tough guy tight ends—and a few more scantily-clad women, but for the most part, football parties don't get out of control. Coach keeps us on a tight leash. Nobody wants to risk getting kicked off the team for one night of hedonistic pleasure.

Frat parties, on the other hand…

Mason turns to me, a question in her eyes.

"Hm?"

"Nothing," she says, then kisses my cheek. "I just really love you."

One of the girls surrounding us swoons. "Aw. You guys are so cute."

I close my eyes and press my forehead to her temple. "I love you, too, Princess."

Even if she's keeping secrets. Even if she's lying to me. Even if our entire relationship is a lie. I still love her. I'm always going to love her, whether I want to or not.

"I want what you guys have," another girl says, wrapping her arm around the girl beside her. "They're adorable."

I don't tell them that relationships are hard work. I don't tell them that sometimes I hate myself for how much control she has over me. I don't tell them about the struggles we're having, in and out of the bedroom. I don't tell them anything.

"Thank you," I say instead, and I kiss Mason's forehead. She curls into me and rests her head on my chest.

"Oh, gross," Micah says loudly. "I forgot how much you two are always all over each other."

"Fuck off," I tell him again, and the bastard laughs.

I won't tolerate any big brother bravado. He lost that right when he stopped being my friend. Mason and I see each other nearly every day; he lives all the way in South Carolina. He's not part of our everyday lives. He knows nothing about our situation. Right now he's being a dick just because he can, and that doesn't sit right with me.

She rolls her eyes and tightens her grip around me. "Don't fight. You know I hate when the two most important men in my life fight over me. I'm not a doll. You can share me."

"Gross, Mase," Micah says. "We're not going to share you."

She gags. "Don't make an innocent statement into something that it isn't. I love you both in very different ways."

"I'll say," he mutters. He takes a hefty gulp of his beer. "Your cup empty?"

She nods, handing it to him.

"Your boyfriend is failing in his duties to get you drunk," he says accusingly.

"She has a meet tomorrow," I remind him. Besides, I don't want her to get drunk. I keep that little fact to myself.

"So only one more, and then I'm done," she says patiently, ever the mediator. "Thanks, Mic."

"Anything you need, sunshine," he says, chucking her chin.

Mason growls and bares her teeth. He laughs.

"You're a riot," Micah says, shaking his head. "Let me get you that beer."

thirty-four

. . .

Mason

MICAH LASTED HALF an hour on the floor before he crawled into my bed. It's not weird to share a bed with my little brother. Those seventeen minutes I was an only child were the best seventeen minutes of my life. We shared a womb for nine months; we took baths together as children and shared a room until we were seven and a half. We can spend one night in the same bed. It's a double bed: there's plenty of space for both of us.

Other people have never really understood our bond. We have a half dozen half-siblings and step-siblings, but he's my only full blood sibling. He's the other half of my heart, whether I want him to be or not. I know the way he thinks. He knows me nearly as well as I know myself. It doesn't matter that we've spent the last two and a half years in separate states: he's still my brother, my twin, my rock.

That's not to say we don't fight. We do. All the fucking time, like cats and dogs. At the end of the day, I know he has my back, and I have his. Whether he's right or wrong, I'm on his side, and he's on mine.

There's some kind of tension between him and Tucker, and I think I'm the cause of it. I don't like it. They are the two most important men in my life. I'd love it if they got along. I'd love it if they were friends again. I'm not sure why their friendship dissolved. Neither of them have said a word about it. It's like they're content to pretend nothing has ever happened, even though they're both clearly upset by it.

I can't fix them. I can't lock them in a room and force them to kiss and make up. As much as I'd like to, I think it will only make it worse. Neither of them have ever responded well to forceful manipulation. I'll have to be more discreet.

Meet day with Micah visiting starts the same as any other meet day. I roll out with a foam roller, getting at my tight hips. I do a little yoga and stretching routine to get my body limber.

My brother wakes up around eight. His eyes go wide at the sight of me in my sports bra and running shorts. "Jesus! What are you wearing?"

"Oh, shut up." It's not like he's never seen me in a bikini before. If anything, my sports bra covers more skin than a bathing suit does. I covered up this morning solely for his benefit. "Go take a shower. We need to leave in twenty minutes."

Grumbling under his breath, still half-asleep, he pads to the bathroom. He opens the door and lets out a girlish shriek.

I sit up in a hurry. "What's wrong?"

"Naked." He shakes his head and closes the door. "Your friend is naked."

"Fred?"

He nods, his tan skin flushed a dark pink. He looks shell-shocked.

"It's not like you've never seen a naked woman before."

Slowly, his lip curls into a smirk. "Sunshine, when I'm with a woman—"

"No! Stop! I don't want to hear it." I throw my yoga block at him, and it falls limply to the floor between us. The porous foam block is not an ideal throwing device. "I get it, you get laid a lot. That doesn't mean I want to hear about your conquests."

Micah smirks. He's awake now. "You sure about that?"

I raise my eyebrows. "I can tell you all about the times Tucker and I hooked up. You want to hear what happened in this bed on Monday? Be glad I changed my sheets."

He shudders. "All right, all right. You like to play dirty, I get it."

The shower starts. I can hear the curtain get pulled aside as Fred gets in on the other side of the wall.

"You're going to have to wait now," I tell him. "She takes forever."

Eventually, he gets his turn in the shower and dresses in warm clothes. He's still bitching about the weather. Fred, Melissa, and I hustle him to the dining hall, where Melissa uses a guest pass to get him in. We fuel up for the day. He stares miserably into a coffee-flavored protein shake. He's going to get his workout in at the ASC gym while we're getting ready for the meet. Afterwards, he'll find his way to the indoor track to cheer us on.

I don't know if he'll meet up with Tucker. I don't know what's going on there. I'm a little afraid to ask. I don't know that either one of them will give me a straight answer.

Tuck sent me a brief good night text last night, and I woke up to an early good morning message. Normally there's a little more substance to his text messages beyond perfunctory sentiment. I like that he's the last person I talk to before I go to bed, and he's the first person I talk to when I wake up. I like it even better when he sleeps in my bed, but when life gets in the way and we're in our own beds, I like that he's still there with me.

I don't know what our issues are. Clearly we have a few. He's still refusing to sleep with me. I don't know how to make him understand that sex isn't as big a deal for me as it is for him. So what if sometimes I'm withdrawn after? I need my space. So what if sometimes I don't feel good about myself after? That's on me. It has nothing to do with him.

There are a number of reasons why I transferred to Newton. Tucker is only one of them. Never in my wildest dreams did I think we would get back together so easily. Sure, I had to spend a semester basically pursuing him from afar, but now we're together and everything is hunky-dory.

Except for this little sex disagreement.

There has to be a balance. I'm not sure where the middle ground is, but we have to find it. There has to be something between celibate and where we are now.

Tucker is in the stands within the first ten minutes of the meet. He's joined by Amir and Barrett. Wes is there, too, reading a book. Miles, Greg, and Sam aren't there—nope, there they are, in the row behind them. Greg has an enormous backpack with him. As I stretch, I watch him pull a multitude of snacks out of the bag and assemble it on the empty bench beside him.

Between events, I jog over to the stands. Tucker makes his way down to the front row. He leans over the railing and kisses me. I melt into him, wrapping my arms around his neck. He chuckles and pulls away.

"Good morning, Princess," he says, a smile on his face.

"I missed you last night."

His thumb caresses my cheek. "Missed you, too."

"Tomorrow night we'll have a sleepover?" At the worried look on his face, I quickly add: "No sex. Just a sleepover. I like when you're in my bed."

He softens. "Yeah, sunshine. That sounds nice."

"And you'll look out for Micah? I haven't seen him yet."

"He's not here?" Tucker frowns. "Isn't he supposed to be visiting you?"

I scratch at his beard, and he relaxes, nuzzling into the contact. "He went for a workout. I don't run until later. He'll be here when it counts. I'm not sure when."

He sighs. "Yeah, I'll keep an eye out."

Fred calls my name.

"Got to go." I kiss him one last time. He cups my cheek and presses his forehead to mine. "Love you."

"Love you, too," he says quietly.

Coach is gathering the sprinters into a semi-circle for a pep talk. The waiting is always the hardest part. We have another two hours until our races. It doesn't matter that we've been doing this for years, some of us half our lives; the waiting never gets easier. Nervous anticipation flutters in my stomach. Adrenaline pumps in my veins. I wait for my three or four races all week, and then they're over in the blink of an eye.

Micah is standing at the top of the bleachers. He waves at me, and I wave back, pointing three rows over to where Tucker is sitting. He frowns at me. I point again. Tucker is watching me, confused. I point back to where Micah is standing, and he turns, following my finger.

His happy smile fades as he sees my brother. Yeah, there's definitely something up with them. Nevertheless, Tucker stands and waves at Micah, who spots him in the nearly empty student section. Amir and Barrett scoot down, clearing a space.

Neither of them look happy to be sitting next to each other. Micah is nervous; he's chewing on his cheek, something he only does around people he doesn't know. Tucker is withdrawn, an empty shell of himself.

The three of us were attached at the hip in high school. Micah is my ride or die, my other half. Tucker has my heart. Together, the three of us formed a cohesive unit. Micah is still my best friend, whether he admits to it or not. Tucker is my boyfriend again, no matter the issues we're currently having. But the boys' previously strong friendship has splintered— because of me, because of the breakup. I don't think that we can repair it. Not if they won't help. Not if they won't both put the effort in.

Fred bumps my hip with hers. "Your cheering section sure is pretty."

I laugh. "You still can't sleep with my brother."

"I didn't say I wanted to."

I roll my eyes. "All of my female friends have slept with him or tried to. I'm used to it. Just know that all he wants is sex. He's not the type to stick around."

"So basically he's the male version of you," she laughs.

"I've changed. I'm not like that anymore."

"No, you've got yourself someone you *want* to stick around for. I still think you're going to get bored sooner or later," she says.

I hate that I think she's right. I hooked up with plenty of guys at Georgetown. I've had flings. Nobody has captured my attention the way Tucker has.

But I didn't expect us to settle down into a comfortable relationship again quite so quickly. Where are the sparks? Where are the fireworks? I want to be romanced. I want to be courted. And maybe it's a function of modern college dating, but I can't help to feel cheated that I don't get the fairytale romance I see in movies or read about in books.

I love Tucker. I'm in love with him; a part of me always has been, even when we were apart. But he's so set in his ways. He doesn't like to go out. He doesn't like to socialize. I can tell that while he's making an effort to get to know my friends, he would much rather stay in and watch a movie and cuddle than go out and have a good time. He doesn't want to party. He doesn't seem to drink.

Our lives are just so different these days. I don't know how to make this work anymore. And as much as I don't want to live my life without him, I don't want to sacrifice my youth and my Saturday nights to stay in and watch Jeopardy!

with his roommates. That's fine every once in a while; it's not my idea of a fun Saturday night, week after week.

Yeah, I can see a future with him. Yes, I can see us getting through grad school, getting married, having babies. I can see a life with him. Growing old together.

But I'm *so* not ready for that. I'm only twenty; I have my whole life ahead of me. I don't want to be boring and settled at this point in my life. I want to stay up all night and dance with my friends. I want to go to parties and meet new people. And, yes, I want to have crazy drunken sex.

I want to have crazy, drunken sex with Tucker, and he will barely touch me when I'm sober. He seems to have no issue abstaining. Aren't we supposed to be in the honeymoon phase? Aren't we supposed to be all over each other? Instead, he won't touch me. Sex is supposed to be meaningful, he says, an extension of our love for one another. I love him; I love when he fucks me.

But it's still just sex to me, and I can't seem to wrap my brain around the difference between what he wants and what I want. We had sex often enough before the break-up that I know what he likes. He's not as vanilla as he might claim. The dude is downright kinky, and considering how young we both were when we were together the first time, I can only believe he's grown into himself exponentially since then. He knows what he likes.

I've learned more about what I like since then. I'm not the same sheltered kid I used to be. I've been with enough other guys to know what definitely doesn't work for me. He hasn't experimented. He hooked up with one girl, one time, and when it wasn't what he wanted—me, asking him to take me back—he decided he was done with dating for the rest of his life. He's a teetotaler in the extreme.

I'm not like that. I like to drink. I like to have a good time. I like to kick back with my friends and relax. And he...

doesn't. There's no middle ground. There's no in between. I don't know how to compromise between all or nothing. I don't know if we can.

thirty-five

. . .

Tucker

WE SIT in silence during the longest track meet of my life. Beside me, Barrett and Amir talk amongst themselves. Wes grunts occasionally, contributing as he sees fit. Behind us, Sam and Miles are making out, and Greg is patiently third-wheeling with them.

Micah is silent. So am I. I have nothing to say to him that wasn't said last night. Yelled, whatever.

Greg leans forward, his head between ours. "So what's the plan for tonight? Are you guys going to the Delta party?"

"I think so," I tell him. She said she wanted to go. I don't think I can convince her we should do something else instead.

He whistles. "Damn, son, you have changed."

"Not that much."

"In a good way," he's quick to reassure me. "She's good for you."

Micah hums. "She's great."

Greg claps him on the shoulder. "So you guys are siblings?"

"Twins." Micah is extraordinarily tight-lipped.

"Well, she's awesome. We're glad she's here," he says.

"We've been trying to get your boy here out of his shell for the last two and a half years. She's been good for him."

He hums again, politely disinterested. His eyes are trained on the field. There's a brief lull between events. Nothing is going on. He doesn't want to talk to my friends. Or to me.

Greg hands me a sandwich from his backpack. It's turkey and havarti, which is my second favorite type of sandwich.

Micah raises his eyebrows. "Seriously?"

Amir and Barrett get turkey sandwiches, too, and a container of apples and peanut butter to split between them.

"It's a long day," Barrett says, unwrapping his sandwich. "Got to get our protein in."

"The concessions have shitty food," Amir adds, dunking an apple slice into peanut butter. It does nothing for me. If it's not slathered between two pieces of whole wheat bread, I'm not interested. "You can get, like, a hot dog or a microwaved burrito. It's nasty. And it's expensive. My meal plan doesn't cover concessions food."

Micah looks between us. "And all ya'll are football players?"

"Defensive squad," Barrett confirms. "You play for Patterson?"

"Running back," he says, and both of the guys nod. There's a very big difference between offense and defense.

Micah is a shrimp compared to us. He stands at five foot ten, maybe five foot eleven if he grows his hair out, and is about seventy pounds lighter than us. We're built to block, to defend. He's built for speed. On top of that, there's the entirely different mindset we have to have. One guy wants to protect the team, defend against encroaching intruders. The other guy just wants to score and have a good time.

No, I'm not bitter at all.

Greg offers Micah a sandwich. "Turkey and cheese."

"No peanut butter?" He shoots me a sly grin, taunting.

"Nah, that's just for special occasions," he says, clapping

me on the shoulder. "Eat your fucking sandwich. Her race is coming up soon."

The sandwich isn't bad. Sam and Miles were volunteered into making a dozen of them this morning while Wes cut up apple slices and Amir peeled and segmented oranges. Last week, Barrett and I coordinated the snacks for everyone. We all take turns, we all contribute. We're a family.

That's what Mason doesn't get. My roommates are more than just my friends. They're my life. Good and bad, I suppose. I like hanging out with them. I like spending time with them. So what if that time is spent watching movies or playing video games? We enjoy our time together. We get along. Sure, some of the guys like to go out and party—they aren't all reclusive freaks like Wes and I—but we all know when to kick back and have a good time, just us. Sam joined our ranks last semester, and now I can't remember a time that she wasn't part of our group. She's like the kid sister I never asked for and got anyway. She's amazing. And she's really brought Miles out of his shell, so I can't complain about that.

Mason has been good for me in the same way that Sam is good for Miles. She forces me out of my comfort zone. She makes me want to try new things. And not only in bed. I find myself agreeing to go to parties, agreeing to spend time with her friends, agreeing to hang out with her brother. She can get me to agree to just about anything with a sweet smile and an even sweeter kiss.

Going to parties will probably get easier over time. I'll learn to tolerate socializing with drunk people. What I don't know if I can tolerate is Mason getting drunk every weekend —or multiple times every weekend. I don't want to be around that kind of lifestyle.

Mason comes in second in her first race. I can see her disappointment in the set of her shoulders, the tension in her spine. She's not happy.

"You've got this, Mase," Micah cheers, clapping.

She gives us a half-hearted wave. Fred looks upset, too—she came in fourth. None of the Newton sprinters look happy.

Her second race gets called, and Mason lines up on the blocks. Micah chews his cheek as she steadies, readies, waiting for the starting gun to go off.

"Come on, sunshine, come on," he mutters under his breath. He links his pinky fingers together and tugs outward, putting tension on his wrists. "Come on, you've got this, you can do this."

The starting gun fires and then they're off, chasing down the two hundred meters to the finish line. Mason is in the middle of the pack, keeping pace. As she nears the end, she kicks into high gear and pushes past Fred. She motors past the girls from UNH. She crosses the finish line half a breath before the next girl.

Micah lets out a heavy sigh. He rubs his hands on his pants a few times.

Mason is all smiles now. Fred pats her on the back, and she shakes hands with the girls from UNH. A race well fought.

She has a bit of a break before her third race. She takes a drink of water and stretches her arms before she turns back to us. Her elation is written all over her face.

There's no time for her to come over to us. She hooks her fingers into a heart and holds it up to me. I meet her eye and clap a hand over my chest, over my heart. Her face melts into a smile.

Barrett and Amir snigger beside me. Barrett swoons, sagging against me, and I shove him away.

Micah laughs outright. "Man, she is so fucking gone for you."

"I love her." There's a lump in my throat the size of Rhode Island. "She's it for me, man. She's the one."

He turns to me, incredulous. "You're twenty years old. How the fuck do you—"

"When you know, you know. I'm positive. She's the one."

My mom knew within six months that Mama was the one for her. It took Mama a little bit longer to put it all together.

Whatever momentary awkwardness Mason and I are dealing with is just that—momentary. It's a blip. In the grand scheme of our future together, we can work through her weird hangups with sex and her drinking. We'll make this work.

Or we won't, and I'll have to let her go for good.

thirty-six

. . .

Tucker

AFTER THE MEET, Mason jogs over to the stands. I rush down the stairs to get to her. Micah follows a step behind me. She wraps her arms around me and draws me into a kiss. She's hot and sweaty. I don't care. I pull her into me, pull her close.

"You did great, baby," I tell her, smoothing a strand of her sweaty hair out of her face. "I'm so proud of you."

First in two races, second in the other two. Not a bad showing.

She beams at me for a few beats. Something heavy passes in the air between us.

I *love* her. I love *her*. I don't want to live my life without her in it. If we can't make this work, I might not survive it again, and that terrifies me.

Micah elbows me aside and wraps his sister in a hug. He tugs on her ponytail. "Good job, sunshine."

I frown. That's my nickname for her.

"Let me go shower and get changed," she says. "We'll grab something to eat, yeah? I'll meet you guys at the ASC in forty-five minutes."

"Sounds like a plan," he says.

I head back towards my friends. Greg is packing all of our trash into his trusty backpack. Wes puts away his book. Miles and Sam have already left. Barrett and Amir linger awkwardly in the stands.

"You guys have plans?"

"Going to grab food."

Amir waggles his eyebrows. "Is her hot friend going to be there?"

"Yeah, I think so?"

"Count me in."

Barrett laughs. "She won't look twice at you."

Wes and Greg head back to the house. With Amir and Barrett still playfully bickering, we make our way to the ASC. Micah follows in our wake, quiet. I use one of my guest passes to get him in. Who else am I going to save them for, Jamal? My brother has bigger and better things to do than visit a college campus. When my moms visit, we go out to eat in town, we certainly don't eat at the dining hall.

It's still early. We grab some food—a light snack, really—and find a big table at the back of the room. Micah is chewing on his cheek again. I don't know what's up with him. Normally he's the life of the party, social and outgoing. Mason's the same way. She's never met a stranger she didn't immediately befriend. It used to drive me crazy: she could simply walk up to a person, start talking, and immediately feel comfortable with them. I'm not like her. It takes me a while before I get comfortable with someone.

The ladies join us after almost an hour. Mason's smile stretches from ear to ear. She bounds toward us, her freshly washed hair in a long braid down her back.

"My two favorite guys!" She wraps her arm around Micah's neck and beams across the table at me. "You two getting along okay?"

"Oh, yeah, we're great, sunshine," he says, giving her a charming grin.

Behind her, Fred and Melissa giggle. He's always been good with women, with getting people to feel at ease. He's charismatic as fuck.

"I'm starving," Melissa announces.

Dutifully, we follow them across the dining hall. We take plates and wind our way through the different food options on offer. The salmon looks good tonight, the chicken a little dry. The vegan entree looks like it's been sitting for about three hours—and, considering it's only five o'clock, is probably not far off. It's way too early for most people to be eating dinner, but when you've just expended an incredible amount of energy on the field, it's time to eat. And these girls definitely know how to eat.

Mason settles in beside me, Micah on her other side. I set my hand on her thigh, and she beams at me for the easy affection. He coughs.

"Really, dude?"

I refuse to let him get to me. We're in a safe, committed relationship. We love one another. There's nothing wrong with an innocent hand on her leg. It's not like I'm fingering her in the middle of the dining hall. I'm certainly not about to do anything with her overprotective brother sitting two feet away.

She elbows him. "Leave us alone, Mic. I don't say anything when you hook up with all of my friends. We live our lives differently than you do."

"I'll say," he mutters, taking a bite of his chicken breast.

I lean over and kiss Mason's temple, just because I can. She smiles at me, her fingers scratching through my beard.

The girls dissect the meet. Coach is pleased with them for the most part. Some of the long-distance runners are under fire for their performance today. The field athletes performed beautifully, earning several first place finishes.

"Okay, so game plan," Melissa says, pushing away her tray. "Delta?"

"Delta," Fred confirms.

"Pregame?"

"Not this time," Mason says with a dark look I don't understand. Wait—Melissa is the one that always makes a mess of herself. "Let's reiterate: neither of you are going to sleep with this asshole." She nudges her brother. "They're off limits."

"I get it, I get it," he says, lifting his hands into the air. "I'm here to spend time with you, not hook up with your friends."

I snort out a laugh. It's not the first time I've heard that from him.

Micah looks at me, his jaw clenched. "What's that supposed to mean?"

"I didn't say anything."

Mason sets her hand over mine on her leg. "Let's not fight. We only have a little bit of time left together."

I kiss her temple. "Anything for you, babe."

The Delta house is an enormous monstrosity of wealth and privilege. It's the kind of place that a guy like me shouldn't be caught dead in. I'm too big, too tall, too Black to fit in here. I won't pretend to be someone I'm not. I don't know why Mason wants to be here, except that it's the only decent party on any given night in our small, sleepy college town. The fraternity welcomes non-members and underage students alike. They really don't give a shit who shows up to their parties as long as they're packed full of scantily clad women and dudes trying to get with them.

Micah is a top-ranked football player at a big party school. He probably has women all over him all the time, trying to get with the elite athlete. It's a little different at Newton. The frat brothers are the big draw, not the athletes. Or at least I'm not a big draw. I don't put myself out there; I have no interest in being out there.

If Mason wasn't Mason, I wouldn't be with her. I don't see the need to date. I don't see the need for casual sex. I'm not searching for that deep, lasting emotional connection with everyone I come across. I'm not ready for the rest of my life to start right now. But Mason is Mason. She's the one for me. I don't need to date other people to figure out that nobody else compares to her. She's perfectly imperfect, and I love her for it.

Sure, we're having some growing pains, but I'm confident that we'll be able to figure it out. We love each other. We're meant to spend the rest of our lives together. We'll get to the bottom of this blip and get past it.

Her hand is in mine as we walk into the party. Immediately my senses are assaulted by the odor of stale B.O. and pot. The shitty rap music is set to a decibel above deafening. People are packed in everywhere like sardines. Girls are wearing short skirts and impossibly high heels. Guys leer at them.

The track girls are all wearing a combination of leggings or jeans, long-sleeved sweaters, and tall boots. They're effortlessly casual. I had to ask Greg what to wear to this stupid party—a simple button-down shirt and jeans, a dash of the cologne Jamal got me for Christmas, no tie, no sweater. We hand our coats to the freshman running the coat check and enter the actual party.

"I'll get you girls some beer," Micah announces.

I guess that's my cue to join him. I kiss Mason on the temple and together we shoulder our way through the crowd to the line of kegs in the kitchen. It's only slightly less crowded in here. I feel like I can't quite catch my breath. There's an elephant sitting on my chest.

"So this is Newton," Micah says as we wait for our turn.

"I guess so."

He hums. "You really don't party much."

"I don't really see the appeal." I shrug. "Mason likes this kind of stuff, so I guess I'll be coming to more of these things now."

"You don't drink, you don't hook up," he says, shaking his head. "I'm sorry, man, but I just don't see this lasting. You and my sister are too different. Why the fuck won't you sleep with her?"

"That's between Mason and me," I tell him shortly. "I don't go asking you about your sex life."

"Come on. That's my sister. I deserve to—"

"You deserve nothing," I say, more sharply than I intended. "Our private life is just that—private. I don't go blabbing about our sex life to anyone who asks. Some things are personal."

He laughs and claps me on the shoulder, a reaction I didn't expect. "You're a good man, Tucker Kingsley."

"I'm still not good enough for her."

"On that, I'll agree with you." He shakes his head again. "Then again, I don't think there's anyone else in the world who is. As long as you make her happy, I won't stand in your way."

"How gracious of you," I say dryly. He doesn't go here. He doesn't see her every day. To think he has any control over who she dates, who she spends her time with… It makes my blood boil. This isn't the 1950s. He doesn't get to control her life. He doesn't own her.

They're twins. She values his opinion. Of all people, she's going to listen to him first. Maybe I shouldn't antagonize him…

We reach the front of the beer line.

"Five," he says to the guy running the keg.

I do a quick count. "Four. I don't want one."

Micah laughs. "I'll drink yours."

"Fine, five."

With two cups in hand, Micah with three, we make our way through the party to where we left the girls. Beer sloshes over the side of the flimsy plastic cup, the putrid scent stinging my nose. Mason, Fred, and Melissa are talking to two guys—Mark and another guy I think might be a pole vaulter.

Mark gives me the nod as I hand Mason the cup. She takes it with a smile, wrapping her arm around me and resting her head on my shoulder.

"You guys are cute together," he says.

"Thanks." She looks at me with her heart in her eyes. She rises onto her tiptoes to brush her lips lightly against mine.

Conscious of her brother beside me, her friends surrounding us, the enormity of this party, I keep the kiss chaste. She tastes sour like beer and a little sweet like the protein brownie she had after dinner. Her tongue runs along the seam of my lips, requesting entrance. I cup her face in my hand and run my thumb across her cheek.

Micah gags theatrically, like he has every time I've kissed her this weekend. I flip him off, and the girls laugh.

Mason wraps her arm around my neck, melting into me. I let her deepen the kiss and a burst of affection threatens to overwhelm me.

"Fuck this party," she murmurs against my lips. "We should go fuck somewhere."

I force myself to pull away. She whines deep in her throat, and I run my nose along the shell of her ear, pressing a kiss to the place right in front of her ear, memorizing her scent.

One of the guys whistles. "Damn, son."

I tip her face up, her eyes meeting mine. "Did you get your issues worked out?"

She bites her lip. "King..."

I sigh. "You know I want to, baby. You don't know how badly I do. But until we figure this out..."

"It's just sex," she sighs.

Ice flushes through my veins, putting a quick damper on any potential there was for sex.

"You know it's not to me," I tell her quietly. "It's so much more than that."

thirty-seven

. . .

Tucker

"IT DOESN'T HAVE TO BE," she says. She toys with her lip again. I reach out and pull her lip from between her teeth, running the pad of my thumb across it.

"I don't know what to tell you, Mase. This is a hard no for me. I don't want you to ever not feel good with me. That you're okay with it worries me."

"That's what sex is like. Sometimes it's good. Sometimes it's not."

"The sex not being good isn't great either," I tell her. Her friends are clearly listening in. I block them out, focusing only on her. "But what I'm talking about is the emotional component. Your mental state. If you're not in a good headspace, we shouldn't be having sex. It's as simple as that."

"There doesn't have to be a big emotional component."

"There does for me."

She throws her hands into the air, sloshing beer onto the carpet. "It's not like that with other people, Tucker. It's about sex. Dirty, mindless fucking because it feels good. It doesn't have to be complicated."

My heart is in my throat. I disentangle myself from her,

taking a step back. "Maybe you should be having sex with other people, then. People who aren't me."

"I don't want to have sex with other people," she shouts, catching the attention of half the party. "I only want to have sex with you!"

"You mean you want to fuck me," I snap.

She takes a step back. Some of the fire goes out of her eyes. "What's the difference?"

"I don't want to fuck. I want to make love to you, and have you love me."

"Isn't that what we're doing?"

"No, Mason, it isn't." I step towards her and cup her cheek again. "I don't want a fling. I don't want to toss you aside after I've had my fill. I want to be *with* you. And you just want me to fuck you."

"Tuck, no. That's not what—"

My breath comes in rapid bursts, like I've just run up and down the stairs of the arena in full pads. "It feels like you're using me. And that's not cool with me. I'm not some toy you can turn on and off with the flick of a switch. I'm a real person and I have real feelings."

She frowns. "Of course you are—"

"You treat me like I'm just some guy, any guy with a dick desperate to fuck you. Like you don't care that it's me, that it's us."

She flinches.

"I've been up front about what I need the entire time," I tell her carefully. "I need that emotional connection, and you aren't giving it to me. So either we don't do this, or you figure out what's going on with your head and fucking talk to me."

Her eyes flutter closed. She bows her head, sagging against me. I wrap my arms securely around her, steadying her. If she needs me, I'll be her rock. I wish I could expect the same type of support in return. I don't know that I'll get it.

"I'm scared," she whispers.

"Of what?"

"Of us." She swallows. "I didn't want to do it, King. I never wanted to hurt you."

"I don't care about the past," I lie. "We can only worry about our future."

"I don't know how to have a future with you. You want all these big things for us, and I'm just trying to get through the track season." She forces a laugh. "I can appreciate that you're sure, that you know you want a future for us. After college, after grad school. But right now I have to focus on the here and now, and the scale of your feelings is sometimes too much for me to deal with."

I can't help the pang of hurt that ricochets through me. I thought we were on the same page. I thought we were building a life together.

I swallow. "What do you need?"

"I need a partner, in bed and out of it. And you're not here with me." I flinch, and she amends: "You're here, but you don't want to be. And I can respect that. I won't force you to do something you're not comfortable with. But don't expect me to sit idly by while you—" She breaks off, breathing hard.

"While I what, Mason?"

She takes a deep breath. "While you waste your life away." She meets my eye. "You lock yourself up and don't let anyone in. Even me. You hide away in your room, or you sit on the couch with your friends. And I don't want to be a reclusive shut-in at twenty years old."

My heart pounds a thousand beats a minute. "I'll open up more. We're still getting comfortable with one another again."

"We are, but you aren't," she says quietly. "We're too different. We have different interests. That's not to say it can't ever work. I'm saying that it's not working. Not for me. I'm not ready for forever. All I want is right now. And you're not the right now kind of guy."

I take a step back. "Okay then."

Her brow wrinkles. "Okay?"

"I love you, Mason. I want you to be happy. And clearly that means that I'm not doing my job. So if you want to party with your friends, if you want to go out drinking every night and slowly kill yourself and all your brain cells, I won't stop you. I'll live my life the way I want to, and you'll live yours. But we won't be in each other's lives. And I just want you to know that it's because of you. Because I was trying. I was putting in the effort. But you refused to meet me halfway. You wouldn't give me an inch."

She flinches. "King…"

"No. Mason, no. You don't get to call me that, not anymore. I won't be your King anymore. You won't be my Princess. We'll just be two people who used to know each other."

Her face crumples. "I don't want to lose you. I love you."

"Clearly that's not enough." I shake my head. "Have a nice life, Mason."

Turning on my heel, I push my way through the crowds of people. She doesn't chase after me. She doesn't try to get me to change my mind. She lets me go.

Maybe my moms were right when they said love can't conquer all. Maybe they were right when they said sometimes love isn't enough. There are simply some mountains that are insurmountable.

And it doesn't feel good—it feels downright shitty.

thirty-eight

· · ·

Mason

MY BROTHER WRAPS his arms around me. I stand there, a little shell-shocked. I don't know what to think, how to react. I'm just numb.

"It's okay, sunshine," Micah says, and that's the straw that breaks the dam.

Tears run silently down my face as I stare at my brother. He curses and tugs me closer.

"It'll be okay." He pets my hair.

Tucker ended things. He doesn't want to be with me. He would rather end what we have than continue on as we've been.

Because I can't give him what he needs. Because I'm broken.

"He's an asshole," Fred says.

"Fuck him," Melissa adds.

I cling to Micah's shoulder. My brother holds me, rocking slowly from side to side.

"It's okay, sunshine," he says again. "Let it all out."

Mark brings me a fresh beer. Bryce brings me two shots of tequila.

I don't know how we get past this sex thing. I want to

have sex with Tucker. I do. It's just that sometimes the enormity of our situation hits me like a brick wall, and I don't know how to cope with that weight. We're too young to be this serious.

This is the time in our lives we're supposed to go out and meet new people. Experiment. Kick back with our friends and have a good time.

Except that as much as I want to spend time with my friends, I want to spend time with him more. He's the last person I want to see when I go to sleep every night and the first person I want to see every morning, even before I've had my coffee. He's the only person I want to have crazy, dirty sex with. Or crazy, emotional sex. Or any kind of sex.

He's it.

I sob harder and cling to my brother. He holds me tight.

"He's a jerk," he tells me. "You deserve better than him."

"I love him," I say through my tears. "I only want to be with him."

"He'll come around," Melissa says.

He won't. I know Tucker. He's stubborn to a fault. I hurt him. Again. My unwillingness to play by his very fair rules cuts him deeper than I realized. He's not going to take that lying down. He's not going to welcome me back with arms wide open a second time.

He's going to retreat and lick his wounds. Maybe this time he'll actually get over me. Maybe this time he'll actually move on.

Micah is my rock, my other half, but Tucker has my heart. For better or for worse, all I want is Tucker. And I pushed him away. I wouldn't talk to him—couldn't talk to him. I let my past, our past, blind me to the realities of our present.

And the reality is, we weren't perfect. We had real struggles. He wanted to work through them, and I clammed up.

I don't know how to talk about these things. With him, with my friends, with other people. I'm not a prude. I've slept around. I've been with other people. Some of those experiences have been good, and others have been rather lackluster. That doesn't make them bad: it just means they weren't great.

He's never really put himself out there. We started dating so young. He's only ever been with one other woman, and by all accounts, it was less than satisfying for him. He doesn't know that sometimes you have to kiss some toads to find your prince.

I found him, and he's a King. He's the one for me.

Except that he doesn't want to do the same things I want to do. He doesn't like hanging out with my friends. He doesn't like going to parties. He seems to have an issue with my drinking and having a good time. I don't get it. He wasn't nearly this repressed and uptight in high school.

Maybe we're just too young. I don't want to pretend that he's going to wait around for me; I know better than to think lightning will strike twice. This is the end of the road for him and me. And I just have to be okay with it, because there is no way I'm going to be able to change his mind and convince him to take me back.

I don't have some secret trauma I've been hiding from him. I don't have any deep, dark secrets. I'm not a prude. It's just that sometimes after sex I get overwhelmed and need some time to process. And when I'm sleeping with real people, they tend to want to do things like cuddle and indulge in an afterglow together. Vibrators don't have expectations. Vibrators don't ask more of me than I'm able to give.

Maybe he's right that I was using him. Maybe he's right that I was treating him like a dildo, like a dick on command.

But I like the person that dick is attached to. I like the human as much as I like the cock. I liked having sex with him, partly for the equipment, partly for the person operating it. He has a pretty penis, and he knows how to use it to make me feel good. We have a chemistry that goes beyond just the physical, a bond that's deeper than attraction.

He loves me.

Tucker accepted me, all of me, even the parts of me he didn't like. He didn't try to change me. Not once did he suggest I not have another drink or that I stay in. He didn't try to convince me that spending time with my friends was a bad idea. No, he made his displeasure known in other ways: judgmental glances when I filled my cup, folding in on himself in a crowd of people, withdrawing when people tried to befriend him.

It's the way he copes, a tiny voice in the back of my head says. It sounds like him. He's never been crazy about big crowds of people. He showed up: he came to parties with me, parties where he knew nobody, and if he stuck close to my side, at least he was there. He didn't try to manipulate me into leaving early. He didn't try to monopolize my attention. He wasn't controlling like my ex or manipulative like other guys I've hooked up with. He showed up. He put the effort in.

And I refused to talk to him. I couldn't verbalize my issues. I still don't think I can.

Micah maneuvers us to a couch. He pulls me against his side and lets me cry on his shoulder until I'm a snotty, sobbing mess. He doesn't care. We've been here before, him and me. Somehow, I think we'll be here again.

"What do you want to do, Mase?" My brother tucks a strand of hair behind my ear. Tucker used to do that. I sniffle. "Do you want to drink or do you want to talk about it?"

Neither. Both. I don't know.

"I don't want it to be over," I admit to the sanctuary of his arms.

"I think he's pretty adamant that it is," he says. I tighten my arms around him and he curses. "Mase, I didn't mean it like—"

"No, no, you're right. I don't—I can't—" I struggle to get breath into my lungs. "He doesn't want to do this. I can't give him what he wants. There's no way to move forward. We're at the end of the road."

"He's a dick," Micah says.

"Yeah, but he's my dick."

He doesn't even gag at the insinuation that we have sex. "If you really want to be with him—if you want to prove to him that you're ready for this—"

"That's the thing. I don't know that I am," I tell him. "We're too different. We want different things. We live our lives in completely opposite ways. He wants to stay in all the time. I don't want to be locked away on the couch for the rest of our life together."

"That's bullshit." He shakes his head. "He's trying. He's showing up to parties you and I both know he wouldn't be caught dead at. He's putting in the effort. And you're not even meeting him halfway, you're not showing up. You know he has issues with dealing with sex. You know he has problems with drinking. And you getting blitzed and not talking about anything—"

"What do you mean, problems with drinking?" I blink at him. "He doesn't have any issues."

Micah stares at me. "His mom is an addict. Both of his grandfathers died of alcoholism. Don't you remember going to his Grandfather Kingsley's funeral in ninth grade?"

My breath catches in my throat. I do. It's a vague memory, hazy from time and the tequila I've had tonight. We had only been dating for about five weeks, not doing much more than holding hands and occasionally kissing on the cheek. He was a stoic rock while his Mom sobbed during the funeral. Jamal was holding his Mama, who refused to cry for her father.

He doesn't drink. I don't know that I've seen him with anything stronger than Gatorade at one of the handful of parties we've been to the last few weeks. He didn't touch the wine I brought him. He doesn't *drink*.

And I got drunk and called him because I was sad and

lonely. I got drunk and called him from the track party at the last away meet. My decision to go out and drink with my friends is hurting someone that I care very much about.

"Clearly he loves you," Micah says. He touches my shoulder and I curl into my brother. "You have to decide if this is fixable."

I swallow. "I—I want it to be. I want to be with him. He drives me crazy, and I hate half the decisions he makes, but..." I sigh.

"But you love him," he says quietly.

"I do, yeah."

"Are you ready to spend the rest of your life with this guy? Because he's serious. He knows what he wants, and what he wants is you."

"The rest of my life is a real long time."

"He's sure," Micah tells me. "He's ready to lay it all down on the line for you. So you have to decide if you're willing to do the same for him. Because otherwise, you need to walk away. Don't play him around. One way or the other, you have to be sure."

thirty-nine

. . .

Tucker

I WALK HOME in the bitter cold. My heart isn't broken. I'm devastated, yeah, but a part of me is resigned. There was no way Mason and I were ever going to work out. We had too many problems. It wasn't simply the sex and her negative reactions to it. It wasn't only her overindulgence in alcohol. It's a lot of tiny little fissures, things I could chalk up to personality differences. When I'm honest with myself, I can admit they're incompatibilities. We're too different.

Besides, there's no guarantee we would have made it through college and then grad school. Maybe it's better that we break up now. I can try to actually get over her this time. I can try to actually move on this time.

This time will be different.

Wes is sitting in his armchair when I get home from the party. He grunts at me. It's only ten.

"I don't want to talk about it."

Barrett appears in the doorway, two bowls of popcorn in his hand. "Talk about what?"

"Nothing."

Wes grunts again.

"I thought you'd be out with Mason and her brother," Barrett says. "He doesn't seem like a dick."

"I really don't want to talk about it."

The downstairs toilet flushes and Amir exits the bathroom. "Talk about what?"

"I'm going to bed."

Wes looks up from his book. "You two have a fight?"

"It's over."

All three of them stare at me, shock written all over their faces.

"But you, like, loved her," Barrett says.

"Yeah, and sometimes that's not enough."

"You were perfect together," Amir says.

"Nobody's perfect. There were problems. I just decided I can't ignore them anymore."

"You should call her," Barrett says.

"There's no fixing this. It's over. It's done. I'm going to go to bed."

Amir rolls his eyes. "Come watch this movie with us."

"I'm really not in the mood."

"Do it anyways."

He claps a hand on my shoulder and not so subtly maneuvers me into the living room. He shoves me onto the couch. Barrett puts a bowl of popcorn and a Gatorade into my hands.

"Hydrate, motherfucker," he declares. He hands the other bowl to Wes and flops onto the sofa beside me. Amir takes one of the armchairs, stretching out his long legs in front of him.

Wes turns on the movie, an Irish spy thriller from a no-name production company with a cast of no-name actors. I sit there and try to concentrate on the plot. The fight echoes in my head, replaying over and over again.

The defeat in her voice. The resignation in the pit of my stomach.

My moms said it best: sometimes love isn't enough. I can't force her into a box, shoehorn her into my life. I went to her parties, but she refused to meet me halfway. She would rather drink and have a good time than concentrate on being with me in the here and now. She would rather clam up and refuse to talk than try to explain her hangups.

I want forever with the Mason I used to know, not the current shell that simply looks like her. I want to build a life with her, I want to have children with her, but not at the expense of my own wellbeing. I can't sacrifice my future for someone that doesn't want the same things I do, that hides away instead of talking out her problems.

I sigh. It's time to call someone. Between my stress eating induced-revelation last night, the realization that Mason has made no effort to resolve her issues, and doesn't *want* to resolve them, I'm in over my head. I can't handle this on my own. First thing Monday morning, I'll go to the student counseling center and sign up to talk to someone. I don't know what kind of specialist I'll need to see; that's their job to decide. Clearly I can't do it on my own. I need help.

The last time I tried therapy, I was too heartbroken to make an honest go of it. I had too many unanswered questions. Well, I have those answers now. I know exactly why the wheels fell off the wagon on this one. Now I just need help working through all of it.

I'm too numb to feel anything more than resigned. I want to scream or yell or punch something. I want to curl up into a ball and cry. I want to do something, anything, except sit here in silence and watch a shitty movie with my best friends.

In the morning, I'll be heartbroken. Once the realization that it's really over finally hits, I'll be devastated. But I trust myself enough to know that this time I'll work on moving on. This time I'll try harder. Sam and Miles are certainly happy: clearly love is possible at this stage in our lives, regardless of what's going on with me. Maybe Sam can set me up with some of her softball teammates, help me get my feet wet. I'll sign up for a dating app. I'll put on a brave smile and try.

But not yet. First I have to mourn this. Mourn the future that won't be, the life Mason and I were building for ourselves that's crashed spectacularly to the floor. I thought I knew what I wanted. I thought we wanted the same things. Now I'm starting from scratch.

Put one foot in front of the other. Finish this movie. Go to sleep. Stay in bed all day tomorrow, because I fucking need it, and it's Sunday, and I have nothing better to do. And then first thing Monday morning, call student counseling services. Get help.

I don't know what the future will look like, but I've got a plan. That will have to be enough.

———

I make Barrett come to Jamal's game with me. He's originally from the greater Boston area, from a small suburb to the northwest of the city, so he knows his way around the city pretty well. This is only the third time I get to see my big brother play professional ball. He flew us all out to Detroit for his first game, where he got a whole twelve minutes of playing time in a preseason exhibition game. He had us out for another game over my winter break.

It's kind of cool, knowing the kid who used to tease me and protect me from bullies in equal measure is now a professional basketball player. The guy who was there for me whenever I needed him, the big brother I turned to for advice—about school, about girls, about football, about everything—is making his dreams a reality.

Pro football isn't in the cards for me. I'm not like Jamal. I'm not like Micah. I'll be content with grad school and then a nice little life. A house in the suburbs. Maybe a dog. Eventually some kids.

A pang ricochets through me. I thought I'd have Mason beside me in that future. I thought we were building something together. Instead, I stand alone.

I've had two sessions with my new therapist, Dave, a doctoral candidate with a Marriage and Family Therapy degree—the same degree Mason wants to pursue. He's in his mid-twenties, single, and rocks some pretty sick dreadlocks falling halfway down his back. He's exactly the type of therapist I never knew I needed. He listens well, he doesn't condescend, and he lets me talk. I didn't know how badly I needed to just *talk* it out until I unloaded on his couch.

My moms had me in and out of therapy all through childhood. My brother too. I had a mild crisis of conscience in my preteen years about being adopted and puberty and who even am I if I don't know my biological family. The therapy helped. I tried it again after the breakup, but things were still a little too raw for me to process at that time. Sometimes, people need a little extra help. I'm man enough to admit when I can't do it on my own.

Jamal arranges for us to sit in a private suite with the rest of the team's private guests. Two players have their wives in for the game. One player has what seems like his entire family there.

Barrett gets a beer—because he can, because it's something to do with his hands—and I drink a bottle of water. My brother is actually getting some good playing time in. He's not half bad.

Of course he's not bad. He wouldn't be playing in the NBA if he was terrible. Still, it's a little weird to realize the kid I grew up with, the big brother who slept two doors down from me our entire lives, is now a professional athlete in the prime of his career.

I take a few videos of the crowd, of the arena, and post it to social media. I don't pretend to think Mason still follows me. I know she hasn't removed herself as my friend. I'm not posting to brag about how cool my life is. Okay, maybe I am a little. Mainly I'm posting because the only other things on my page are football highlights, and I need a little brightness in my life. I have my camera trained on the hoops when Jamal sinks a basket. I send that video to my moms. I'm sure they're watching the game at home—they try to watch all of his games, even the late-start west coast games—but it's nice to "see" it live.

Detroit takes a significant lead late in the second half, so of course Jamal gets some more playing time. His minutes are protected, playing against the second string guys instead of the top players. The Celtics fans start getting restless. We're in enemy territory, a wave of red, white, and navy blue amongst a sea of green jerseys. It's a precarious position. Detroit pulls ahead in the last five minutes. It's a close score, 113 to 110.

After the game, we follow the rest of the suite's inhabitants to meet my brother and his teammates in the friends and family room off the side of the locker room. The players are all wearing suits and ties, the ladies are dressed to kill, and then there's Barrett and me in grubby jeans and sweatshirts.

"There you are!" Jamal starts towards me. He slings his arm around my neck. "Haven't seen you in ages, Tucky."

"Don't call me that."

"My little Tucky-poo." He pinches my cheek. I try to fling him off of me, but he holds tight. He grabs me into a headlock and gives me a noogie. "My little baby brother."

I manage to evade his grasp. I tackle full-grown men on the field every day. Jamal is no trouble for me—even if he's two inches taller, I'm close to fifty pounds heavier. We grew up wrestling and tussling. Now I'm afraid to exert too much pressure lest I injure the multi-million dollar hands he's blessed with.

Barrett laughs. "You mean I can't call you Tucky-poo?"

"Fuck you."

He snorts and shakes his head. "Oh, all the guys are definitely going to hear about this."

Jamal releases me and brushes down his suit. I straighten my clothes.

"No, they're not."

"Not that I'm totally thrilled you brought a dude with you," Jamal starts, and I groan. "I thought you were bringing Mason? I was looking forward to seeing her."

My easy smile fades. My brother sees the answer on my face.

"I'm going to kill her," he says. He cracks his knuckles. "I have time to make it out to Newton and back before the flight takes off."

"It was me. I'm the one who ended things," I admit. The ache in my chest isn't so all-encompassing anymore. I'm not ready to move on, but I'm not stuck in that paralyzing numbness. We've been apart again almost as long as we were together. "It wasn't working."

"Bullshit," he says. "I haven't seen you as happy as you were with her in—years. Since she ended things the first time."

"Yeah, but we gave it an honest try. At least, I did. There were problems. She wouldn't talk to me, wouldn't open up. And I couldn't keep pushing. She wanted something I can't give her."

Jamal frowns. "What? A lifetime of happiness?"

"Meaningless sex."

"But you guys are, like, together. You love each other and shit." The furrow between his brows deepens. "It's the very definition of not meaningless. And you're demi—"

"Yeah, let's not share my personal shit with the entire room," I tell him quickly.

Barrett's eyebrows quirk. "Fuck, dude, you are the most closed off person I know."

"No, I'm not."

"Yeah, you are," Jamal says. "You've always been like this. It's nothing new."

"Fuck you, I'm not—"

He holds up his phone. "Want me to call Mama for a second opinion?"

"It's past her bedtime." I'd be surprised if she stayed up to watch the end of the game. She goes to sleep at ten o'clock, sharp, in order to be at the dental practice for seven a.m. patients. She might start watching at tip-off, but she falls asleep early.

"I'll wake her up."

"You wouldn't."

"Try me," my brother taunts. "You hide away in your little shell. You're like a turtle. You turtle."

"I'm not a turtle."

"Why did you and Mason break up?"

"Because she—she—" I take a deep breath. "She couldn't give me what I needed, and she made choices that I disagreed with. I didn't want to surround myself with negative influences."

"It sounds like you're making a lot of accusations," Jamal accuses. "You disagreed with her decision making?"

"She's getting drunk every weekend."

"So? She's in college. She's allowed to."

"I know she is. I'm not trying to get her to stop," I explain haltingly. "I just don't want to be around that kind of lifestyle."

My brother's face softens. "You're not going to turn out like Grandaddy. She's not going to be like Mom."

"Yeah, but I don't want to start down that path. I don't want the temptation. It's easier if I cut it all out."

"I drink. Mama drinks," he says. "I understand why Mom doesn't. That doesn't mean you need to abstain entirely."

I shrug. "I have no interest in it. I don't like the taste. I don't need the empty calories. If I'm going to blow my diet,

I'd much rather eat ice cream than drink a gallon of jungle juice."

Jamal sighs, shakes his head. "Okay. So she's drinking. What else?"

I check my watch. "How much time do you have?"

forty

. . .

Mason

MY CHEST PHYSICALLY ACHES. I went to the student health center. They found nothing wrong with me. So it's just my heart that's breaking.

Tucker was supposed to be my end-game. I wanted a life with him. I just wasn't ready for that life to begin quite yet.

I don't know what to do. I live my life on auto-pilot. School. Practice. Homework. At night, I curl up in my cold, empty bed and cry. I screwed up the single greatest thing in my life—for the second time. Except this time it was him walking away. This time it was him giving up. I didn't try hard enough. I couldn't tape us back together with glue and a prayer.

I love Tucker Kingsley. I want to spend the rest of my life making him happy. Even if that means that sometimes we stay in. Even if that means cutting back on the drinking. Even if it means admitting the real reason why I transferred to Newton.

I don't know how to make him talk to me. The Friday after the breakup, I have an away meet at Amherst, and the next shift at the assessment center feels like forever away. He ducks past me in sociology class. He won't meet my eye.

My friends are no help.

"Fuck him," Fred says. "Fuck someone new."

"He's an asshole," Melissa says.

"Forget about him," Mark says.

I don't want to fuck someone new. He's not an asshole just because he ended things. I don't want to forget about him.

I love him.

I didn't realize how poorly prepared I was to be in a relationship at this stage of my life until I was confronted with the reality of it.

My Saturday nights are my chance to relax after a long meet. I need that time to unwind. I like to kick back with my friends and have a good time. Can I spend the time with them without drinking? I honestly don't know. Being around drunk people is significantly more fun when I'm drunk, too.

I don't mind the occasional night in on the couch. I don't want to spend every night watching TV or playing video games—or watching as other people play video games. Every once in a while is fine. I don't even mind spending time with his roommates. I like his friends.

What bothers me is that he doesn't put himself out there. He hides. He cowers in on himself and hides away from the world. He went to one party, decided it wasn't for him, and never went back. He slept with one other girl, didn't have immediate soul-shattering chemistry, and decided he didn't want to have casual sex. Which—fine. It's not for everyone. But he didn't even *try*. He didn't put himself out there. He hid in his dorm room, he hides in his house now, and he doesn't seem to want to change that.

There's no middle ground. We tried to compromise. He went with me to a few parties. I stayed in with him and his friends. Neither of us were particularly happy.

But fuck, if I'm not miserable without him.

My self-worth is not dependent on who I may or may not be dating. My self-esteem isn't predicated on who is or is not in my bed. I'm not the kind of girl who falls to pieces because my boyfriend breaks up with me.

Except now I am. And as much as I hate that this is what he's reduced me to, mainly I hate how much I miss him. His stupid smiles and his unhealthy coping mechanisms and his inability to unwind. I miss it all.

For three nights straight, I eat a peanut butter sandwich for dinner. It helps soothe the ache of missing him ever so slightly. Maybe he's onto something here. The first night, I do it because I miss him. The second, I'm genuinely craving peanut butter—I must be about to get my period. The third night, I see him making one and want to know why. Why does he need to emotionally eat today? What triggered him? Is he okay?

He sits at the far end of the dining hall, his back to the rest of the room like usual. He hunkers down in his regular seat and slowly eats his meal. I watch the muscles in his broad back jump and bustle.

He won't look at me. He won't talk to me. Not that I've really tried—I know better than to press my luck. He's hurting.

Neither of us wanted to break up. Neither of us are happy.

The guys pack up and leave the dining hall, leaving behind only Miles and Sam. They coo at each other and stare into one another's eyes from across the table.

This is my chance.

Interrupting Fred's monologue about Sullivan the football player—they're back on again, which worries Melissa—I make my way across the room. I pull out the seat beside Sam. Tucker's seat. The hard plastic is still warm from his body heat.

"This spot taken?"

She tears her eyes away from Miles to stare at me.

"Uh, yeah?"

"Right this minute?"

Miles clears his throat. "You can sit." Sam turns to glare at him and he shrugs. "She's not the devil."

"Thanks, I think."

His eyes are hard. "Let's be clear, I don't like you."

"Duly noted."

"But you wouldn't be here if you didn't have a reason."

"I miss him," I say flatly. "I messed up. I ruined the best thing that ever happened to me."

"Yeah, you did," Sam says harshly.

"I need to know…"

"We're not your go-between," she snaps. "You can't use us to—"

Miles kicks me under the table. I think he meant to get her. I wince and he frowns.

"Let's all take a breath here," he says, ever the peacemaker. "What do you need to know?"

I swallow. "How… how is he?"

"He keeps his cards pretty close to his chest."

I wince. That's what I was afraid of. "Has he… talked about it?" My friends have made me talk it to death.

"We know the jist of what happened," Sam finally says. "You're not making yourself many friends here, are you?"

Annoyance bubbles up within me. "Why the fuck do you hate me so much? What did I ever do to you?"

"It's not what you did to me, it's what you did to *him*," she snaps. "You broke his heart."

"He's the one who dumped *me*! He's the one who ended things."

"I'm not talking about right now," she says hotly. "I'm talking about however long ago you were together. You destroyed his soul. It's only in the last few weeks that we've seen a hint of his real personality. I hate you for turning him into a shell of a person. I hate that you had to come back around just for us to see who he really is. I hate that he's so broken up over you that he's still barely coping two plus years later."

My heart is in my throat. "Barely coping?"

"He's miserable," Miles says gruffly. "He misses you."

"I miss him, too. I miss him a lot."

It's not the prize of having a boyfriend. It's not the warm body in my bed.

It's having a partner in this life, someone by my side. Someone who supports me and lets me lean on them when the going gets tough, and lets me support them when they need a hand. Someone who believes in the same things I do, someone whose values and ideals match up to mine. Someone who wants the same things in life that I do.

No, not someone. *Him.*

We're a perfect match on paper. Our chemistry is out of control. It's just our current lifestyles that are out of sync.

I'll sacrifice nights out with my friends. I'll give up drinking if it makes him happy. I don't know how to get better at the coping with the emotional overload that comes with sex.

But I can talk to him. I can let him hold me and believe him when he says it will turn out all right.

"I want him back," I announce to his friends.

Sam's eyes are hard. "Why should he even agree to talk to you again?"

Miles kicks me again. I flinch, and he flushes.

"Because she loves him," he answers for me. "And sometimes we do crazy things for the people we love, like ambush them in the middle of disciplinary hearings."

She frowns. "But—"

"When a friend asks for help, you help them," he says slowly. His eyes lift to meet mine. "You are asking for help, aren't you?"

I nod. "I need a plan. Here's what I have figured out..."

forty-one

. . .

Tucker

THERE'S an insistent knocking on the door. Wes pauses the movie and, being on the end of the couch, I get up to answer it.

Mason is standing on my front porch. She hugs her arms to her chest.

I stare at her in surprise. The cold February wind whirls around her.

"What are you doing here?"

"Happy Valentine's Day, Tuck," she says, chewing on her bottom lip.

"You shouldn't be here."

"I don't care." Her chin lifts up as she meets my eye.

"Mason."

"It's not over until we both say it's over," she announces.

My laugh is bitter. "It doesn't work that way, Princess. You made that pretty fucking clear the first time."

She throws her hands up in the air. "I was eighteen! I was an idiot! How long are you going to keep punishing me for a mistake I made two and a half years ago?"

I roll my eyes. "Have a good night, Mason."

Closing the door, it bounces open. She's stuck her foot in the jamb.

"I'm not leaving until we talk about this," she declares. From her backpack, she pulls out a bag of whole wheat bread and a jar of creamy Skippy. "We're going to work through this shit, Tuck. I don't care how many sandwiches we need. We're going to get to the bottom of this."

My heart gets lodged in my throat. "There's nothing to talk about."

"I love you." Her eyes are locked on mine. "I *love* you, and you love me, and we've come too damn far to give up like this. So yeah, we're going to talk. We're probably going to fight. But I'm still going to love you. That's not changing any time soon."

"Mase…"

"Close the fucking door," Amir yells from the living room. "You're letting all the warm air out."

I sigh. "Come in."

Stepping aside, she follows me into the small foyer. She unzips her coat and hangs it over mine on the hook. She pushes the bread and peanut butter into my hands.

"Do your worst, baby."

"I'm not hungry."

Binge eating disorder, that's what Dave called it. I haven't binged since the breakup. I had a peanut butter sandwich the other night—one—and that was more because I missed the taste than any desire to emotionally eat.

I'm not going to magically be cured with the help of a label. It's something I've struggled with for a long time, and will probably continue to struggle with for the rest of my life. But naming it, making it real, makes it not so scary. It's controllable. With the help of therapy and Dave and some extra support from the nutrition staff, it can maybe not control my entire life.

It's hard. I need to take in so many calories a day to maintain weight. Most of my diet is lean protein, whole grains, and healthy fats with the occasional peanut butter sandwich thrown in. There's a metric fuck ton of vegetables in there, too. I'm already hyper-aware of my caloric intake. Now my food log will be shared with the nutrition counselors and with Dave. It's okay if I binge. It's not the end of the world. We're working to curb the behavior that leads me onto that path in the first place.

Mason pins me with a look. "Tucker. I'm trying."

I'm painfully aware of the guys behind me. Miles and Sam are up in his room—I can hear the rhythmic thumping of his headboard against the wall, her muffled moans. Greg is out with a girl from the gymnastics team he's been casually seeing. Amir, Barrett, and Wes are watching a zombie robot movie.

I swallow and head towards the stairs without comment. Mason scurries to follow me. I open the door to my room and gesture her inside.

She sets the food down on my desk and turns to face me. She links her pinkies together and tugs, putting pressure on her wrists. She only does that when she's nervous, a habit she picked up from her brother. I hate that I know that about her.

"You wanted to talk," I tell her roughly. My heart catches in my throat. "So, talk."

"Okay." She takes a deep breath. "I think we should renegotiate."

My eyebrows go up. "What is this, a relationship or a business deal?"

"We'll treat it like whatever we need to in order to work this out," she says. She perches on my desk. "I can admit that I have problems being vulnerable after sex. I'm aware. I'm working on it."

Crossing my arms over my chest, I lean against the door and study her. "And what are you doing?"

"I'm going to start journaling," she announces. I roll my

eyes. "If I can't get more comfortable, I'm open to seeing a sex-positive therapist, but—"

"I'm seeing someone."

She chokes. "Like—you're—"

"A therapist," I amend quickly. "I'm not dating anyone else, no. I started seeing a therapist. He's cool."

"That's good," she says. She presses a hand to her chest. "I hope that helps."

"Yeah. Me too."

"What are you… I mean, do you want to…"

"I need a little extra help right now," I tell her. "I never got over you. I need to this time."

"Or you could not." She pushes off the desk, a sultry half-smile on her face. "We could—"

"You're doing it again. Right now. You're trying to manipulate me with sex." I shake my head. "We can't."

"I love you, Tucker," she says quietly.

"Sometimes that's not enough."

"I didn't realize how much my drinking was affecting you. I can—well, I won't stop entirely, but I can agree to dial it back."

"Don't do anything on my account."

She swallows. "I want to. I want to count on your being in my life. I don't want that to end."

"Mason…"

"No. I know that I messed up. I know that I should have talked to you more. But there's no magic reason why my head is fucked up when it comes to sex. I wasn't traumatized. I wasn't assaulted. I just can't deal with it sometimes. That doesn't mean I want to stop having sex with you. It just means that sometimes I need some space. I don't always want to cuddle. I don't always want to be touched. I just need some space."

"You can have your space," I tell her. "You can have all the space you want."

Her laugh is bitter. "I don't want space from you right now."

I throw my hands up in the air. "Well, fuck, Mason, that clears that up."

"I want to be with you," she tells me. "I want to spend my life with you. And, yes, sometimes it's scary. Sometimes your feelings are too heavy for me. That doesn't make them wrong. I'm working through it on my end. But you can't keep hiding away."

"I don't hide."

She pins me with a look. "It's a Saturday night. When I knocked on your door, what were you doing?"

"It's Valentine's Day. Date night. I don't have anywhere to go."

"There's a singles' party at the ASC."

"I'm not ready to date other people," I tell her flatly. "Eventually I'll get there. I'm not ready. That's not to say I won't be. Dave thinks it's a good idea if I'm single for a while."

I need to learn how to function on my own again, without her ghost watching over my shoulder. I need to move on. As much as I don't want to, I think I need to.

I thought Mason and I were going to spend the rest of our lives together. Now that that's not happening, I have to figure out what I want for myself. Not only when it comes to a romantic partner, but also as a partner in life.

"I don't think you should date anyone else," she says. "I think you should date me."

I laugh. It isn't funny. "We've tried that. Twice. It doesn't work, baby."

"We didn't date," she corrects me. "We jumped straight into a relationship. We can start with casual dating. We can agree to being together, that we won't see other people, and still feel each other out all over again. We won't have sex until my head's on straight. We'll date. We can date."

"Mason…"

"And besides," she says, shooting me a saucy grin, "the third time is always the charm."

"We can't date."

She pouts at me. "Why is that?"

"Because you waited. You let me believe I was going crazy, imagining you on campus, and all this time you were right here in front of me."

forty-two

. . .

Mason

"YEAH, I DID," I admit freely.

"And you never mentioned it," he accuses.

"I didn't know how."

He spreads his arms wide. "You've been on campus since August. Why the fuck did I not know about you being here until January?"

"Because I wasn't ready!"

He blinks at me.

"I came here for you. Is that what you want to hear? I transferred to Newton because of you," I snap. "There were other reasons, this is the program I wanted to begin with and the coach is awesome, but that was one of the big reasons. And then I chickened out. I saw you hanging out with Sam and this other chick and—"

"What other chick?"

"I don't know, she was tall and skinny and gorgeous."

He frowns. "I don't know who that is."

I wave a hand. "It's not important. It was in November, right after midterms."

"Wait a minute…" He scratches at his beard. "Do you mean Mackenzie?"

"I don't know? You were in the dining hall, and she was sitting next to you, and you looked so happy…" My stomach churns remembering how awful that moment felt.

"Mack is Miles's sister. She was visiting for a weekend," he says slowly. "She'll be a freshman here next year."

"Well, I got jealous and freaked out. So I didn't say anything."

"She's in *high school*." He sounds disgusted. "How could you think that Mack and I…" He shudders. "No, Mason, I was not dating my friend's younger sister. I wasn't dating anyone."

"I know that now." I chew on my lip. "I don't want you to date anyone else. I only want you to date me."

He sighs. "It's not that simple, sunshine."

"It is, though." I approach him, and when he doesn't flinch, I set my hands on his hips. Slowly he meets my eye. "I love you. You love me. We're both going to try some counseling. We'll grow together. It won't be easy, but we can work through this. I believe in us."

Tucker swallows. "I—I believe in us, too. And I know that I can't let you break my heart all over again. I can't give you that power anymore."

"You have that same power over me, King. You always have." I step closer, my hands tightening on his hips. "You've always held my heart in your hands."

Pain clouds his eyes. "Mason…"

"This isn't going to be easy," I tell him. "There isn't some magical cure. But I think we can work past this. We both want to be together. We need to get out of our own way and just fucking *be together*."

He lets out a heavy sigh. He slumps against the door, bowing his head. "I—I can't."

"Why not?" I run my thumb across his cheek, and he automatically nuzzles into the contact before he remembers he's not supposed to anymore. He turns away. "Tuck, it's just me. You can talk to me."

"I've spent my entire adolescent life in love with you, Mason." His eyes meet mine, brown and soulful. "You're all I've ever known. What if I'm settling? What if—"

I swallow. "If you want to date other people…"

"I don't, though. That's the thing. I don't want to date other people. I only want to be with you."

"So what's the problem?"

He sighs. "I thought I was sure. I thought I knew what I wanted."

"And now you don't?"

"I'm so confused." His head bows. "I want to be with you, I do, but I don't know if it's a good idea."

"Because…"

"Because of everything. Our past. The sex. I just—" He takes a deep breath, then another. His hands curl into fists.

"What's wrong?"

"I really want a fucking peanut butter sandwich right now," he mutters, shaking his head. "I know I shouldn't, but I do."

"That's why I brought it. I can make you—"

"No. I don't need it. Thank you. I want it, but I don't need it."

"I need you." The words are quiet in the stillness of the room. "I know I'm supposed to stand on my own two feet, I'm supposed to be a strong and capable woman who don't need no man, but Tucker, I need you in my life. I want to spend my life with you. We don't have to go out and party all the time. We don't need to stay in all the time. There's a happy medium here. We can both get what we need out of this."

He swallows, his eyes slowly rising to meet mine.

"I have a lot of work to do," he says. "Therapy is—"

"I know. We both have to put in the work, separately and

together." I step closer, so his broad belly brushes against my flat one, our toes touching. "I'm trying, Tuck. All I can do is try."

He lets out a blustery sigh. "Mase…"

I rise up onto my tiptoes. Slowly, I brush my lips against his. "King."

His lips crash into mine in a forceful kiss. Before I can so much as blink, we're twisted, he has my back pinned against the door, and his tongue licks into my mouth. His thick body presses against mine in all the right ways. His fingers bury themselves in my hair.

It's like my world shifts slowly back into place.

Our tongues tangle, speaking the words neither of us are able to convey verbally. Our bodies speak a language only the two of us understand.

I love you. I want you. I need you.

Tucker's teeth scrape against my bottom lip. He soothes the sharp ache with his tongue. Abruptly, he pulls away.

"No. We can't."

"We can, and we should." Tightening my arms around him, he bows his head, his forehead pressed to mine as he takes a deep, shuddering breath. "King, we owe it to ourselves to try again. A real, honest try. We'll both put in the work. We've both made mistakes. But we can get past this."

His eyes squeeze shut. "I want to. I want to so fucking bad. But I don't think it's a good idea."

I cup his cheek, forcing his eyes to meet mine. "Why?"

"We crash and burn. We—"

"We lasted three and a half years before I got insecure and freaked out," I remind him. "We made it three weeks now before our worlds imploded. If it doesn't work, it doesn't work, but at least we'll know for sure."

"You broke something in me. You destroyed everything that was good about my life," he tells me. "I stopped being a functional person when you left. I don't want to ever go through that again."

"And yet you had the strength to walk away when it wasn't working," I remind him. "You drew a line in the sand and refused to let me compromise your boundaries. That's healthy. That's exactly what you're supposed to do, baby. You got yourself help. There's no magic cure. There's no prescription you can take or button you can press to make everything all better. It takes time, and work, and maybe a few tears along the way. We're going to have fights. We're going to have disagreements. But that doesn't mean we give up. It means we work through them."

Tucker swallows. "I love you, I do, but Mason…"

"We can work through whatever it is."

He sighs, straightening his shoulders. He seems to realize he still has me pinned to the door because he takes a step back, then another, until he's crossing the room and sitting on his unmade bed. He pats the spot beside him.

I cross the room and take a seat next to him. We sit cross-legged and stare at each other.

"The drinking," he finally says. "It concerns me."

"I can dial it back," I admit readily. "I don't like blacking out. I don't enjoy hangovers. I need to learn how to have one or two and still have a good time."

He nods, swallowing again. "I really don't like the drinking the night before a meet. You can't run your best, baby, if you're—"

My heart aches. I didn't realize it was weighing so heavily on him.

"I can try to abstain the night before a meet," I tell him. "I really do try to limit it to one or two."

Tucker chews on his lip. "I'm not trying to control you. I don't want to tell you how to live your life. But maybe a little less drinking and frat parties?"

"As long as I get to spend those nights with you, I'm okay

with that." I reach for his hand and am mollified when he takes mine, lacing our fingers together. "I don't want to stay in every night. We need to go out on dates. I'm not asking you to wine and dine me. I just need—"

"I know," he says. "I need it, too."

"We should date. Get to know each other again as the people we are now and not the kids we used to be. We jumped directly into a serious, committed relationship. We need to keep things more casual for a while."

He doesn't look nearly as upset by this prospect as I expected. "I don't have a lot of money. I can't keep a job while I'm playing football. We start spring camp in three weeks, and then I'm going to have even less time."

"I can deal with that. We can have picnics in the library for all I care. All I want is to spend quality time with you. I don't care if that time is limited. I don't care if we keep all our clothes on. I just want to be with you."

He kisses the back of my hand. "Yeah, clothes are staying on. For a while."

I frown. "King…"

"No. I want your journaling to work. I want you to feel better. And I won't pressure you into doing anything that makes you uncomfortable. I can wait. It will make it all that much better when we finally get there."

"You can wait?"

Slowly, a smirk spreads over his face. "I mean, I'm not suggesting abstaining entirely. We can still fool around. But if you start getting squirrelly, if you start withdrawing, yeah, I'm not afraid to pull the plug on happy naked time."

forty-three

. . .

Tucker

SHE STARES AT ME. "Did we really just negotiate our relationship?"

I have to laugh. "I think so?"

Mason launches herself at me, tackling me to the bed. Her body lays across mine, her lithe form like a weighted blanket on top of me, solid and comforting and familiar. Her face is inches from mine.

"Hi," she says, biting her lip.

Not for the first time, I tug that lip loose. "Mine."

She swallows, her eyes darting to meet mine. "All yours."

And then her lips are on mine, and my fingers are in her hair, and her tongue is in my mouth, and everything is right in my world.

I can do anything with this woman by my side. That's not to say I can't do it without her. I can. I just don't want to if I don't have to. I would much rather go through life with her than on my own.

Down the road, we'll work out this sex thing. We'll figure out grad school. We'll get real, grown-up jobs. Maybe a post-grad degree. And then marriage. And babies. Lots and lots of babies. My moms are itching to be grandmothers. I can't wait to have a little girl with her eyes and my frizzy hair, a little boy with my dimples and her bad attitude. Or maybe we'll adopt. Foster a bunch of kids until we find our forever kids.

It's a simple life, a simple dream, but it's mine. Ours.

I maneuver us until Mason is stretched out beside me on the bed. Drawing her leg over my hip, I let my hands explore her strong thighs, her pert ass, the strength of her back. Her hands are all over me, touching my chest and my shoulders. She rolls onto her back, pulling me with her. Her hand slides down my belly to palm my cock through my joggers.

Arching into her touch, I cup her face and lick into her mouth, taking what I need from her. She slips her hand beneath the fabric of my sweatpants and wraps her hand around my dick. Slowly, tortuously, she glides her hand over my shaft.

"Mason…" I press a kiss to the pressure point in her neck, scraping my teeth over the delicate skin there.

"Please," she says, panting. She squeezes me firmly. "Please, can I suck your cock?"

I pull back to meet her eyes. "You really want to?"

She runs her thumb over the sensitive head. "I really do."

Shifting, I adjust us to a better angle, and she doesn't waste any time. She tugs my joggers down my thighs and wraps her fingers around me again. I thrust into her tight little fist. Mason moves down in the bed until her head is at an appropriate level. She runs her tongue up the underside of my shaft, sucking on a bulging vein near the tip.

I think I must have died and gone to heaven. And then she sucks the head into her mouth.

"You really like this?"

She nods, taking more of me into her mouth.

"I love you."

She smiles around my cock. She takes my hand and places it on the back of her head. I thread my fingers through her hair. It's like an out-of-body experience, watching the woman

I love willingly, gladly suck my cock. The center of my chest feels heavy, even more so when she takes me all the way in, until the head meets with the soft pressure at the back of her throat.

I lose myself in the push and pull. Her mouth on my cock is like a drug, sending me floating through the air on waves of pleasure. She bobs and sucks and licks. Her hands stroke the parts of me she can't fit in her mouth.

My balls draw up tight. She cradles them in her hand, as if testing their weight. Her fingers slip beneath the sack to rub at my perineum.

"Stop. Mason."

She stops immediately. She lifts her head and releases my cock at once. "What's wrong?"

"You need to take your pants off and come sit on my face," I tell her.

A pleased smile spreads over her face. "I can do that."

"You should suck my cock while you do it."

She pulls off her hoodie and t-shirt in one swift motion. My cock twitches at the sight of her in that electric yellow bra. Slowly, I touch myself as she shimmies off her pants and her matching electric yellow panties and climbs back onto the bed.

I catch her hand and pull her on top of me. She straddles me, her hot, wet heat pinning my cock to my pelvis. Her hands fist in my shirt as she rides me, bucking against me.

"Holy shit," she breathes, her head tossed back. "I think I could come just from this."

"Sit on my face, sunshine," I tell her. "I'll get you there."

She crawls up the bed and situates herself on top of me. I grab her hips and bring her into closer range. I touch the tip of my tongue to her clit, and she tenses. I part her folds and suck at her in earnest. She moans, throwing her head back. I adjust her positioning over me, and she sucks the head of my cock into her mouth.

It feels even better from this angle. I spread my legs as far as I can with the sweatpants around my knees and she takes the hint, running her tongue along the sensitive seam in the middle of my balls.

She smells amazing, like musk and honey and salt and perfection. With my fingers, I gather the wetness pooling at her core and tease her entrance, slowly, slowly. Mason groans around my cock, and the reverberating echoes vibrate within me.

I slip a finger into her tight, wet heat. She grinds onto my finger, onto my face. My lips and tongue are coated with the pearlescent evidence of her desire. She tastes a little bit salty, a little bit sweet, a little bit perfect. I could do this all day.

Her fingers play with the sensitive line running up my balls. She slides back to rub against my perineum again and that's it—I'm done. I come with a shout, muffled by her perfect pussy. She swallows around me, taking it all, taking all I have to give her.

Renewing my attention on her, I slip a second finger inside of her, scissoring and stretching her. Her fingers dig into my thighs, her nails sending little pinpricks of pain and pleasure directly to my tired cock. I curl my fingers against her front wall, pressing against that spot that makes her sit up in a hurry, her channel sending a fresh burst of wetness onto my tongue.

Her walls clamp around me with a vise grip. I suck at her clit, and she grinds on my face, taking what she needs from me. A few more thrusts and her walls start to flutter around me, clenching my fingers in a tight grip.

"Holy fuck." Mason collapses onto the bed beside me. She wiggles around until her head is level with mine again. She meets me for a sweet, sated kiss. "King, I… you…"

"Yeah?"

"Holy fucking fuck."

Pride blooms deep within me. We've always been good at this.

"You're okay? Your head is—?"

She meets me for a messy kiss, more tongue and teeth than lips and finesse. She tugs me on top of her, until I'm pinning her with my hefty bulk.

"Mason…"

"My head is great," she tells me, wrapping her arms around me. "It's not all the time. There's no trigger. Sometimes it just happens."

"I only ever want you to feel good with me." I brush some of her hair out of her face and kiss her temple.

"I do," she says quietly. "I feel my best when I'm with you."

epilogue

. . .

Tucker

A YEAR AND A HALF LATER...

———

"So, this is the place."

I wave my hand at the small student apartment. It's not much. Two bedrooms, one bath, small kitchen. A tiny little speck of a living room. But it's mine.

Ours.

My mom clutches her heart to her chest. "My little baby's all grown up."

Mama rolls her eyes. "He's been a grown up for awhile."

Jamal laughs. "He'll always be my little Tucky-poo."

Growling, I tackle my brother onto the couch. He fights against me, and I pin him down. I might be done with my football career, but I haven't forgotten how to tackle.

"All right, all right, break it up," Mom says. "Honestly, you two."

"He started it," I mutter, kicking my brother's shoe.

He kicks me back.

"Boys. Enough," Mason says from the tiny kitchen. She wipes her hands on a dish rag. "I swear, you two are worse than me and Micah."

My brother perks up at the idea of another guy being here to round the group out. "Where is he? I thought he was supposed to be here for this."

She rolls her eyes. "He can't get away in the middle of the season. He has a game on Sunday."

Jamal reports to training camp next week. We have two weeks before classes start, two weeks to get acclimated to our new digs. It's our last chance to spend some time together before we get busy with our everyday life.

Micah was drafted the spring of our junior year, in the middle of the second round. We all expected him to ride the bench for a few seasons, pay his dues, but when San Diego's star running back tore his ACL, the back-up broke his clavicle in a bad tackle, and the number three and four dudes couldn't keep up, he stole the show and the starting squad job.

He keeps in touch. He came out for spring break, sleeping on Mason's floor and cheering her on at her track meet. He would stay for longer, but a week is enough time for all of us to be in the same room. He and I get along better from afar, and after a few days, he and Mason fight like cats and dogs. We were both glad to see him go. He came back for graduation in June with both of her parents and their new families. *That* was fun. Her mom is still a judgmental bitch, but her dad likes me now, especially once he heard about my plans to propose as soon as we're done with grad school.

Mason claps her hands together. "Sit down, sit down. Eat."

She's been stressing over this meal for weeks. I told her to relax, that my moms don't expect her to cook or pull out all the stops, but she insisted. I did most of the prep last night, before they got here, and she put on the finishing touches this morning. It's the first chance we've really had to use our new kitchen. The first real guests we've had.

Most of our friends have graduated and moved on. Wes is still around, starting grad school in a few weeks. We had him and Mack over for dinner the other night. We might have a few of the football or track people over next week. We'll see. It's weird seeing the people we went through undergrad with, still stuck in school like nothing's changed.

We're about to embark on a new phase in our lives together. Grad school looms over us like a storm cloud on the horizon. We both applied to a half dozen schools—we applied to all of the same programs, and we agreed to only consider places that accepted us both—and Newton was the best combination of academics, community, and aid package. Jamal has graciously offered to cover my tuition and living expenses, whatever my scholarships don't cover. Micah insisted on paying for hers. I have a job working in the student resource center. It's not much, but it pays the bills.

She's going to be working with the track team as a graduate coach and in the social services assessment center two days a week. I spent the summer helping out with the football team, but I think I have to bow out after this season. I'm ready to close the book on that stage of my life. I'm ready to focus on my future: graduate school, getting my substance abuse counseling certifications, clinical internship, Mason.

We've both agreed to hold off on marriage until we're done with school, until we're financially on our feet and relatively stable in our new careers. She's going for an MFT degree while I'm going for a master's in clinical psychology, which will allow me to take the certifications I need to become an addiction counselor. We haven't decided what city we'll end up in, whether we'll go back to DC or move to Boston proper or pick another random city on the map. It depends on where we can both find jobs. I don't care where we live as long as I'm there with her.

Mason ushers us all to sit at the little table. My moms generously helped us furnish the place with all of the discarded furniture that used to be in their house; they wanted all new furniture for this new kid-free stage of their lives. Jamal's knees knock into mine underneath the table, Mom needs to use an unmatched desk chair from our guest room/office, but we're all together.

It's relatively simple fare. My brother brought bagels from the shop in town. We made blueberry pancakes, hash browns, bacon and sausage, and a baked omelette. I prepared a platter of sliced fruit and a veggie tray. My moms picked up a berry cheesecake. We all contributed.

I feel like a grown-up, like a proper adult, hosting my family in my new apartment for the first time. I've lived in student housing for the last four years. Sure, we could have guests, but it was very much shared student housing. Now Mason and I are living together in a real, grown-up apartment with real furniture. We don't have to eat in the dining hall anymore. We're on our own.

She beams at me. She's always gotten along well with my moms. She and Jamal get along nearly as well as I do with Micah. She always joins in on my family's weekly video chat calls. She's part of my family.

Mason sets her hand on my thigh. "I made a couple peanut butter pancakes, just for you," she says, pointing at the platter.

I lean over and kiss her cheek before helping myself to a few. "Thanks, Princess."

The binge eating is… well, it's not entirely under control, considering I'm about to embark on the most stressful year of my life, but I'm working on it. I'm still seeing my therapist, Dave, now in what he hopes to be the final year of his doctoral program. Mason sees her therapist every other week, though she's had to bounce around to find one she liked. We're… stable.

There's no magic cure. There's no instant fix. It takes work. We've both put in the effort. We don't stop just because we got to a good place: we're still working, still trying.

The little apartment is warm with love and laughter. Mom teases Mama for picking the blueberries out of her pancakes until Jamal reaches over and eats them for her. My brother drinks nearly an entire gallon of orange juice in less than an hour. Mason and I play footsie under the table.

It's easy and comfortable. Surrounded by all of the people who matter most in my world, I'm embraced in a cocoon of love and affection.

It still hasn't sunk in that this is what the rest of my life will be like. Sure, my moms won't be here every week. Jamal is busy with his own life. We have grad school about to suck up all of our time.

But looking past that—at our future, at Thanksgiving and Christmas at our house, our families mingling and combining. Her mess of step- and half-siblings running around, growing up before our eyes. Our brothers with their inability to date women they want to bring home for the holidays.

And, eventually, babies of our own. A whole house full of babies, adopted or fostered or born to us. I don't care. All I care is that they're ours.

Mason and Mama are talking about—something, I don't know. Interrupting them, I lean over and kiss Mason's temple.

"What's that for?"

"Because I felt like it," I tell her, brushing a strand of her hair behind her ear and indulging in the easy affection that's become so natural for us again.

She turns to me and kisses me properly. Her teeth scrape over my bottom lip, and I nearly groan out loud. I can't wait for our guests to leave, until we have the place to ourselves again. We've christened half of the surfaces in our two weeks in the apartment. There's plenty of time for us to get to the rest of the place.

"What's that for?" I run my thumb across her cheek.

Mason grins at me. "Because I can."

afterword

Thank you for reading Blitz. This book is my baby and I absolutely love it to pieces.

You know what would make it even better? A review!

Reviews are more important than readers realize. If you liked this book, please leave me a review!

Want more about Tucker and Mason's Happily Ever After? Click here to read the bonus epilogue!

xoxo,

Allie

about the author

Allie is a queer and AuDHD writer with a hyper-fixation on inclusivity and representation. She loves the color purple, Michigan football, and the Boston Bruins. When she's not absorbed by a book, she likes to spend time with her nephews.

Born and raised in Southern California, she now calls South Carolina home. She is allergic to the cold, rain, snow, and mosquitos.

also by allie lasky

Want to see how it all started? Read THE GAME PLAN to meet sweet cinnamon roll football player Miles and the feisty sorority girl who stole his heart.

———

The story continues with END GAME. When Diana's world falls apart, she goes to the only person who makes it make sense — her best friend, Barrett, who's been in love with her forever.

———

Meet the Neurospicy Book Club in THE THOUGHT OF YOU: Falling for my Grumpy Roommate, where Johanna finds out she's autistic… because her happy-go-lucky new roomie (and reformed playboy ex-football player) has to tell her.